CONFESSIONS OF A DIVA

CONFESSIONS OF A DIVA

Jessica N. Barrow

iUniverse, Inc.
New York Lincoln Shanghai

Confessions of a Diva

iUniverse books may be ordered through booksellers or by contacting:

iUniverse
2021 Pine Lake Road, Suite 100
Lincoln, NE 68512
www.iuniverse.com
1-800-Authors (1-800-288-4677)

ISBN-13: 978-0-595-39676-4 (pbk)
ISBN-13: 978-0-595-84082-3 (ebk)
ISBN-10: 0-595-39676-3 (pbk)
ISBN-10: 0-595-84082-5 (ebk)

Printed in the United States of America

To My Father

Dad, I miss you and I love you more than life itself. If you can see me now, I know you're smiling down on me. If Heaven gets too full, make sure you hold me a spot.

Your daughter,
Jessica

CHAPTER ONE

"This has been one of the worst days of my life."

"Because of me?" Jonathan asked, momentarily removing his eyes from the road to glance at the young lady sitting in the passenger seat of his car.

Scratching between her braids and angrily wishing that her sister hadn't plaited her hair so tight, Tomi ignored her ex-boyfriend and stared out at the star-filled sky as they sped down the freeway.

"So that's it? You don't have nothing else to say to me?" Jonathan asked.

Smacking her lips, Tomi rolled her eyes and ignored him even more. The only reason why she had chose to go out with him in the first place was because all her other options were exhausted. Her home-girls were out clubbing, and because she had bombed her chemistry test today, her parents wouldn't let her go; her oldest sister, Niya, was bugged down with studying for her college exams, and her other sister, Kelise, was out on a date with Ricardo.

In other words, if she didn't want to spend a beautiful, warm Friday night cooped up in the house with her parents, she figured hanging out with Jonathan would be the next best thing. Before agreeing to hang out with him, she had made him give his solemn vow that he wouldn't try to come on to her, he wouldn't beg for her to take him back, and he wouldn't so much as mention their previous relationship period. He had agreed and no sooner had they pulled out of her driveway, he had already reneged on his promise.

All day long, all she had heard was, "Tomi, I love you", or "Tomi, we feel so right together", or "Tomi, don't you remember how good things use to be"— Tomi, Tomi, Tomi! Damn, she was tired of hearing her own name.

"What are we pulling over for?" she asked as he made a sudden unexpected turn and came to a stop in the abandoned parking lot behind Ronald's Food Market.

"What are we pulling over for?" she repeated again as he killed the engine.

"Tomi, we need to talk."

"I ain't got nothing to say to you. You've pissed me off for today."

"Three years, Tomi. Three years and you're going to let it all go, just like that?"

"Oh Lord, here we go again." Tomi rolled her eyes towards the sky. "Jonathan, how many times do I have to tell you that I don't feel the same way about you like I use to. It's not there anymore. Can we just please—"

"—I can make it be there," he interjected. "I can change whatever you need me to change. I can do it, I swear I can. Just give me one more chance. Is that too much to ask? Just one more chance?"

Tomi rubbed her throbbing temples in slow, circular motions and wished again that Kelise hadn't braided her hair so tight. "Take me home, Jonathan."

"Tomi, baby, please; I'm begging…"

Tomi didn't say a word, but her irritation was obvious in her movements and facial expression.

With an abysmal sigh, Jonathan pressed his forehead against the steering wheel, trying to gather his haywire emotions. Finally, his every body part resolute in his unspoken decision, he reached beneath his seat, fumbling for something. Seconds later, his hand resurfaced with a black steel revolver, .38 caliber.

Tomi's first reaction was a shrill, surprised scream; she backed herself against the passenger door, trying to put as much space as possible between her and the gun. With eyes void of emotion, he pointed the gun at her temple, the same temple that she had recently massaged. As Jonathan pressed the hard, cold metal against her warm flesh, her voice escaped her lips in a thin, wavering whisper. "Jonathan, no. Please, no."

"I don't want to do this—don't make me do this."

"I'm sorry, Jonathan. We can be together. I love you, too, baby. We can be together, I promise. You don't have to do this." She was crying, now, and willing to say anything that it took to get him to put away that black piece of metal, freeing her from Death's cold, relentless grip.

"Can't you see, Tomi? Without you, I am nothing. My life doesn't make sense; it has no meaning. I just need to—I need to get away. If I can't be with you, there's no reason to live."

He swallowed deeply. "When you look back on this night, remember that you could've saved us, Tomi. I gave you the chance. You could've saved me. Good-bye. Maybe we'll get our second chance on the other side."

Before she could stop him, he removed the gun from her head, placed the hollow barrel in his mouth, and pulled the trigger. Tomi opened her mouth and screamed.

Six years later

"Who is Destiny? Your old lady?"

"No, that's my daughter's name."

"Oh." Tomi paused, lifting a perfectly arched eyebrow at the man before laying out all the necessary tools on the tray. "I was just asking. I've lost count of how many times someone has rolled up in here, got their lover's name tattooed on them, only to return in two weeks or less asking me how to get it removed."

"I wouldn't get a chick's name tattooed on me if someone paid me to do it."

"Good. You're one of the smart ones."

"Guess so."

She washed her hands at the sink behind her, then proceeded to open each wrapped tool. "Destiny's a pretty name. How old is she?"

"She would've turned two today."

Would've.

Tomi cursed herself for not knowing when to keep her mouth shut. "I'm sorry," she said sympathetically. She wanted to ask him how had she died, but she knew it was none of her business.

Once she had finished unwrapping all the tools, she pulled on a pair of latex gloves and positioned the large machinery. Leaning close to him, she meticulously outlined the name that she had stenciled on him earlier. He sucked in a quick breath when the burning needle made initial contact with his sensitive skin, but that was the only sound or reaction that he made.

As she finished the outline and leaned closer to fill in the letters, she couldn't help but notice the cologne that he had probably dabbed behind his ears before stepping out his car. It was Eternity. The same kind of cologne that Jonathan used to wear when…

She shook her head, discarding those painful memories before they had a chance to crawl up from the darkest corners of her mind and render her immobile.

Quickly but carefully finishing the tattoo, she filled the cursive letters and pulled the machinery back, removing both her gloves in one quick, adept movement.

"All done." She gave him a mirror, allowing him to observe her handiwork.

The skin around the tattoo was red and swollen, so she informed him, "Don't worry about the swelling; it should go down in two to three days."

"This shit is tight," he admitted, returning the mirror and rising from the reclining chair.

She handed him a piece of paper. "This has everything on it that you need to know about how to take care of your tattoo. Use cocoa butter; it will keep it from scaling, plus it will heal faster. And I'm," she looked away from him, "I'm sorry about your little girl."

"Don't sweat it. You didn't know."

"I know, but still…"

"Don't sweat it," he reiterated, anger and frustration furrowing his brow.

"Dang, I'm sorry," Tomi apologized, holding her hands up to gentle him. Obviously, the subject of his deceased daughter was out-of-bounds.

"Listen, I ain't mean to raise my voice at you like that. It's just a sensitive issue—one I don't like talking about. You forgive me?"

"If you forgive me for nosing in your personal life in the first place, then I forgive you for getting loud with me. Truce?" She held out her hand.

He looked down at her hand—slender fingers, long and thin, a sterling silver ring on every finger, square acrylic nails with a pink and purple flower design on the pinky and thumbnail. He stared at her hand so long that Tomi almost self-consciously pulled it back. But at the last minute, he took her hand in his. His large dark hand dwarfed her smaller, lighter one. Where his hand was rough and callused, hers was soft and silky like pink rose petals.

At that small of a touch, an electric shock went through both of them, and Tomi snatched her hand out of his, shaking her hand as if it had been burned by his touch. When she chanced a glance at him, she knew he had felt it too, because he was looking at her as if he was seeing her for the very first time.

Without being inconspicuous, he looked Tomi up and down. She was a very attractive woman. Her thick, milk-coffee hair was braided in a design at the front, and the rest of her shoulder-length hair was pinned back with a honey-nut colored, turtle clip. Her eyebrows were perfectly arched; her cat eyes were almost the exact same color of her hair. She had a small diamond stud in her left nostril, and on her lips, she wore a thin coating of tan shimmery gloss.

A spaghetti-strapped white camisole that drooped low teasingly flaunted her generous cleavage; a name was tattooed in thin cursive letters across her left breast. Her shirt stopped short of her navel, which was adorned with a silver belly ring that dangled a diamond angel. Jeans, low-cut and wide leg, loose at her tiny waist and hugging her wide hips and thick thighs, were the perfect accompaniment to make her outfit. Her arched feet were encased in white, strappy heels, and her little cotton-candy pink toe nails peeked out from beneath the cuff of her pants.

After eyeing her from head to toe, his eyes, on their own volition, returned to that generous cleavage, those two, tanned melons, kissing ever so gently beneath that white camisole. He wanted to dive his face in those ripe melons and caress her warm skin with his tongue.

"My face is here," she reminded him, lifting his chin up until his eyes met hers.

"My bad," he laughed, shaking the image from his mind. "Can't help it. You're a very attractive woman."

"So I've been told." She placed her hands on her hips. "I hate to rush you, but I do have other customers waiting."

Not only her looks, but her personality as well piqued his interest. He liked her feistiness, that spark of a rebel spirit in her eyes. Usually, for him, women fell in three categories: wifey material, booty-call material, or just-friends material. This exotic beauty standing before him could easily be placed in all three categories at once.

"What's your name?" he asked.

She lifted her eyebrow at him again. After the way he had just stared her down, practically eating her for dessert with his eyes, she figured he was going to ask her if she had a man, ask for a piece of ass, or, at the least, ask for her phone number. But he wanted her name. Interesting. Maybe he was different from all the other lame asses who had tried to spit game. Or, maybe she was trying to read him too much too fast.

Slow your roll, Tomi, she admonished herself. He was just a man; maybe cuter, more attractive, and more interesting than all of the other men she had become acquainted with, but yet in still, a man. That was the one thing that she didn't need complicating her life any more than necessary. Their little interlude had become too personal for her, so she decided to change the pace.

"You don't need to know my name," she snapped at him, noticing that her other customers had taken interest in their conversation. "This is my place of business, okay? I'm done with your tattoo. Unless you want a body piercing or another tattoo, the door is right there. I do have other customers waiting."

Her words hit their mark with perfect precision. The amorous smile fell from his face, and his cinnamon eyes, which had been so enticingly warm, turned cold. "Nice meeting you," he said in a business-like tone before turning towards the door.

"Look, I didn't mean it like—" Her words were cut short by the slamming of the door, which swung madly back and forth on its hinges. It couldn't have been any worse than if he had slammed the door in her face. Not only had she been embarrassed in front of all her customers, she also felt three feet tall with the way her words had wounded him. She hadn't meant to hurt him, only dissuade him from pursuing her. But she believed in her heart that what she had done had been done in the best interest of both of them. If she ended things before they had a chance to begin, she could never be held accountable if things went awry. She couldn't carry a weight like that on her shoulders again.

Jonathan's words floated up from her memory: *You could've saved me, Tomi. I gave you the chance.*

It had been her fault, not his. She might as well have had her own finger on the trigger. She had failed him. She hadn't been there for him when he needed her the most. Not again. She couldn't go through that again.

Finishing up quickly with the other three customers there, she did a name tattoo down a man's forearm, a blue and purple butterfly on one girl's ankle, and she finished her last customer with a nose piercing. When she walked into the waiting area and saw that she didn't have any more customers, she grabbed the phone and dialed Kelise's number. She had to talk to somebody about the guy who had made such an impression on her. He had been the only thing on her mind every since he'd left.

"Hey, trick, what you doing?"

"Nothing," Kelise replied, smacking into the phone, "just eating this turkey bacon club sandwich and editing the Dear Iesha part of the magazine. Why? What's up?"

"Girl, I just had this customer not too long ago, and I can't stop thinking about him."

"What?" Tomi could picture her sister pausing in mid-chew. "What makes him so special?"

"I…I don't know. But there's something there; there really was. We had this type of…of chemistry, I guess."

"Chemistry?" Kelise was shocked to hear her sister talking like this. Niya and she had both thought that Tomi was probably diking since she never brought up a topic concerning a man, and never even looked at one hard—no matter how attractive the guy might be. Every since that incident with Jonathan, Tomi just wasn't Tomi anymore. She couldn't fault her completely though; anybody who had witnessed their boyfriend blow his face to smithereens, up close and personal, would be traumatized, too.

"So what did he look like? Was he cute?"

"Fine as hell. He was a dark pecan color, and he had a close-cut fade. About six-two, medium build, thin sideburns, a goatee—and a sexy ass voice!"

If Kelise's jaw could've dislocated and fell on her desk, it would've done so at that very moment.

"But what got me the most, Keli," Tomi continued, completely unaware of her sister's astonishment, "was his eyes! His eyes were like a cinnamon-brown color, and they were so deep. It was like I could see into his soul. He looked at me, and I could feel that we were connecting on another level, serious up. We touched and there was enough sparks flying to start a barn fire."

Kelise put her pen down and looked at the phone incredulously. She could *not* believe that Tomi was saying this. "Oh, my God, Tomi, you are really feeling this brother!"

"Do you think so?"

"Do I think so? Do you hear yourself? Do you hear how you're talking about him? Sounds to me like he might have boyfriend potential."

"Oh, Kelise—"

"Oh, Kelise, nothing. What's his name?"

"I don't know."

"Wha—what do you mean you don't know?"

"I didn't ask."

"You didn't ask? Tomi, I'm going to put you over my leg and beat you with barb wire. Let me guess, you don't have a number to get in contact with him either?"

"…no…"

Kelise sighed heavily into the phone. "What am I going to do with you, girl?"

"It doesn't matter, anyway. I completely messed things up."

"I'm scared to ask. How?"

Tomi described in detail everything that had happened from the time he strolled into her parlor to the time he walked out, slamming the door ear-splittingly loud as he made his departure.

"So you talk about his deceased daughter, snatch your hand away from him, refuse to give him your name, and tell him to leave. Yeah, Tom, I think you need to go ahead and wrap that one up. If that man has any sense, he's not going to want anything to do with you. Probably don't even want to be in the same room with you. Way to go Tomi!"

"Kelise, now is not the time for jokes."

"Hey, you ruined it, not me. Maybe another one will come along, and this time, you won't mess it up. But look sis, hate to rush you, but I have to finish up this section of the magazine by four, and I have to make one more phone call."

"To who? Ricardo?"

"No, to Niya. Phillip was over at the Blue House yesterday."

"No he was not."

"Yes, he was. Seen him with my own two eyes. Girl, it's time for her to draw a line through his no good, trifling ass. He's back on that powder, and to be honest, I don't believe he ever quit."

"Me neither. A'ight, girl. Tell Niya I'll call her later."

"Sure thing. Bye sweetie."

Tomi hung up the phone and sat there, thinking about what Kelise had just said. 'Maybe another one will come along, and this time, you won't mess it up.' To her surprise, she realized that she didn't want someone else to come along. She was only interested in this one guy, and the sad part was that she didn't even know his name.

CHAPTER TWO

"Either step outside, now, or I will say what I have to say right here, right now, in front of everybody."

"Niya, if I lose my job—"

"Oh, wow! Five dollars and sixty-five cents an hour! We would hate to lose that, now wouldn't we, honey?" Some of his co-workers snickered behind them, but she didn't care. She was pissed off and she wanted the truth.

"Give me five minutes," he told her.

"Two." She crossed her arms and rolled her neck to the side to show him that she was not playing.

"Okay, then. Two minutes." He hurried off to the back, and she stood there, tapping her foot impatiently. He returned almost exactly two minutes later. "Let's go outside."

He took her by the elbow and led her out back, near the dumpsters. "What in the hell is so important that you had to come to my job and embarrass me in front of all—"

"You're doing that shit again, aren't you?" she cut in, getting straight to the point.

"What shit?" he asked confused.

"Don't play dumb with me, boy. You know exactly what I'm talking about. Coke, powder, cocaine—whatever the hell you want to call it!"

Phillip placed his hands on his hips and shook his head. "I can't believe you. I can't believe you actually think that I would go back to doing that mess. I told you I was done with that, Niya. Is that what this is all about?"

Niya held up a hand to stop him. "Phillip, no more lies, okay? Somebody told me that they saw you at the Blue House yesterday."

"Who told you this? Was it Tomi or Kelise?"

"It doesn't matter who told me—"

"It was Kelise. I know it was Kelise. She always got her nose up in somebody's business when she needs to be worrying about her own relationship. She's been engaged for how long? Two, two and a half years? And—"

"Phillip, don't try to change the subject. I don't care what's going on in her life right now. She allegedly saw you at the Blue House, and all I want to know is if it's true or not." She laughed at herself and shook her head, looking away from him. "Why am I asking you this anyway, huh? I know you're not going to be honest with me. I know you're not man enough to actually admit—"

"Niya, it was me."

Stopping in mid-sentence, Niya cleaned her ear canal with her pointer finger. "Sorry, I think I heard that wrong. Can you run that by me again?"

"I said it was me. I'm not trying to hide anything because I wasn't doing nothing wrong. Kelise is right. I was at the Blue House yesterday."

Biting her lip to hold in her anger, Niya finally let out some of that pent up emotion by throwing him a hard punch to his chest. "You fucking liar!" Her accusation was full of rage. "You told me that you had quit snorting that powder. I should've known all along that you were full of shit."

"No, baby, listen to me." He held her firmly with her arms pent to her side. "I didn't go over there for drugs."

"Let me go, Phillip," she hissed at him.

"Not until you calm down and listen to me."

"Let me go!"

"Is everything alright?" a white man asked, pulling up beside them in his Ford navy blue truck and eyeing Phillip with distrust.

Phillip released his wife, and she took several steps away from him. "Everything is fine, sir. I'm just having a discussion with my wife. Is that a crime?"

The man gave Phillip a dubious look, then looked at Niya for her approval. She had to physically shake off her anger, but finally managed a nod. "Everything's okay."

Looking at her skeptically, he said, "If you say so," then put his truck in drive and drove off.

"Okay," Phillip continued, toning down his voice, "like I was saying. I went over to the Blue House to get this." He dug into his back pocket and retrieved a ten karat white-gold ring with four diamonds intertwined. It was the same ring he had bought her for their anniversary two years ago, the one that had "just so happened" to come up missing from her jewelry box. After much pestering, fussing, and fighting, he had finally admitted that he had pawned the ring to handle his drug habit.

"When I pawned this ring," he told her, "June Bug promised me that when I could repay him, he'd give it back. That's why I've been coming up short on the bills lately, because I've been saving up so I can buy back your ring. Can I see your hand?"

Niya stared into a pair of sincere hazel eyes. Phillip was a handsome prince to her, even now in his black and red Arby's outfit. His naturally curly hair was shining in the sunlight, and his goatee was perfectly trimmed. He seemed to tower over her with his height and broad chest—he had played quarter back for NCCU during his college years. It wasn't his natural good looks that had drawn her to him (although they had played a major part); but it was the look that he was giving her now; that look of adoration and open sincerity. It was as if he was laying his heart on a table before her.

"Your hand?" he asked again, softly.

Begrudgingly, Niya held out her right hand. He slid the anniversary ring on her right ring finger, then kissed the palm of her hand.

All feelings of antipathy melted away. "Oh, Phillip, I love you, baby. I'm sorry for ever doubting you." She wrapped her body in his, reaching up to kiss his lips.

"I love you, too, Niya," he told her, strengthening his warm hold around her tiny waist. "I've loved you from the first time I laid eyes on you, and I love you even more with each passing day." He kissed her again, this time holding the kiss long enough to feel her passion ignite by the sudden restlessness of her hips.

"What time do you get off?" she asked, allowing her hands the pleasure of roaming down his hard chest.

"I have to work to closing. I'll probably be home no later than—"

"Phillip!" A tall, slim, light-skinned girl with a pretty face and a cherry-colored, short-cropped hairstyle hollered his name from the back door. "Maggy said to tell you to get your ass in here now. She needs you to work the front."

"Tell her I'm coming, Cassandra." He turned back to his wife, giving her another deep kiss. "I'll be home no later than one. Are you going to wait up for me?"

"With nothing on except for that black silk robe you bought me." Her voice was a purr.

"Don't even wear that," he told her, feeling his penis harden with the thought of her bare macchiato skin against those white sheets.

"Don't even wear that," he repeated with a growl, pulling her close so that she could feel his erection.

She giggled. "Phillip, you better put that up before you go inside. I don't want those little girls eyeing my goodies."

He laughed and shook his head. "I'll tuck it to the side. I love you, babe."

"Love you, too." She gave him a quick kiss and he swatted her butt before jogging back inside the restaurant.

"I can't believe I let Kelise get me that worked up over nothing," she told herself as she headed to her car. But she would have to ask her sister if she could keep the kids overnight. She didn't want anyone or anything to interrupt Phillip and her when he got home from work. An anxious smile touched her lips as she revved up the engine.

CHAPTER THREE

Laying sideways across her fluffy, King-sized bed, Tomi ended the entry in her diary with a kiss, something she had been doing since her sweet sixteenth birthday when she had received the ten-year journal from her mother. This diary wasn't just her best friend, it was a memoir of her life; she had even given it a name, *Confessions of a Diva*. The entry she had just completed was about all the things she would've done if she could relive the incident in her parlor with the man whom she had found so uncannily attractive.

For the life of her, she couldn't figure out what made him stand out from all the other men who had tried to spit game at her. All they got from her were rolled eyes, a cold shoulder, and if one of them got brave enough to touch her, a black eye.

Rolling over so that she was facing the ceiling, she sighed and pictured him in her mind. Tall, dark caramel-chocolate skin, cinnamon eyes, trimmed goatee, sexy sideburns. She wondered how he would look stepping out of a warm shower, water dripping down his muscled legs, his manhood standing up straight, unashamedly pressing against his hard stomach—

"Oh my God, what am I doing?" she asked, pushing herself up to a sitting position and wiping a hand across her eyes, as if by doing so, she could wipe that disturbing image from her mind. "You are never going to see that man again. Let it go. Think about something else."

As if in agreement with her statement, her stomach growled, long and loud. It was only then did she realize that, besides a strawberry and cream granola bar for breakfast, she hadn't eaten anything all day. With one hand pressed against her stomach, she made her way into the kitchen. Her mind had been so occupied with her fantasy-filled journal entry that she hadn't noticed the degree of her hunger.

Pulling open the refrigerator door, her eyes were blessed with the sight of a half-stick of butter, a box of Arm and Hammer baking soda, a pitcher half-full of strawberry Kool-Aid, and a bowl of spaghetti that was starting to mold. *This is what happens when you go spend a week with your sister and forget about your own apartment,* she scolded herself. But she didn't have a choice. She *had* to go stay with somebody because those nightmares were starting up again, and she didn't have the funds to afford a shrink. She threw the bowl of spaghetti away and snatched her car keys off the hook. It was way past time to do some grocery shopping. Better now than never.

Hopping into her champagne Nissan Altima, she headed for Food Mart. Inside the store, she dropped a head of lettuce into her shopping-cart, followed by two tomatoes, a cucumber, a bag of carrots, a can of olives, a bag of shredded cheese, a bag of croutons, and a bottle of blue cheese ranch dressing. That should handle her salad.

Then, she headed down the meat aisle. She picked up a tray of ground beef, planning to make her meatloaf specialty, but remembered that a few months ago, she had threw her casserole dish away because it had turned into a breeding ground for mold. Even with gloves on, she had been reluctant to touch it.

"Oh, well. I'll just buy another casserole dish." She placed the ground beef in her shopping cart and headed down the aisle that shelved the cooking utensils and cookware. To her dismay, the casserole dish that she wanted was on the highest shelf. Standing at five feet six inches, she knew she couldn't reach it. She looked around for a nearby employee and when she didn't see one, she stepped up on the bottom shelf and began to reach for it herself.

"Let me get that for you," a male voice offered.

Someone reached over her and easily lifted the ceramic casserole dish from the top shelf. "Here you go."

With the words 'thank you' already forming on her lips, Tomi turned around to face her helper and was greeted with the startling sight of those familiar, cinnamon-brown eyes. "Oh, my God."

Her unexpected appearance had startled him, too, because he dropped the ceramic dish on the tile floor. It hit hard and broke in half.

"Oh, shit!" he exclaimed, looking around to see if anyone had witnessed the accident. No one was on the aisle and, before someone could come over to inspect what had caused the loud noise, he picked up the two halves and stuffed them behind some frying pans on a lower shelf. Using his shoe, he scooted the rest of the ceramic debris beneath the rack.

"You are going to hell," Tomi told him jokingly.

"In gasoline drawers," he admitted. They laughed, and then he took the time to look at this magnificent beauty who he had thought he would never see again. She was just as beautiful as he remembered, wearing a white wife-beater, a pair of holey, paint-splattered, dark blue jogging pants, and a pair of black, fuzzy bedroom shoes. Her hair was in a wrap, and she had a blue silk scarf holding the wrap in place. Her face wore not a single stitch of make-up, but her skin seemed to glow.

"Oh, my God, don't look at me like this," she told him, covering her face. She was so embarrassed. "I just ran out the house to do some late-night grocery shopping. I didn't think I would run into anybody." *Especially not you*, she thought to herself.

"I don't see nothing wrong with how you look. Actually, I think it's kind of sexy." He lent credit to his words by gently caressing her high cheek bone with the back of his hand.

"Don't." She pulled back from his touch, but even that small a caress was too much. Already, those erotic sensations, which came to life only when she thought about this man, were beginning to stir between her legs. It was as if these feelings that had been dead inside of her for so long were starting to come to life…and the thought simultaneously scared and excited her. The part that scared her the most was that she was experiencing such intense feelings for a man whom she didn't even know his name.

"What's your name?" she blurted out, and his face broke into a smile.

"My, how the tables have turned."

"What are you talking about?" She was perturbed.

"If I'm not mistaken, I recall asking you the same question not too long ago, and got the third degree for asking. 'My name ain't none of your business,'" he mimicked her in a high pitched voice, one hand on his hip, the other waving in the air, head rolling on his neck, and eyes rolling in his head.

Tomi couldn't help but laugh at his impersonation of her. He mimicked her so well.

"See, now that's what I like to see," he said, holding his arms out to either side of him, "a smile. Was that too hard?"

"Oh shut up," she laughed, shoving him playfully. "I guess I kind of flew off the handle a little bit."

"A little bit?"

"Okay, well, maybe a little more than a little bit."

"Don't even sweat it, shorty. How 'bout we start over? We're going to wipe the slate clean and become properly introduced." He held out his hand. "Dante McKoy."

Finally, she had a name to go with the face of this man who had affected her like no other. Tomi hesitantly viewed his proffered hand. She remembered what had happened the last time they'd held hands, and she wondered if they'd feel that same current of electricity this time.

Slowly, she let her hand slide into his. And the electric shock was still there; it was like an exposed wire waiting to be touched. The electric spark flowed from his hand into hers, went up her arm, and down her spine, settling somewhere in her stomach, where it metamorphosed from electricity into hyperactive butterflies. But this time, she didn't pull her hand away. In fact, she tightened her grip, holding his hand firm in hers.

"Tomi Thompson."

"Tomi," he repeated, testing her name out on his tongue for the first time. "A unique name for a unique woman." Maintaining eye contact, he leaned forward and kissed the back of her hand. "It's a pleasure to meet you."

She licked lips that had become strangely dry. "The pleasure's all mine." Damn, if he didn't have her wetter than the Mississippi River. And the way he was looking at her, with those sexy, oval-shaped cinnamon eyes. She didn't have to be Einstein to know what he was thinking, and her thoughts were paralleling his.

The store intercom broke the magic of the moment: "Food Mart will be closing in ten minutes. Please select your final items and bring them to register three for purchase. Thank you for choosing Food Mart." The employee sounded like she was tired and wanted the shoppers to hurry up and get the hell out the store so she could go home.

"Look," Tomi said, gently removing her hand from his instead of snatching it away like she had done earlier, "I want to apologize for how I talked to you that day at the shop. I was completely out of line."

"Don't sweat it, shorty."

"No, I feel really bad about the way I treated you. You hadn't done anything wrong. You forgive me?"

Craning his neck to inspect the contents of her shopping cart, he replied, "I'll forgive you under one circumstance."

"And what's that?"

He held up the spaghetti TV dinner in his hand, then looked back inside her shopping cart full of food. "I got the munchies and an empty fridge. This right here ain't gonna cut it. You gotta feed me."

"Feed you?"

"Feed me for forgiveness." He scrunched his face and poked out his lips, giving a terrible impersonation of a sad puppy dog. "Please."

Invite him over.

That thought seemed to materialize out of nowhere. It was disturbing how easily the thought had come to her—and how persistent it was.

Invite him over.

Tomi was shaking her head no, whether mentally or physically, she wasn't sure, but she knew she was rejecting the idea. Using her mind as the battlefield, an inner war raged between her id and ego.

Invite him over, now, her mind demanded.

No, she told herself, *I'm not ready for a male friend. I'm not ready to make that step just yet.*

What are the odds that he and you would end up at the same place, at the same time, for the exact same reason? It's not a coincident; it's receiving a second chance. Go for it.

I don't want to be responsible for him, she tried to rationalize. *I can't do it again.*

The smile on Dante's face was starting to recede, and he nonchalantly tapped the side of her shopping cart with the spaghetti dinner in a departing manner. "See you around, Tomi," he said, somewhat abjectly turning to leave.

"Wait!"

He turned to face her. "Yeah?"

"I, uh, uh…" Tomi didn't know what to say. He was looking at her expectantly, almost hopefully. She was speechless. All she knew was that she couldn't let him walk out her life again—not without a fight (and what she was fighting for, she had no idea). She said the words before she could stop herself. "Do you want to come over to my house tonight? You know, for dinner." He didn't say anything, so she quickly added, "I mean, only if you don't have anything else to do, because if you do, I completely understand and I—"

"Tomi."

"Yes?" She was so glad he had stopped her from having to embarrass herself anymore than she had already done.

"You go grab the rest of your groceries; I'm going to go put this back. I'll meet you at register three."

"Okay."

As he jogged off down the aisle, she watched him go, and wondered what and the hell had she gotten herself into.

"You have a nice place."

"Thanks." She still could not believe that he was actually in her house, standing in her kitchen.

Dante looked around, missing nothing. Her kitchen was small and sufficient with a black, smooth-surface stove, a black refrigerator, a chrome, two-sided sink, and a black, marble-topped island surrounded by three stools with jungle-print cushions. His eyes traveled into her living room. Her living room was small and compact consisting of a cream-colored chair and love-seat, a small, circular wooden table with a glass top, and a 32-inch screen TV setting on a TV stand that matched the wooden table. The only decorations were tall, plastic jungle plants strategically placed in each corner of the room, and matching jungle print wall-paper in her kitchen. A beautiful, live bamboo plant was the centerpiece of her dining table. She had framed pictures of brown tigers, and white tigers with blue eyes decorating her walls, and an enlarged family portrait hung on the wall above her brick fire place.

"We took this picture last year," she told him when he walked over to the picture to get a better look. "That's my sister Niya; she's the oldest of us all." Niya had shoulder length hair, almost the color of Tomi's, but a little darker. She wore small silver-framed glasses.

"That's Kelise." She pointed to the woman with short brown-tipped locks. Tomi and she could go for twins if it weren't for their different hair-styles. "Ever read the magazine BSC, *Brothas and Sistaz of Color*?"

"Nope. Heard about it; why?"

"That's her magazine. She runs it."

"Word? That's what's up."

"And that's our mommy and daddy," she told him, pointing to the older woman and man seated with smiling faces in between the three sisters.

Dante decided that she looked more like her father than mother. She had her mother's cat eyes, but everything else were attributes from her father. They had the same long, slim nose and the same facial structure. Her mother's face was short and round, while her father's was long and lean like all his daughters'.

"You have a beautiful family," he told her. "I can see a lot of love there."

His statement was complete, yet it sounded unfinished, as if those few words only skimmed the surface. Instead of questioning him, she let it go. She didn't want to 'nose' into his personal life. If he wanted her to know more, he'd tell her.

"Thanks," she said, and her stomach growled loud and long, one of those 'I refuse to be ignored' growls.

"Let us start cooking before you fall dead of starvation," Dante teased, eyeing her stomach warily.

She threw a light punch at his chest. "You always got something to say," she complained, washing her hands after he had finished washing his.

"Hey, don't get mad at me. That's your stomach over there speaking in tongues."

Tomi shoved him again, and he stumbled into the island, laughing at her lighthearted anger. "You's a violent little somebody, ain't you? Why don't you handle the meat; I'll cut the vegetables. I don't think you need to have possession of a sharp knife right about now."

While engaging in small talk, Dante chopped up the vegetables for the salad, and Tomi made the fixings for her meat-loaf. About an hour and a half later, seated on black cushioned stools, they indulged themselves with a delicious salad, topped with walnuts and raspberry vinaigrette, juicy meatloaf, which contained onions, garlic, and bell peppers, and buttermilk biscuits that Dante had made from scratch.

"So," Tomi began, "what do you do for a living?"

"Construction work." He bit into the tender meat-loaf. "God, this is good," he exclaimed, and his appraisal of her cooking skills made her smile. "Right now," he continued, "we're building a new housing complex behind South Brooke High School."

"Oh, so that's what's going on over there? I saw all those felled trees and I thought they were building another shopping center or something. You know how it is down here in Sunny Side, Georgia. Every time you turn around, they're either knocking something down or putting something up."

"True dat, true dat. What about you?" He took a sip of sparkling white grape juice from his wine glass. "What made you decide to be a tattoo artist?"

"Well," she stabbed at her salad before continuing, "I've always liked to do hair and draw, so it was either a tattoo artist or a barber."

"You can cut hair?"

"Can a dog bark?"

"Damn, girl! You can cook, do tattoos, cut hair—what can you not do?"

"There's not much I can't do," she admitted without sounding the least bit cocky or conceited.

"How 'bout you give me a shape up when we finish eating."

Tomi smiled. "I can do that," she told him. "You need a haircut, bad. Head looks like day-old taco meat." She burst out laughing.

"Oh, you got jokes now, huh?"

"Hey, you started it."

"Okay, okay. I'll let you have that one."

They finished up their meal and washed dishes together: Tomi, the washer, and Dante, the dryer. Then, Tomi went in her room and got her hair-cutting kit. She sat a chair in the middle of her living room floor.

"Sit," she told him. He obeyed. She pulled out the plastic blue cape and tied it around his neck, then she started cutting. "You want a fade like the one you had at the shop?"

"Yeah."

As Tomi clipped away at his hair, he thought about how much fun they were having, laughing and joking, and just getting to know each other. He didn't have this type of fun with Denise. If you looked up the word 'boring' in the dictionary, you would see a picture of them right beside it. They had been together for five years, but after their daughter's death, they'd gradually begin to fall apart. Denise wasn't solely at fault for the deterioration of their relationship. Dante wasn't blind to the fact that the guilt of their daughter's death had caused him to draw inward. His guilt had become a sore, and like a dog with an injured paw, he'd wanted to crawl into a corner and lick his wounds until the pain subsided.

Deep down inside, he felt as if he was betraying Denise by enjoying Tomi so much, but, technically, they weren't an item. He had no ties to Denise, but she refused to accept that fact. Many a times he had told her he wanted out, but she refused to let him go. It had never mattered before because there was no other woman that attracted him to the point where he wanted to get to know her on any level besides a quick toss in the sheets…until Tomi.

It didn't take Tomi a full fifteen minutes to hook him up. She went in her room and returned with two hand held mirrors. Handing him one mirror, she held the other behind his head. "What do you think?"

"Damn, girl. You're better than my barber. How 'bout if I start coming to you to get G'd up?"

"It's going to cost you."

"How much?"

"Twenty."

"A deal."

"Now," she said, setting the mirrors aside and standing in front of him, "I've got to get a hold of this face. It looks a pure mess."

"Guess my face and your attire have something in common."

"Thought you said I looked sexy."

"Meant every word."

Tomi glanced down at him and caught the heated gaze that he directed at her. Lighthearted teasing, she could accept; desire-laced innuendos, she couldn't. She didn't know how to respond to those. She chose to pretend as if she didn't understand the meaning of that look.

"Tilt your head back," she ordered, inclining his head at a forty-five degree angle. She trimmed him up and smiled at her handiwork. "Take a look."

She handed him one of the mirrors and he nodded his head, rubbing his chin between his thumb and pointer finger. "Nice. Nice. You got skills for real."

"Don't I know it."

She reached around him to remove his cape, unintentionally pressing her breasts against his chin. Dante inhaled the scent of her peach perfume and felt his penis harden.

"I'm sorry!" She jumped back as she realized that her breasts had been pressed all in his face. "I didn't even realize…" Her face turned red, and she looked away.

"It's okay," he assured her with a laugh. "I didn't mind it at all."

"I'm sure you didn't."

He leaned forward. "Why are you always so apologetic, Tomi? Relax. I'm not going to bite."

"I know," she told him, folding the cape carefully so that no hairs would fall on the carpet. "It's just that…I'm not use to being around males like this. To be honest, you're the first male, outside of family, to ever step foot in my house. Usually, I don't let men get this close."

"You want to talk about it?"

She shook her head. "No." Her reply was a whisper.

Trying to change the subject, she told him to turn his head to the side so she could see how his tattoo was coming along. She dropped to her knees and held his chin at an angle as she studied her artwork. The tattoo looked perfect. The swelling was gone, and it was completely healed.

"Looks good," she told him.

"Not better than you." He took the hand that was holding his chin and kissed the pad of each fingertip before placing a soft kiss in her palm.

"Dante…" his name was a gasp of air on her lips.

"You are so beautiful, Tomi." He was staring at her with those intense, sincere cinnamon eyes. She couldn't look away if she tried; she was hypnotized.

She felt him leaning towards her in his chair, knew that he was about to kiss her, and was frozen to the floor. He locked his fingers through hers with one hand, and held her chin in place with the other. She wasn't trapped; she could pull away if she wanted to.

"God, you are beautiful." He was close enough that she could feel his breath on her lips. Her stomach was jumping with anxiety and fear. She wanted this kiss, but she didn't. She wanted him, but she couldn't.

Her cell phone ring was loud, shrill, and totally unexpected. *Saved by the bell*, she thought as she scrambled to her feet and ran in the kitchen where her phone was located. She answered it on the third ring.

"Hello?"

"Girl, you sound breathless. Did I interrupt something?" It was Niya.

"No, Niya. What's up?"

"You wouldn't believe me if I told you."

"What? What happened?" Tomi placed her elbows on the counter and leaned forward. She wondered what could be important enough for her sister to call her at one o'clock in the morning.

Dante entered the kitchen, stood behind Tomi, and wrapped his arms around her small waist. He pulled her apple bottom against his manhood and held it there. She swatted at him to leave, but he buried his head in her warm neck and held her, turning them around so that now, he leaned against the counter, and she leaned against him. Tingling sensations started in her belly and made their way up her body, settling in the spot where his wet lips brushed against her neck.

"Tomi Lietta Thompson, are you even listening to me?"

"Yes. I mean, no. I mean, start over. I wasn't listening." She couldn't think straight, not with Dante's soft lips kissing down her neck and across her sensitive shoulders. Covering the mouthpiece with one hand, she mouthed at Dante to go away, but he ignored her request.

"I know you don't have a man over there," her sister accused after listening to her sister's background for a minute.

"No, I don't," Tomi lied with ease. "What are you doing calling me this early in the morning, anyway? And why are you whispering?"

"I called Kelise, but Ricardo is over there. You know when he comes home, it's all about him. I had to talk to someone about this."

Tomi felt Dante sink his teeth into the soft skin just behind her right shoulder—one of her erogenous zones; she bit her lip to keep from making any sound. He pulled her closer to him, and when she felt that hard rock pressing into her back, her heartbeat accelerated at a mile per minute.

"Tomi, I think Phillip is cheating on me."

"Why…why do you think that?" She was breathless. Dante was rubbing that hot, wet place through the front of her pants, and she felt like she was melting in his hand.

"He's in the bathroom right now, talking on his cell phone. His cell started vibrating, and I guess he thought I was sleep. I have my ear against the door right now, but I can't hear anything. He has the water running to cover up his voice."

"Oh." Dante was nibbling on her ear while rubbing between her legs, and it took all her willpower not to moan aloud.

"Oh? That's all you have to say? Oh?"

"Niya, I…I gotta go. I'll call you back, okay?" She flipped her cell phone closed, tossed it on the counter, and turned to face Dante.

"I didn't invite you over to have sex," she informed him, tracing his bottom lip with her finger.

His voice was low and deep as he said, "No one said anything about sex."

He had hot desire written all over his face as he pulled her against him and fused her mouth to his. She did moan this time, and she kissed him back with a passion that she never knew existed. He held her head in place as his tongue thrust deep inside her mouth, mimicking the moves that his lower body was making against hers. Tomi felt her knees go weak, and she held on tightly to him in order to remain standing.

Maneuvering them around so that she was backed against the stove, he sucked on her tongue until she felt her panties melt into a pool of nothing. Finally, he released her lips only to kiss down her neck. She held the back of his head while he sucked on her skin, so many thoughts racing through her mind. She knew what was happening, and she knew she'd probably hate herself in the morning, but for now, she would throw caution to the wind, clear her thoughts of any inhibitions, free her mind.

Dante was aware of her release of control, because her body became acquiescent in his hands; wherever he touched her, her body responded accordingly. He lifted up the edge of her wife-beater, revealing her black laced bra.

"Dante," she moaned his name, unsure if it was encouragement to go, or a plea for him to stop.

"So beautiful," he said once her breasts were free from their lacy cups. That day at the parlor, he had wondered how she would look minus the white camisole, and he wasn't disappointed. Her breasts were round, firm C-cups; her areolas were dark circles against her butter-toned skin, and her nipples were erect, pointing at his lips in a tempting invitation.

When he enveloped one hard brown nipple in his fiery mouth, Tomi thought she would pass out from sheer pleasure. Her sex life had been none existent for so long, too long, and she didn't know if she could take what he was giving her; the sensations were too intense.

As he suckled her breast, a flashback went through her mind.

She was eighteen, and she was sitting in the passenger seat of Jonathan's car.

Dante released that nipple only so he could pleasure the other one.

The cold black metal of the gun's barrel was pressed against her temple.

Tomi moaned as his tongue worked its magic; she couldn't think straight as he nibbled on the sensitive skin beneath her breast, then used his tongue to trace a path to her belly ring.

Fear was not only a feeling but a bitter taste at the back of her throat. She remembered all the times Jonathan had playfully told her that if they ever broke up, he couldn't take seeing her with anyone else. She thought about all the times he had said, "If I can't have you, no one can."

As Dante placed wet kisses down her flat, smooth stomach, edging closer and closer to the waistband of her pants, her vaginal muscles clenched in anticipation. His tongue dipped into her navel, and he tugged gently at her hanging belly ring with his lips. She was as wet as the Atlantic Ocean. He could smell the womanly scent of her wetness, and it made his penis become even more erect.

Jonathan took the barrel of the gun and stuck it in his mouth.

"Oh my God, Jonathan, no. Please don't do this. Please don't—"

Dante reached for the waistband of her jogging pants, and Tomi didn't stop him. She couldn't have stopped him if she wanted to. If he didn't touch her there soon, she felt like she would explode.

Tomi watched as he squeezed his eyes shut and pulled the trigger.

It sounded more like a deafening boom of thunder than a gun shot. She had her eyes squeezed tight, but at the booming sound of death, her eyes flew open, and the contents of her stomach boiled, threatening an upheaval.

As she took in the sight of his concave, gore-filled head, bile rose in her throat and, holding her stomach with one hand, she vomited on the passenger floor. Once she had finished, she opened her mouth again, expecting another flood of vomit, but instead, a shrill scream escaped her trembling lips. She staggered out of Jonathan's car, fell on the ground beside the front tire, covered her face with shaking fingers, and screamed, and screamed, and screamed, and screamed.

"Tomi, what's wrong? Did I hurt you?" Dante couldn't understand why she was screaming. He had reached for her waistband and, as he had started to lower her pants, she had started screaming and wouldn't stop. He pulled her to him and held her protectively against his chest. "Tomi, baby, what's wrong? What's wrong?" But she wouldn't stop screaming.

"The blood," she screamed. "Get it off me." She rubbed at her face, arms, and hands. She kept wiping her hands on her jogging pants, back and forth, back and forth. "Get it off me. The blood!"

"What blood?" Dante asked, looking all over her, but he didn't see a spot of blood anywhere.

Finally, Tomi looked at him, really looked at him, and realization settled on her face. He was not Jonathan. She was not eighteen. And she wasn't covered in blood. It was all in her mind.

"Oh, God," she said, realizing that she'd just had one of her flashback episodes. "Oh, God." She covered her face and began to cry.

Dante grabbed the hand-towel off the stove handle and used it to conceal her bare breasts. She held the towel in place as he pulled her into his arms, kissing her forehead gently.

"It's okay, Tomi. I got you. I won't let anybody hurt you, okay?"

Tomi cried in his arms until she didn't have any tears left to cry. Once she had regained some type of control over her emotions, she pulled away from his comforting embrace. "I'm sorry, Dante. I didn't mean to…I'm so embarrassed…I'm sorry…"

"No, I'm sorry," he cut in. "It's my fault. I shouldn't have let it get this far. You want me to go?"

"No," she told him, shaking her head. "Can you spend the night, please? I just need you to hold me."

She sounded like a frightened child, and Dante felt the overwhelming urge to kill whoever it was that had caused her this pain. He picked her wife-beater up from the floor and pulled it over her head. Then, he lifted her in his arms and, cradling her as if she were a baby, carried her to her room. He placed her on the tall, King-size bed and lay down beside her. She rolled over to him, laid her head on his chest, and was fast asleep in no time. Dante, on the other hand, didn't get a wink of sleep. He stayed up all night, holding Tomi, kissing her forehead, and comforting her whenever she awoke from a bad dream.

Chapter Four

"I was so embarrassed," Tomi told Kelise as they headed to Kelise's candy-apple red Chevrolet Cavalier. "When I woke up," she opened the car door and slid into the passenger seat, "he was gone, and he had left a letter on my pillow. It said that he knew I wouldn't want to see him when I woke up, so he left before I was fully awake. He told me that he was sorry at how far he had allowed last night to go, and if I wanted to talk, he would be willing to listen. He left his phone number."

"Did you call?"

"No."

"Call him."

"No!"

"Why not?" Kelise asked, giving her sister a hard stare. "Why do you have to be so stubborn?"

"I'm not being stubborn," she argued, "I'm just…embarrassed." She ran a hand through her curls. "I mean, damn, Kelise, I can't look him in the eye ever again. He probably thinks I'm easy, how far I let him go, and then with my little flashback episode, he probably thinks I'm psychotic, too. A psychotic, easy chick. That has a nice ring to it, don't you think?"

"No, you're full of shit; that's what you are."

"Whatever. Enough about me. I heard that Ricardo is home—"

"Was home."

"He's gone again? That fast?"

"Yeah. He has a meeting in Toronto, Canada. He had to leave at five this morning so he could catch his plane on time."

"When is he coming back?"

"At the end of this month."

Tomi didn't say anything, but Kelise could read her sister's mind. It seemed like Ricardo and she spent more time apart than they did together. And it seemed that whenever they were together, all they did was have some quick, I-missed-you sex before he disappeared for another month or two.

She had brought up their wedding date again last night and, as usual, all Ricardo had said was, "As soon as I take vacation, we'll get married. I promise, baby." He had been saying that for the pass two years, now, and he still hadn't taken his vacation. There was no doubt in her mind that she came second to his job, but she understood how much his work meant to him. He was the one who had helped her get her magazine started. He had backed her up on her dream career, so it was only fair for her to do the same. But sometimes, she got lonely.

Kelise turned into Niya's driveway and parked behind Phillip's gray, 1979 pick-up truck.

"Damn, Phillip's here," Tomi complained as she stepped out the car. "I don't know what Niya sees in him."

"Must be his good looks and the way he throws it to her. I can't see any other reason."

They walked to the door and rang the doorbell once before letting themselves in.

"Aunt Tomi and Auntie Kelise is here!" Kadeesha exclaimed, running to get a hug from both of them.

"It's 'are here,'" Niya corrected her daughter, "Aunt Tomi and Auntie Kelise *are* here."

"This is not grammar school," Tomi informed her sister while picking up her four-year-old niece.

"My daughter is not going to go around speaking that Ebonics mess. If she's going to talk around me, she's going to talk right."

"Whatever." Kelise dropped her purse on Niya's crimson-colored sofa. "I have to use your bathroom. Girl, I have to piss like a race horse." She disappeared down the hallway, practically running to the bathroom.

"What are you doing today?" Tomi asked her niece, putting her down.

"Grandma is coming to pick me and Elijah up—"

"Elijah and me," Niya corrected from the kitchen.

"—and we're going to the fair. I already went once, but I'm going again. I won two gold fishies, but they're already dead, and I won a big brown and black stuffed doggie, it's really soft, Aunt Tomi, you want to feel it, it's in my room.

And I rode four rides, but I couldn't get on the rest 'cause the man said I wasn't tall enough, I'm tall enough Aunt Tomi—the doctor said I've grown three inches taller. And one of the rides I got on was *sca*-ry; it turned upside down and went in circles, round, and round, and round, Aunt Tomi, I was so scared, I thought I was going to fall out, but I didn't and—"

With her talkative niece two steps behind her heels, Tomi headed into the kitchen where Niya was washing dishes.

"Where's Phillip?" Tomi asked her sister.

"Upstairs taking a shower. He has to work today."

"I don't get it," Tomi said, taking the drying towel off Niya's shoulder and drying the dishes. "Why in the world did he go to college and get a degree in accounting only to work white-collar jobs for the rest of his life?"

"Who knows?" Niya shrugged her shoulders. "I don't even want to talk about him right now. Kadeesha, go get Elijah from the basketball court. Tell him I said to shower and be ready by the time Grandma gets here."

"Yes ma'am." She slid into her sandals and hurried outside.

"Anyway, I want to know what in God's name had you so busy last night that you couldn't talk to me?"

Tomi blushed and placed the dried silverware into their allotted places. "I had a little company over."

"Company? Not Tomi!" She looked at her little sister in disbelief. "So who is this guy?"

"His name is Dante, and we're just friends."

"Just friends?" Niya gave her a dubious stare. "If he was just your friend, he wouldn't have been in your house at that late an hour."

"I had a flashback while he was over."

Niya paused while washing dishes and looked over at her sister sympathetically. "Was it bad?"

"The worse one yet," she admitted.

"Oh, God. What did he do?"

"He spent the night over and held me until I fell asleep."

A genuine smile spread across Niya's face. "He's a sweetheart. He might be the one," she said with a wink.

"We're just friends," Tomi reiterated.

"Hey, Tomi," Phillip acknowledged her presence as he strolled into the kitchen wearing his Arby's uniform. "How you doing?"

"I'm good," Tomi replied without enthusiasm.

Phillip went in for a kiss on his wife's lips, but Niya turned her head to the side. He settled for a kiss on her cheek. "I get off at six," he told her. "You want to go somewhere and talk then?"

"I have nothing to say to you, Phillip." Her words were clipped and cold.

Phillip glanced over at Tomi, an embarrassed expression on his face. He leaned over and whispered something into Niya's ear. She shrugged her shoulders. "Whatever."

"You have a good day, Tomi," he told her, placing his cap on his head. He headed outside.

Kelise entered the kitchen and went straight for the fridge. "Who made this Kool-Aid? You or Elijah?" she asked, removing a pitcher full of red liquid from the refrigerator.

Niya replied, "Elijah."

"Never mind," she said, returning the pitcher to its spot in the fridge, "that's not Kool-Aid; that's strawberry syrup. So what happened last night with you and Phillip? I got your message, but I was a little…busy."

"I bet you were. Seems like everybody was getting their freak on last night except for me; and I'm the married one!"

"Hey, I was two months backed up."

"And that's too much information," Tomi informed her.

"Girl, he had me speaking in Spanish."

"Eww!"

"Okay, guys," Niya cut in, "enough about Kelise's sex life. Back to me and my problems." She used the sprayer to clear the sink of all the soapsuds. "Phillip lied his ass off last night. He's claiming that it was his sister on the phone. I asked him if it was his sister on the phone, then why did he have to go in the bathroom to talk to her; he said he didn't want to wake me up. I asked him why did he have the sink on full blast; he claims that he was brushing his teeth. Brushing his teeth at two o'clock in the morning. How dumb do I look?"

"Lies. All lies." Kelise rolled her eyes. "He is so full of—"

"Mommy, Mommy, Mommy! Grandma's here," Kadeesha exclaimed, running into the kitchen.

"Where's your brother?"

"Upstairs getting ready."

"Well, come give me a kiss. And tell Grandma that Mama said to call her later."

"Okay." Kadeesha kissed her mother and both her aunts before running out the door.

A few moments later, Elijah came stampeding down the steps.

"What did your father say about running in the house, Elijah!"

"Sorry, Ma." The boy slowed down from a full run to a fast-paced stride. "Hey Aunt Tomi and Auntie Kelise. Bye Aunt Tomi and Auntie Kelise."

"That boy is a mess," Tomi said, smiling at her nephew as he closed the front door behind him.

"Be good," Niya called out after him. "So, girls," she turned to face her sisters, "we have a whole Saturday all to ourselves. What do you want to do?"

"First, we've got to go to the mall. I saw the cutest shirt that I have to have!" Kelise told them.

"I need a manicure," Tomi said, looking down at her nails.

"Me, too," Niya agreed, reaching for her purse. "Okay, first we'll go to the mall, then we'll all go get a manicure and pedicure, and we'll end the day with a trip to the spa."

"And who's paying for all this?" Kelise asked.

"Girl, please. Incase you're forgetting, a sister did just get signed partner. Hello!"

CHAPTER FIVE

Dante awoke with a climax from his wet dream of Tomi…or so he thought he did.

Denise collapsed against his chest, completely out of breath. "Damn, Dante. We haven't done that in a while! But it was well worth the wait."

"Denise? What the hell are you doing here?" Dante was pissed. The whole time he thought he was giving Tomi the best of him, he was actually throwing it to Denise? And unprotected at that! He pushed her off him and stood to his feet, holding the black and white striped comforter against his waist. "What the hell are you doing here?" he asked again.

"Calm down, shit." She sat up, and the white sheet fell from her shoulders, exposing her small, brown-tipped breasts. "What's the big deal, anyway?"

"What's the big deal?" Dante roared. He picked up a pillow that had fallen to the floor and threw it at her. "Cover yourself up." She did so grudgingly.

"What's the big deal?" he asked again. "You broke into my house and made me have sex with you."

"In other words I raped you?"

"Pretty much."

Denise made a face. "First off, nigga, I didn't break into your house; I do have a key. And secondly, I did *not* make you have sex with me. You did that on your own free-will, and it was damn good, if I might add." He might've been moaning another woman's name, but if it took him calling out another woman to get some more of that good-loving, she would not object.

Dante sat down on the edge of the bed and looked at her. "Did I nut in you?" he asked. She nodded her head, and he dropped his. "Oh, shit. Oh, shit."

"I mean, damn, what's the big deal?" she asked again, starting to get angry. "We're together now, and we might as well—"

"What makes you think that we're together?" he interrupted her. "We are not a couple, but you can't seem to get that through your thick ass head."

"Then why do you still call me 'baby'? And why do we go places holding hands?" she asked, her eyes tearing up. "And why do you still kiss me? Incase you're forgetting, our daughter is dead, Dante, and—"

"Denise, don't start that again—"

"No, you listen to me." She stood to her feet, but covered her nakedness with one of the bed sheets. "I was at work, Dante, and you were supposed to be watching her."

"It's not my fault." He wanted to cover his ears and yell at the top of his lungs to block out her words. She was saying everything that his conscience accused him of, and he didn't want to hear it. In his mind, he knew that there was nothing he could've done to prevent his daughter from dying of SIDS, but that still didn't stop him from feeling guilty.

"I'm sorry, Denise," he told her, pulling her to him. He kissed her forehead, her lips. "I'm sorry, baby."

"It's okay, baby," she told him, rubbing his head as he silently cried on her shoulder. "As long as we have each other, it'll be okay."

After they had both calmed down, he jumped into the shower, and she went into the kitchen to make him breakfast. Wearing only his boxers, Dante sat on the edge of the bed, thinking. He didn't know what to do. There was a possibility that Denise could be pregnant by him, and he still hadn't heard a word from Tomi since the night that he went to her crib, got freaky, then witnessed her lose it.

He looked over at the answering machine to see if the red light was blinking. It was not. No new messages; no message from Tomi. He checked the caller ID to see if he had any missed calls. No missed calls; no call from Tomi.

What's going on? he wondered for the umpteenth time, setting the cordless phone back on its base. It had been a whole week now since their unplanned rendezvous, and he still hadn't heard a word from her. He didn't know if she wasn't calling him because she was mad at him for taking advantage of the situation, or if she was just too embarrassed to face him. Whatever the reason, he was missing her like crazy. Every since the day that he'd gotten a tattoo, not a day went by that she didn't cross his mind. Too bad the feelings weren't mutual.

But they had to be on the same page, he thought as he headed into his kitchen. Why else would she have responded to his kisses and caresses the way she had? He felt himself getting hard just thinking about the way she had responded to him, and he quickly changed his train of thought.

Denise was standing in front of the oven with sausage frying in one pan, and cheese eggs cooking in the other. She had on a pair of his Garfield boxers, and she wore her black tank-top. Denise wasn't an ugly woman—she was far from that. She had a fair complexion; if she had been a born a shade lighter, she could've passed for a white woman. She had naturally gray and hazel eyes, and her hair was black, silky, and long; those long curly locks hung low enough to caress the middle of her back. She was a beautiful woman, but Dante wasn't feeling her like that anymore. He wished she would accept the fact and stop throwing their deceased daughter in his face every time he tried to let her go for good.

There was a time when he had loved her more than life itself, but once their daughter had died, it seemed as if the part of him that adored her had died as well. Their daughter's death had caused him to open his eyes and really see Denise for what she was—a conniving, scheming, stubborn woman who was more in love with herself than anything else, and who thought the world revolved around her middle finger. Inspite of her negative personality traits, he still cared about her, but love wasn't a part of the equation. Not anymore.

She hummed as she pulled a plate from an above cabinet and filled it with two sausages, a steaming pile of eggs, and two Pillsbury biscuits from the oven. As she sat the plate in front of him, she asked, "Who's Tomi, Dante?"

Her question caught him off guard. He looked up at her, wondering how she knew Tomi's name.

As if reading his mind, she said, "You kept calling out her name while you were fucking me. Just wanted to know who she was."

Saying nothing, Dante dug hungrily into the pile of eggs and took a big bite from one of the juicy sausage patties. Denise placed her plate on the table and sat down directly across from him. She crossed her arms against her chest and asked again, "Who is she, Dante? One of your hoes?"

He gave her a warning look, non-verbally telling her to watch herself.

"Then who is she?" Denise demanded, determined to get an answer out of him one way or another.

He washed down the food with a swig of orange juice before replying, "She's a friend."

"How serious are y'all?"

"Damn, can I eat in peace?" he asked, holding his hands out in a questioning manner.

"Not until you tell me who she is to you."

"Like I said, she's a friend." He finished eating and dropped his plate into the sink. Denise still hadn't touched her food. "I have to get ready for work," he told her. "When I get out the shower, I want you gone; and I want you to leave my house key on the table. And," he added, "I don't want any more surprise visits from you. Do you hear me?"

She didn't say a thing, but her eyes were poison-tipped daggers. Dante stalked off to the back room to take a shower, and Denise watched him as he walked away. His muscles rippled in his broad back with each step that he took, and his boxers hung low on his tight, little plump ass. Even after five years of being together, she could still look at him and get wet. He was *her* man. And no Tomi, Tama, or Tanya would take him from her. If she had to beat a bitch's ass, she wouldn't hesitate to do it. Dante Myles McKoy was her man, and she'd make sure it stayed that way.

*   *   *   *

The boss man called out, "Break!" and Dante could've passed out with relief. It was hot as hell today—that June sun was no play. He was sweaty and tired, and he still had four more hours to go. Jumping into his Camry, he headed to the store and bought the biggest bottle of water that they sold. Then, he headed to the one place he had been thinking about all day. Expressions Tattoo Parlor.

He hoped Tomi wouldn't think he was stalking her, but he had to see her. Inside, two people were sitting in the waiting area. The young white girl was looking at pictures of tongue-piercings while the black girl with micro-braids was looking through a row of tattoo pictures on the wall.

A white man walked from the back with a fresh tattoo of a dragon on his arm. Tomi was following behind him. "Remember to keep your shirtsleeve pulled up; you don't want it rubbing against your tattoo," she reminded him as he left. "Are you next?" Her question was directed to the white girl.

"Yeah," the girl replied.

Dante looked at Tomi and his heart upped its pace. She was the picture of pure perfection. She had her milk-coffee hair in a wrap, and she wore a small amount of make-up on her face. With no bra, she wore a stretchy yellow blouse that clung to her breasts, outlining her dark nipples, those same chocolate pebbles that he had devoured not too long ago. He felt his penis hardening and he changed his train of thought before his woody became evident to anyone who glanced his way.

Her legs were three-quarters covered with a pair of skin-tight khaki capris that had an intricate design embroidered in yellow and green thread down one leg. She wore a pair of wooden stiletto-heeled sandals that laced up her ankles, and displayed her French-tipped, pedicured toes. Dante had the strong urge to back her against the wall and kiss her until his name became a chant on those juicy lips.

"What are you getting?" Tomi asked the girl.

"A tongue piercing."

"Hold on for a sec." She turned and hollered into the back, "Max!"

A few seconds later, a white guy, with a bright purple, green-tipped Mohawk and tattoos on every visible part of his body except his face, appeared from the back. "Yeah?"

"You have a tongue-piercing. Go with him," she told the girl.

The girl curiously eyed the man's strange appearance, shrugged her shoulders, and disappeared into a room with him.

"And what are you getting?"

"I want a tattoo of Pooh bear on my shoulder," the black girl told her. "It's number G32."

"Okay. Walk straight down that little hallway and wait for me in the room on your right."

"Okay." The girl stood to her feet and followed Tomi's directions.

Tomi turned to face Dante. "So you're stalking me now?" she asked, smiling to show that she was only half serious.

Dante's face showed his surprise. "How'd you know I was standing over here?"

She wiggled her nose. "I could smell you. Sweat and Eternity—not a good combination." She couldn't help but tease him. Sweaty, tired, and dirty looking, he still had that underlying sex appeal that she found so tempting.

He stepped from the shadows, and she saw that he wore steel-toed boots and was covered in sawdust. "You must be on break."

"Yeah," he told her, asking her without words if he could take a seat. She shrugged her shoulders, and he sat down in one of the chairs. "I wanted to see you. I haven't heard from you in a while. You never called." He sounded wounded.

"I'm sorry," she apologized, unable to meet his eyes. "I've been meaning to call you...but I've been really busy."

"I bet you have." His voice was dripping with sarcasm.

"Dante, it's not even like that," she started to explain.

"Then what is it?" He was being vulnerable again, those eyes that she loved so much opened to the point where she could see into his very soul. "I thought we both were feeling each other. Was I wrong?"

"No, Dante. I do like you. I just…" She shifted from foot to foot. "Dante, I was embarrassed," she finally admitted. "I didn't want you to see me have one of my breakdowns."

Dante reached for her hand and held it against his lips. "Tomi, I told you, I'm here for you."

"I know, but…" She took her hand from his. "I have to get back here and do this woman's tattoo. Can you give me about twenty minutes?"

"Yeah, I don't have to be back at work until one-thirty."

"Okay. I'll do her tattoo and, if Max can cover for me, we can go somewhere and talk. Cool?"

"Cool."

She headed to the back, and Dante watched, entranced by the curves of her body and the sway of her hips. Tomi was Maya Angelou's definition of a phenomenal woman. She returned with purse in hand. "You ready?"

"Let's go." They headed to his Camry, and he held the passenger door for her as she got inside. "Want to go to Big Scoops?" he asked.

"Mmm," she licked her lips, "I love ice cream, especially when it's this hot outside."

"What kind do you like?"

"Chocolate-chip cookie dough." She licked her lips again. "What about you?"

"Mint chocolate." She made an ugly face. "What's wrong with mint chocolate? I'd rather eat mint chocolate than some nasty, raw cookie dough any day."

"Oh, whatever," Tomi told him. "Don't knock it 'til you've tried it."

"Same to you."

"I tried mint chocolate, and it is not a hot item." She pointed a finger down her throat to show him what she thought about it. "You ain't got no taste."

"I must have a little taste. I'm talking to you, ain't I?" Tomi didn't have a smart reply for him this time. He pulled up at Big Scoops and hopped out the car. "This'll only take a minute," he promised her.

When he returned, he held one waffle cone, and all she could see was a humongous glob of mint-chocolate ice cream glistening on the top. "Dante," she groaned as he slid into the driver seat, "I'm not eating that. Why didn't you get me some cookie dough?"

"I did," he told her. He twisted the cone around, and on the other side, there was an equally large scoop of cookie dough ice cream.

"Dante."

"Come on, Tomi. It's not a big deal. You eat your side, and I'll eat mine."

She was hesitant for only a second more, and finally she placed her hand over his, pulled the ice cream cone near her lips, and tasted the cold treat as he did the same to the opposite side.

"This is too good," she exclaimed, eating the ice cream fast before it had a chance to melt. She hadn't had ice cream since Kadeesha's birthday party in January.

They ate away at the ice cream, talking, and making wise-cracks on each other until the ice cream had disappeared and there was only their cold lips remaining. Tomi's large eyes met his smaller ones.

"You got a little bit of ice cream right there," he told her, pointing at the corner of her mouth.

"Where? Here?" Her small pink tongue darted out to catch the ice cream, and Dante felt the awakening of his right-hand man. The thought of her wrapping that little pink tongue around him was enough to drive any man crazy. He groaned aloud.

"Let me help you." His voice dropped an octave as he leaned over and licked the ice cream from the corner of her lips. She didn't hesitate to find his tongue with hers. Her arms snaked around his neck, and she pulled him close as he kissed her into ecstasy, leaving her breathless.

She was the first to pull away, and she looked out the window while fanning herself with her hand.

Dante's breathing was hard and ragged as he said, "Tomi, what are you doing to me?" His had went down to the crotch of his pants and he rubbed himself, making a face as if he was in pain.

Growing bold, she reached over and pulled his face to hers, kissing him gently. "You taste like mint chocolate," she whispered into his mouth.

"Is that a bad thing?" he asked.

"Nope." She sucked at his bottom lip. "Not one bit."

"I thought you said you didn't like mint chocolate."

"I changed my mind."

Her hand dropped to his belt buckle and he grabbed her wrist to keep her hand still. "Don't go down there," he warned her. "If you so much as touch it, I'm going to bust."

She laughed and pulled her hand away. "Boy, you are a mess."

"Tomi, you honestly don't know what you do to me," he admitted, turning to face her. "You can drive a man wild with your touch." Shyly, she looked down, but made no reply.

He decided to be honest with her. "Tomi, I'm a grown ass man, but sometimes, you have me feeling like a little teenaged school-boy. No woman has ever affected me the way you have. There's something special about you. I like your style, I like your attitude, I even like the way you look at me and roll your eyes when I say something out the way." She smiled and he gently cuffed her chin. "I haven't forgot about that night at your crib either. I've been missing you like crazy."

She looked over at him and took his hand in hers. "I've missed you, too, Dante."

He smacked his lips. "You're just saying that."

"No, I'm for real," she told him. "Serious up."

This would be the perfect time for you to tell her about Denise, his mind admonished him. Tell her.

But he couldn't. He wouldn't try to sugarcoat it; he was too much of a coward to tell her. He barely had her and didn't want to risk completely losing her over something so trivial.

"A penny for your thoughts," she offered.

He chewed his bottom lip thoughtfully, and she could see his mind turning like clock-work. "It's nothing," he lied. He let his head fall back against the head-rest.

The silence between them was a bit uncomfortable. Dante had took the first step to unlocking the door between them, and, now that the door was no longer locked, she felt as if he was waiting for her to say something to push the door on open. But she couldn't reveal that part of herself to him. She hadn't even told her own family the truth about Jonathan's death, and her family was one that was close-knit and caring. If she didn't have the nerve to open up to her family, what made him think that she would open up to him?

The drawn out silence became too tense, and Dante knew he had to say something. After staging a mental war with himself, Dante finally asked quickly before he could take his words back, "Do you like seafood?"

"Yeah. Why?"

"I know this little restaurant; their seafood is pretty good. If you want to, we can go there tonight. If you don't want to, that's cool, too, but if you want to than that's cool, too, but it's all on you—"

Tomi lifted one eyebrow. "You asking me out on a date?" She said it as if the thought itself was offensive.

Dante quickly took his words back. "No! No, I, uh, I wasn't asking you out on a date, ma, I was just saying—"

"Because if you were," she interrupted him, "my answer is yes."

Dante looked over at her, and her serious countenance melted away into a heart warming smile. "Got you," she laughed.

"Jokes, man. You got a bag full don't you?" He leaned over and kissed the curve of her shoulder. "So we're on for tonight?" he asked. "It's a date?"

"Yes, Dante. It's a date."

She felt him smile against her shoulder, and she lifted his head so she could kiss his lips.

His smile widened. "Man, that's what's up. Let me take you back to the shop before you get something started. I have to get to work—I'm already running five minutes late."

"Yeah, and I know Max is wondering where the hell am I at. I told him I'd only be gone for ten minutes." She hooked her seat-belt as he started the car.

He got her back to the shop in a record time of three minutes and twenty-seven seconds. As she stepped out the car, he asked, "Can you be ready by a quarter to eight?"

"Yeah. I get off at six."

"Well, I'll be at your house promptly at seven forty-five; not BP time, either," he added as an afterthought.

Tomi laughed and leaned into the passenger window. "Come here."

He leaned over to her, and she held his face as she kissed him fully on the lips. She caught his bottom lip between her teeth and tugged gently before letting him go.

"Tomi," he said, his face buried in her neck.

"Yeah?" Her voice was throaty and low.

"Don't ever wear that shirt again."

"Why?"

He plucked one hard nipple with his thumb and she gasped. "Cause I don't want any other man seeing what I'm seeing now."

The intensity of his words rested heavily on Tomi's shoulders. Yeah, he had only asked her not to wear the shirt, but he was also letting her know that he had laid claims on her. The feeling of once again being able to feel as if you belonged to someone else swelled in her chest. It was at that instant that she made the decision to have sex with Dante—she didn't know what would happen after that, and she was probably setting herself up for a let-down, and she was probably going to end up hurting him because, although she looked as if she had it together on the outside, mentally, she wasn't quite there yet—but as of right now, she needed Dante the way a woman needed a man.

With that thought in mind, she hungrily sought out his lips, kissing him with a raw, hungry passion, trying to let him know by actions what she couldn't possibly put into words.

For a second there, Dante didn't know how to respond to her unexpected passion, but he quickly pulled himself together, allowing her to be the leader, and him, the enthusiastic follower. This time, Dante was the first to pull away, and he was breathing like a man who had just finished a five-mile race.

"Damn." That was all he could say.

Tomi licked her lips and looked at him; he looked wore out from her kiss, but she felt like she had only just begun. She gave him a look as if she wanted to tear his ass up, licked her lips again, and stepped back from his car.

"Seven forty-five," she said before turning away from him. She couldn't help but add an extra twist to her hips as she made her way back to the parlor. She knew he was staring at her ass.

CHAPTER SIX

"What time did you say she get off work?"

"She doesn't get off until five, baby. Come back to bed." He pulled her back into the puffy, rose-colored sheets and slid his hands up and down her silky thighs. "Why are you in such a rush? We've got plenty of time." He kissed her lips, her cheek, her neck.

"Phillip, you know I've got to be to work by three. It's already a quarter pass two." She didn't stop him as he slid off the black thongs that she had just replaced. She didn't argue as his head disappeared between her thighs. And her moans were the only sounds that filled the room as he stroked that heated, moist place with his tongue.

When she came, he crawled up her body to place a kiss on her lips, but she moved her head away. "I'm not kissing you while you got coochie-breath."

"It's your coochie," he told her.

"I don't care." She moved a hand across her exhausted face. "Phillip, I am so freaking tired. I just want to sleep. Are you sure you don't want to go in for me today?"

"No, Cassandra," he told her, slipping into his boxers. "Today is my only day off, and I promised my brother that I would help him fix his car."

She sighed. "Well, let me go get washed up." She caught sight of her short-cut, fuchsia-colored hair in the bed mirror. It was disheveled almost beyond repair. "Your wife got any small curlers I can use?" she asked, scooping her clothes off the floor.

"She should have something in the counter under the sink."

Cassandra disappeared into the bathroom, and Phillip changed the bed sheets. The clock read two forty-seven by the time she had finished washing up and restyling her hair. She had on her Arby's uniform and her visor was in her hand.

"You ready?"

She nodded.

Ten minutes later, he was dropping her off at Wachovia bank, which was located directly across the street from Arby's. "You got a ride home?" he asked.

"Yeah," she told him, hopping out his truck, "my boyfriend is picking me up."

"You need to break up with that lame cat."

"You need to divorce your wife."

"I can't do that. I love her."

"If you love her that much, why you having sex with me?"

"Because…" He didn't know what to say.

Cassandra shook her head at him. "Thanks for the ride." She hurried across the street before the light could turn green, not once looking back. Phillip stared after her, and even after she disappeared into Arby's, he sat in his pick-up truck for a few minutes more, thinking. Finally, he cranked up his truck and drove off.

✳   ✳   ✳   ✳

"Niya, why in the hell do you have that curling iron stashed in your purse?" Kelise asked, removing her reading glasses and pushing aside the papers that she had been editing for the press room.

"Look at it!" She tossed the curling iron on Kelise's desk. "Look at it."

Instead of looking at the curling iron, Kelise couldn't take her eyes off her crazed-looking sister. She looked like a madwoman; her hair was a mess, and her two-piece suit was wrinkled. Kelise had never seen her sister looking this unkempt in public.

To staunch any speculations or rumors of a scandal, Kelise rose from her desk and quickly twisted the blinds shut, blocking them from the stares of her meddlesome employees.

Returning to her desk, Kelise scrutinized the curling iron, but didn't see anything of great significance. "Okay, so it's a greasy curling iron with hair tangled in it. What's the big deal?"

"Look at the hair that's tangled in it!" Niya ordered her sister.

Kelise examined the hair scrupulously. "It's red hair."

"Exactly!" Niya exploded, throwing her hands up in the hair. "Who has red hair? Not me, not you, not Tomi, not Kadeesha!" She pounded a fist on Kelise's desk. "I used that very curling iron this morning, and there was no hair in it! I even cleaned it when I was finished using it! Where the hell did this red hair come from?"

"Niya, sweetie, I'm going to need you to calm down. We don't need to jump to any rash conclusions here," she advised her sister rationally.

"Keli, he changed the sheets!" Niya took off one of her black pumps and flung it at the opposite wall. "That sneaky, cheating, two-timing bastard changed the damn sheets!" She took off her other pump and it violently followed the same path as the one before it. "Damn shoes hurt my feet!" Niya exclaimed, collapsing into the chair once again.

"Niya, I've never seen you like this," Kelise admitted, walking behind the chair and comfortingly placing her hands on her sister's shoulders.

"It's because I love him so much," she cried out in defeat. "Why do he treat me like this?" She buried her face into her hands, and her shoulders shook with the fierceness of her sobs. Kelise hugged her sister from behind as she cried loudly into her fists. "Keli, I've taken so much shit from him. I swear I have. I mean, I stayed with him even through his drug problem. I married him after my whole family told me not to. I looked passed his second-hand jobs, and all his faults, and loved him for him. And this is how he repays me? Keli, he fucked that girl in our bed. *Our* bed!" Her sobs increased in volume, and her shoulders shook with more force. "I'm supposed to be his wife! He told me he loved me. We made love last night. In that same…bed." The little composure she had left shattered with the word 'bed'.

Kelise said nothing, only held her sister and allowed her to cry on her shoulder. Once Niya's cries had subsided, Kelise reached into her desk drawer and pulled out a box of Kleenex. Thankfully, Niya took a handful of tissues and wiped her face, then blew her nose. She sounded like a freight train.

"Feel better?" Kelise asked.

Niya gave her sister a weak smile. "A little."

"So what are we going to do now?" Kelise asked, returning to her leather swivel chair. "You want me to beat the bitch's ass? Trust me, I can find out who she is; I have my sources. I'm dead serious."

Niya waved away her comments. "No need to get yourself tangled up in the system on behalf of my cheating ass husband. This is my problem, not yours."

"So what are you going to do?"

Niya shrugged her shoulders. "I don't know." She blew her nose again. "I just need some time for myself. I guess Ma can keep the kids for a while, and I…I need a place to stay for a few days. Is it alright if I stay with you?"

Kelise bit her lip and gave her sister an apologetic smile. "You remember when I told you that Angel's house burned down? Well, she and her three kids are staying with me until her mom gets here. Her mom has a flight scheduled in two days, but you need somewhere to stay now. If you want to pack like sardines…"

"What about Tomi? You think I can crash with her? I don't mind sleeping on her couch. I need some alone time, but I don't need to be completely by myself. I'd get to thinking about some things, and if I didn't have anybody to stop me, only God knows what I'm liable to do."

"Are you talking about suicide?"

"Not suicide, baby girl, homicide. I would kill his ass dead."

"Lord have mercy." Kelise scratched a spot between her dreds. "Call Tomi and see if you can crash over there. More than likely you should be able to. She's at the shop now, but she'll be done in an hour or two."

"Okay, I'll do that. Let me get out of here so you can get back to your work."

"Are you going to be okay, sis?"

Niya felt her eyes well with tears, and she snatched another Kleenex from the box. "Yeah. I'll be fine. I'll call you later." She grabbed another Kleenex, and another, and another, then gave in and took the whole box.

When Niya opened the door, about five of Kelise's employees nearly killed themselves trying to return to their stations and put on the pretense of being busy. Kelise gave them a reprimanding stare, returned to her office, and flipped open the section of the magazine that she had been editing before Niya had interrupted. She was editing an article that one of her favorite employees, Trisha Bell, had wrote called "How To Let That Man Go".

Niya needs to read this, Kelise thought to herself, and shook her head again.

Chapter Seven

"And how's my sweet-pea doing?"

"I'm doing fine, Ma," Tomi told her mother as she closed up the shop, balancing her cell phone between her ear and shoulder to free her hands. "How are you doing?"

"Living and loving the Lord." Cathy laughed aloud. Hardly a day passed that her mother wasn't in good spirits. "I just got my hair done. I got it dyed an auburn color; it has curls at the front and a bun at the back. And your father took me to a masseuse." She moaned in memory. "That little white man could do wonders with his hands. He almost made me want to leave your daddy."

"Ma!"

"I'm just kidding, baby. But how have you been lately?"

"Pretty good." Tomi started up her car and backed out the vacant parking lot.

"Did you read your Bible today?" This was one of her mother's routine questions she asked every Thursday, and Tomi routinely lied, "Yes ma'am."

"That's good. Don't you know that it's by God's grace and mercy that He allowed us to see another day?" Another of her routine Thursday questions.

"Yes ma'am," Tomi replied.

"We could've been dead and gone. But we're still here."

"Yes ma'am."

"Ain't God good?"

"Yes, ma'am."

"I said, ain't He good!"

"Yes, ma'am!"

"Hallelujah!" Tomi had to wait a minute as her mother thanked the Lord, and told him how good He had been to her. This was nothing new to Tomi, and today, she knew her mother would be especially religious because it was Thursday—Bible study day. And Cathy Thompson never missed Bible Study.

When Cathy finished thanking the Lord, she resumed the conversation where they had left off. "So how my baby been doing today?"

"I'm good, Ma. My life has been going pretty good lately." *Because of Dante.* She smiled at the thought of him.

"Are you telling me one?" Cathy asked her scoldingly. "Niya told me that you had one of your spells—"

"Niya runs her mouth too much," Tomi interrupted her hotly. If she wanted her mother to know about what had happened, she would've told her herself. Niya could be the town newspaper whenever she wanted to be.

"Don't you get hot with me, young lady. I ain't too old to lay you across my knees."

"Sorry, Ma."

"That's better, Little Miss Attitude. Ain't no need of you getting so mad about it, anyway. She's your sister; she's just looking out for you," her mother said in Niya's defense. "If we need to set you up another appointment with Dr. Palmetto, that won't be a—"

"Ma, I don't need to see a doctor. I had a little episode; it was nothing. I'm fine, now." She pulled into the parking lot of Gatesmore Shopping Center; she had to find her a killer outfit for her date tonight—something that would make Dante lose his mind.

"Are you sure, baby? Because we know you've never completely recovered from that incident."

"I'm fine, Ma!" she barked at her mother, but quickly apologized. "Ma, I'm sorry. I didn't mean to yell. I just get so tired of you and Dad always bringing that up. Trust me, I'm fine. If it ever gets to the point where I need to see Dr. Palmetto again, I'll go. I promise."

"Girl, you gonna make me reach through this phone and snatch your hair straight. What's gotten into you?"

"Nothing, Ma. I just wish people would leave the past in the past. Why do someone always has to bring up Jonathan?"

"Okay, baby. I understand. But you know we're always pestering you about this because we love you, and we're concerned about you."

"I love you all, too, Ma, but dang."

Cathy quickly changed the subject. "Niya also told me about this new young man you're seeing."

Tomi exhaled deeply and counted to ten as she entered the store. She made a mental note to cuss Niya out the next time she saw her. That's why she didn't like telling her anything; Niya ran her mouth too damn much.

"So how serious are you two, Tomi?"

"We're not serious," Tomi told her, heading for the clearance rack. "He's just a friend."

"Friend or boyfriend, we're just happy that you're finally moving on with your life. For a minute there, your father and I thought that you might be a...well, you know, a *lesbian*." She whispered the last word as if it was the worst word in the English language. "But if you're talking to this young man, then obviously you're not a...well, you know. And even if you were one, even though it goes against my every belief, I'd still love you the same. But I'm glad that you're not. That's one less headache I have to deal with."

"Okay, Ma." Tomi pulled a black, spandex shirt from the rack. It tied around the back of the neck and had a large, dark green emerald in the middle of its V-shaped bosom. She liked it.

"May I help you?" the store clerk asked, walking over to her. She was the only customer in the store at the time.

"Ma, I'll call you later, okay? I'm a little busy right now."

"Okay, baby. I love you, and you be good."

"I will. Love you, too." Tomi flipped her cell closed and saw that she had one new message and five missed calls. All the missed calls were from Phillip (why in the hell he was calling her cell phone, she had no idea). She checked the number on the message, thinking it was from Dante, but it was from Niya—the last person on Earth whom she wanted to speak with at the present time.

"Yes, ma'am, you can help me," Tomi told the store clerk, dropping her cell into her purse. "This shirt says $18.99, but it's on the seven dollar rack."

"I can ring it up for you," the clerk told her, taking the shirt from her. The short, black-haired, brown-eyed woman went behind the counter and ringed up the shirt. "It's seven dollars," she told Tomi.

"I want it," Tomi called out while looking through the pants rack. She wondered if she should wear pants or a skirt. She decided on a skirt. Dante hadn't had the chance to view her long, well-toned legs. He would get that chance tonight, and hopefully, he'd be between those legs tonight, too, if he played his cards right. She felt herself get heated at the image in her mind and decided to change her thoughts to something less disturbing.

She pulled a thin, sheer, army-green colored skirt from the clearance rack. It was cut at an angle, high on one thigh and reached just past her knee on the other leg. Wear this with that black shirt and her green and black stiletto heels that strapped up to her thighs, and Dante wouldn't be no more good. A seductive smile curled the edges of her lips.

Approaching the check-out, she grabbed a thick, green, marble-like bracelet, which would be the only jewelry that she wore tonight. Her total came up to a cheap nineteen dollars and fourteen cents.

Checking the time, she noticed that it was half past six. She still had to get home, take a milk bath, and make herself up before Dante got there. She put some pep to her step.

"What the hell is she doing here?" Tomi thought as she turned into her driveway. Niya's white and chrome 2006 Cadillac STS was parked in her driveway, and her living room light was on. Tomi jumped out the car and hurried into her house.

"Hey Tomi. I cooked a broccoli and cheese casserole for us." Niya was sitting on Tomi's sofa, wearing Tomi's favorite silk gold-colored pajama pants, her black spaghetti-strap shirt, and her black, fuzzy bedroom slippers, watching a sitcom and downing a bottle of sparkling white grape juice.

"What are you doing here?" Tomi inquired, shutting the front door.

"You didn't get my message?" she asked, ripping into a bag of Ruffles cheddar and sour cream potato chips. Tomi crossed her arms and shook her head. "Phillip had a bitch in our house today. He tried to cover it up, but didn't do too good of a job. She left her bright red hair in my curling iron." She said all of this matter-of-factly.

"What?" Tomi's jaw dropped. "You're playing right?"

"Nope. I'm as serious as this divorce that we're about to have." She took another sip of the grape juice. "I left my wedding ring on the eating table, right beside the curling iron. He's been blowing up my cell phone, but I won't answer any of his calls."

"So that's why he called me," Tomi stated rather than asked. She sat her purse and shopping bag on the kitchen counter. "How long are you going to crash here?"

"I don't know." Niya let out a heavy sigh. "I dropped the kids off on Ma. Asked her if she could keep them for a while so Phillip and I can spend some quality time together." She practically spat those two words out. "I don't want Ma to know what's going on. At least not just yet."

"Oh, but you can tell her my whole life story?" Tomi asked, remembering her earlier conversation with her mother.

"What are you talking about?" Niya seemed genuinely confused.

Tomi threw her hands up. "You know exactly what I'm talking about. Niya, you run your mouth too damn much. But I don't even want to talk about that right now. I have a date to get ready for. He's going to be over at seven forty-five."

"Well, you'd better hurry it up. It's already going on seven." Niya watched as her sister hurried off into the back-room. It touched her heart to see that Tomi was finally starting to get over the barrier in her life that had kept her depressed for so long. Even if her own marriage was falling apart before her very eyes, Niya was happy for her sister.

After Jonathan's death, Tomi had refused to step foot in a car for a whole year. Because of this, she was forced to walk, catch the subway, or take the city bus every day. Some days, she would seem perfectly normal, while on other days, a simple loud, unexpected noise, like the slamming of a door, would send her in a frenzy. It would be hours later before they had succeeded in calming her down.

Finally, their mother Cathy couldn't take it anymore, and she found Tomi a shrink. Dr. Palmetto. He was a kind old man, gentle in speech and demeanor. With wiry hair, graying at the edges, large silver-framed spectacles resting on his wedge shaped nose, and a warm smile always curving his lips, he put you in the mind of someone's trusted grandpa. After spending five sessions with the psychiatrist, Tomi was once again able to sit in a car without flipping out.

Dr. Palmetto also told them that Tomi would never be whole until she could be honest about what happened, and forgive herself. After two more sessions spent with Dr. Palmetto, Tomi was almost Tomi again...except she took no personal interest in the male species.

Niya and Kelise had almost accepted the fact that their sister was probably a closet lesbian...and then this. Dante. She hoped in her heart that this guy was the one because she didn't want to see her sister suffer anymore. Tomi was too young to be living such a boring, mechanical life. It was pass time for her sister to laugh, let go, and live.

A half-hour later, Tomi walked into the front-room and stood in front of the TV. She twisted around with a big smile on her face. "How do I look?"

"Like a freaking model!" her sister declared, standing to her feet in order to get a better view of her sister. The V-shaped shirt opened up almost to her navel, exposing the inner-sides of breasts that were both high and full. The green skirt was cut dangerously high on her left thigh, but reached down to just below her right knee. The skirt fit perfect around her minuscule waist and hugged her thighs. Her legs were a maze of green and black straps that laced up to her lower thighs, and the heels on the shoe were pencil-thin—they had to be at least six inches in height.

"You are gorgeous!" Niya exclaimed, unable to take her eyes away. "I am so jealous."

Tomi couldn't help but to blush. Her thick hair was done in waterfalls that fell almost to her bare shoulders. She had used as little make-up as possible: some green eye-shadow, a little eye-liner, a soft brush of blush across her cheeks, and a light coating of shimmery gloss on her lips. She knew she looked pretty, but Niya made her feel as if she put Tyra Banks to shame.

"Stop exaggerating," Tomi told her sister, waving her compliments away.

"Tomi, I couldn't be any more serious." And she meant it from the heart. "Oh, I think I'm going to cry."

Just then, there was a knock at the door.

"Oh God! He's here! I didn't even hear him pull up." Tomi patted her hair, pulled at her shirt, smoothed out her skirt. "Real quick, how do I look?"

"Absolutely amazing." Her sister went to the door and pulled it open.

She had expected the man to look decent, but he took her breath away. No wonder her sister was so infatuated with this Mr. Goodbar. He was probably twenty-six or seven, standing at a good six feet and two inches or so. He had smooth skin of a light brown, pecan shade, and some of the most interesting eyes she had ever seen. They were a dark, reddish-brown color; they were eyes that exhibited a seriousness and softness all at once. His hair was cut into a fade and his sideburns, mustache, and goatee were nicely trimmed. He wore all black except for a checkered black and white silk tie. In his hand, he held a bouquet of twelve white roses.

There was a look of confusion on his face. "Am I at the wrong house?" he asked.

"No, not if your name is Dante," Niya told him flirtatiously.

"Move, Niya," Tomi told her sister, pulling the door open and nudging her sister out the way. She smiled when she saw him. "Dante, you look handsome."

His jaw was hanging at the sight of her. "Tomi..." He was at a lost for words. "Tomi, you are...you look...damn, girl..."

She blushed again and took the bouquet from him, inhaling the scent of the beautiful, fresh flowers, while saying, "Dante, I'mma need you to come up with a new word besides 'damn.'"

"When it comes to you, ma," Dante added smoothly, "I often find myself at a loss for words."

"Damn," Niya said, looking at her sister with a 'go head girl' look. "That was deep baby girl."

"And you are?" Dante asked, turning to face Niya.

"Please excuse her inhospitableness," Niya apologized. She held out her hand. "My name is Kaniya, but everybody calls me Niya. I'm Tomi's oldest sister."

"Oldest?" Dante frowned, and placed a gentle kiss on the back of her hand. "You don't look a day over twenty, beautiful. If I would've met you first…"

"Dante!"

Niya turned plum red and fanned herself with her free hand. "Tomi, if I weren't married, I'd give you a run for your money."

Dante stated, "I'm flattered."

"You should be, fine young ass. You couldn't handle me anyway; I'd tear you apart."

"Niya!"

"Well, he is fine. I'm just keeping it real."

Tomi rolled her eyes, placed the flowers into a vase that had been filled with water, and possessively snaked her arm through his. "Well, Dante, you met me first, and Niya, you *are* married so leave my ma—my friend alone."

Niya giggled and Dante smiled contently because they both had caught her Freudian slip.

"Dante, bring your ass before I change my mind and not go on this date period."

"Nice meeting you, Niya," Dante whispered before a heated Tomi practically yanked him out the door.

Niya called out after them, "No excessive kissing, no excessive touching. Don't keep her out too late. By my standards, twelve o'clock should be the latest, and have fun!"

But Niya knew they hadn't heard her. All she heard was tires screeching as they pulled out the driveway and flew down the road.

*　　　*　　　*　　　*

Tomi was laughing hard enough that doing a simple task such as walking in a straight line was proving to be difficult. Grabbing her side with one hand and Dante with the other, she declared between bursts of laughter, "Boy, you are crazy!" Tears squeezed from the corners of her eyes. "You are a mess! I can't believe you said that!"

"Hey," he said, helping her maintain her balance with a proffered arm, "I just call it how I see it. She knew if she walked out the house looking like that, somebody was going to have to say something. She looked like a Madea look-a-like, old grandma-looking ass."

As Dante held open the passenger door for her, Tomi was still bugging from his earlier crack on the manly-looking lady with her floral print dress. Gracefully, she slid into the passenger seat, holding her legs together like a lady should whenever wearing a skirt. Dante fired up the engine.

"So how did you like the food?" he asked.

"Mmmm. It was delicious!" she exclaimed. She had ate a supper that consisted of filleted white snapper with a shrimp cocktail, buttered garlic croissants, and a glass of Merlot. For dessert, she had a delectable strawberry and honey Tiramisu—she ate every crumb. "I feel like a fat hog!" she admitted, rubbing the little pudge protruding from her tummy.

"What do you want to do now?" he asked, cruising down Green Boulevard.

"I don't know. But let's do something!" So far, Tomi was having the time of her life, and she didn't want the night to end—not just yet, anyway. Her body was pumping energy, and she wanted to do something fun. "Let's go to Bananas," she proposed.

He lifted an eyebrow at her. "Bananas? That dead place? Nobody goes to that boring ass club anymore."

"Oh, I didn't know." She hadn't been to a club since she turned twenty-one; that was three years ago. Bananas had been the jump off back then. She didn't know what was hot now. "Well, let's go to a club, any club. I feel like dancing."

"You ain't said nothing but a word." Dante made a sharp right and, holding tight to the passenger door, Tomi giggled. Seconds later, he was pulling into an overcrowded parking lot with a flashing, red and yellow neon sign that screamed Red Light District. "This is the jump off right here," he told her.

She didn't doubt his word. According to the many cars parked out there, there had to be at least five hundred people inside or more. They could not find a parking space. And the music thumping from the building was loud and crunk. Tomi could barely sit still.

They walked to the entrance, showed their IDs, and Dante paid both their ways. Tomi had to give her eyes time to adjust to the dark club. The only source of light came from the flashing red lights positioned over the dance floor, and the dim lighting over by the bar. Other than that, it was dark.

"You want something to drink first, or do you want to dance?" Dante had to yell over the music.

She had a little buzz from the two glasses of Merlot she had downed at Marcellos. Tomi could already feel her body moving to the beat of one of Missy Elliot's songs, but she still needed an extra boost of courage to actually get on the dance floor and let loose. "I'd like something to drink first," she told him. "Preferably an Incredible Hulk or Blue Motorcycle—whichever they have."

"Okay, I'll be right back." Dante headed towards the bar, leaving her standing there by herself. It was only after he was gone that she noticed how many males were poised against the wall behind her, bobbing their heads to the music, and eyeing her down like their breath stank and she was a peppermint Mentos.

She suddenly felt naked and alone. The urge to run after Dante was strong, but she didn't want to look like a frightened child, so she stood her ground.

"Thick in all the right places," she heard a slurred male-voice whisper near her right ear as his hands slid around her waist from behind.

"Excuse you!" Tomi exclaimed, yanking herself free of his unwanted touch. "Keep your filthy hands off of me."

The man's features were obscured by the darkened club, but she could tell that he was brown-skinned, tall, slim in build, and sported a small fro. He was probably somewhat attractive, maybe a little cute from what she could tell, but regardless of his looks, that didn't give him the right to touch her. The tell-tell signs of intoxication, such as the slurring of words and the loss of one's balance, were written all over him.

"Damn, excuse me for looking!" He staggered backwards with his words. "Who wouldn't look at a sexy, fine, tenderoni like yourself. Is it a crime to look?"

"Last time I checked, you look with your eyes, not with your hands."

"Is there a problem here?" Dante slipped a plastic cup filled with a greenish-colored liquid in her hand, turned towards the inebriated man, and rolled up his shirt sleeves, taking a fighter's stance. He repeated his question. "Is there a problem here, sir?"

"Dante, it's cool," Tomi said, placing a restraining arm against his chest, and giving him a small push back. She came out to have a good time, and she wasn't about to allow some man who couldn't hold his liquor to ruin it for them. "Let it go. He's cool."

"You don't want no problem with me, young blood," the man promised him, his eyes brightening with the anticipation of a scuffle. "I'll knock you ten shades lighter than the sun, Dark Vader."

"Dark Va—?" Dante's fist was two seconds from smashing in the other man's face when Tomi stepped in between the two men, risking getting her head knocked off to forestall a fight that was itching to happen.

"Dante, forget him, okay. Let's just move on. I want to dance. Don't you want to dance?" Tomi took Dante by the arm and steered him away from the steaming man. The man made some rude, degrading remarks about Dante, calling him a coward and a punk ass nigga, but Tomi continued to force him to walk away and ignore the man.

"Why did you do that?" Dante asked, once they were on the opposite side of the club.

"Because I came here to have fun, not to watch two niggas beat the living shit out of each other to prove their manhood. That's what's wrong with you black men nowadays. Y'all act like you always have to prove something, preferably with your fists rather than with your common sense."

"I saw that nigga grab you, baby. I was just trying to protect what's mine."

Dante froze, realizing the words that he had allowed to slip from his lips—the words 'baby' and 'mine'. He wondered if Tomi had caught it, and she obviously had because her cup had halted a half-step from her lips.

Dante looked down at the floor, and Tomi could've sworn that if he wasn't so dark, he'd be blushing right about now. Knowing that things were a little tense right now, Tomi opted to lighten the mood.

"You aren't drinking anything?" she asked, taking another sip from her cup.

"Nah. I want a clear head when I get ready to drive us home."

"Oh, yeah. What was I thinking?" She was just happy that the mood had changed, and immediately, she felt at ease again. She demolished half her cup with one big gulp, and made a sour face as the liquid eased down her throat.

"Damn, girl!" Dante exclaimed. "You downed that like a pro!"

"Shut up," she told him, finishing up the cup with two smaller gulps. Already, she was feeling a bit tipsy. As Usher's song, *Yeah!*, blasted from the speakers, Tomi's hands went up in the air and she started rocking her hips from side to side. "That's my shit right there!" She grabbed Dante's arm and tipsily made room for them on the dance floor.

Tomi was about as drunk as she could be as she turned her back to him and bounced her ass like it was a bowl of jell-o. Dante's hands secured themselves around her tiny waist, holding her in place as she bounced against him.

"Damn, Tomi, slow down," he told her, unable to keep up with her fast pace. "You ain't even on beat."

Usher's song ended and was followed by Ying Yang Twins' *Get Low*. Before Dante knew what had happened, Tomi was down on the floor, dropping her ass like she was getting paid to do it. A bunch of dudes crowded around her and Dante quickly pulled her to her feet, making sure that they all knew that she was not for the taking. She danced the rest of the song with him.

Finally, the deejay slowed it down a bit, and D'Angelo's song, *How Does It Feel*, mellowed throughout the room.

"This use to be my jam," she told him, her words slurring together. She wrapped her arms around his neck and pulled him close. His arms locked around her waist, and he tried to help her find the rhythm to the song, which was a futile task.

Alcohol, mixed with adrenaline, mixed with suppressed desire, was too strong a concoction for Tomi. She felt like a horny rabbit, and as D'Angelo's voice invaded her ears, whispering about what he was going to do to his woman once he got her behind the bedroom door, the fire in Tomi blazed hotter and hotter. She looked up at Dante, her eyes focusing in on his, asking him an unspoken question.

Leaning into his embrace, Tomi allowed her lips to hover above his, feeling his warm breath as he shakily exhaled against her skin. She kissed his bottom lip, a butterfly kiss so light, Dante didn't know if it was real or if he was merely imagining it. But that butterfly kiss was nothing more than a tease and Tomi needed more; she had to have the real thing. With a low purr of womanly need, she sought out Dante's full lips with her own. Her tongue delved deep into his mouth, tasting the satisfying flavor of him, and she heard him moan as he tightened his grip on her.

With her teeth, she bit down on his tongue and sucked him deeply into her mouth, turning his head to the side so she could get better access. Dante's knees buckled, and for a minute, she thought they would fall to the floor, since her weight was pressed almost fully against him. But redeeming himself, he regained his balance, grew strength anew, and lifted both her legs around his waist, hiking her up against him and forcing her to hold tight to his neck so she wouldn't fall. His hands immediately went down to her bare thighs, holding her in place. Through the translucent nylon of her sheer panties, he could feel her wetness pressing against his hard manhood, and he almost lost it. She was so hot. So moist.

"Let's go to my place," she whispered into his ear. "I want you. Now."

Dante was hard as a rock, and he didn't have to be told twice. He let her slide down his body to the floor, grabbed her wrist, and all but dragged her outside of the club. Because he was moving at such a fast pace, he fumbled with the car keys and dropped them on the pavement twice before he was finally able to unlock the doors. He was on her before she got in the car good. His mouth was a heated furnace as it found hers, and he passionately kissed her until she was acquiescent to his every touch.

"Dante," she whispered as his hand slid between her thighs. She gasped for air and arched her back high as she felt his fingers enter her without hesitation. "Dante!" He fingered and kissed her at the same time, then dropped his lips to her neck, sucking hard enough on her skin to leave a hickie.

His long fingers went deep inside her, coaxing out her sweet flood. Long and deep, long and deep, one finger...two...deeper...deeper. She couldn't breathe. She couldn't think. She could only...feel. And with a cry of pleasurable release, she came into his hand, screaming his name loud enough to break every window in the state of Georgia.

"Damn, Dante," she gasped, once she was able to catch her breath. He started the car up as her hand found its way to the rock in his lap. "I want to feel it," she told him, clutching his hardness in her hand.

"Please, don't touch it," Dante begged, pushing her hand away, "I can barely think straight as it is." He sped down the highway, breaking every speed limit that ever existed, and pulled into her driveway, only to be welcomed with the beautiful, yet unwanted sight of her sister's Cadillac STS.

"Aww, shit," Tomi moaned, looking at her sister's expensive car. "I forgot she was here." She thought a minute. "Let's go to your crib," she told him.

Without saying a word, he restarted the engine, backed out her driveway, and zoomed down the highway. Minutes later, he pulled into his driveway and killed the engine.

"Come on," he told Tomi, scrambling out of his seat-belt. They rushed to his door, and he cursed as he fumbled through his keys to find the right one, dropping them only once this time.

As soon as they were in the house, he had Tomi plastered against the living room door, and his hands were on every inch of her silky skin. He kissed down her neck and pulled her flimsy shirt to the side, enveloping one erect nipple into his fiery mouth. Tomi couldn't formulate words; she just moaned and made encouraging sounds as he made love to her breasts, equally dividing his attention between those two mounds until her hard brown nipples shined like pebbles that had been kissed with morning dew.

"Tomi," he sighed her name as he kissed down her flat belly, "I've been wanting to do this for so long." He dropped to his knees and hiked her skirt up, then spread her legs apart. His tongue found the center of her wet core, and he reveled in the sweet taste of her juices as she melted into his mouth.

Tomi was practically screaming at the top of her lungs. She had one hand on the door knob, the other reaching for the wall in order to hold herself up. She would call out his name one minute, and scream for the Lord the next. Her left leg shook with the intensity of the sensations.

"No more!" she whimpered. "Please, I can't take…Oh, my God. Oh, my God! I'm going to…I'm fin' to…ahhh!" It was too late to warn him. She came hard into his mouth before collapsing against the door-frame.

But Dante wasn't finished with her yet. He scooped her up in his arms and headed for his bedroom. Kicking open his room door, he all but threw her on his bed. He crawled on top of her like a lion would his prey, kissing her until she was squirming beneath him, begging for him to make love to her. He removed her clothing and kissed every inch of her silken skin.

"You are so beautiful to me," he told her as he kissed down her legs to her ankles, gently biting the arch of each foot. She squealed with delight, and he spread her legs apart.

"Are you sure?" he asked her.

"I've never been surer of anything in my life."

The alcohol had mellowed out her nerves and Dante had mellowed out her body. She didn't want anymore words; she just wanted him inside of her, that minute, that moment, that very second.

"Tomi, are you sure?" he asked her again. "I know you've had a few drinks, and I don't want you to think I took advantage of you when you wake up in the morning."

"Dante, I'm sure," she told him. "Now will you please just…" she reached down and attempted to guide his swollen penis to her wet entrance.

"Hold on for a sec," he told her. He reached over her and pulled out the first drawer of his little black nightstand. She felt him rummaging through the drawer, and then he retrieved a small, metallic square-shaped package. Dante ripped the condom open with his teeth and quickly pulled it on. "Are you sure you can handle it?" he asked her, once he was dressed for action.

"Dante, if you don't stop asking so many damn quest—" She screamed and her nails dug into his back as he entered her deep and strong.

"Baby, are you okay?" he asked, stilling himself within her. His breathing was rough and jagged, and already beads of sweat outlined his brow.

Tomi didn't say a thing. She couldn't. He started moving in her again, slow small movements. She bit her lip, whimpered, and hooked her nails into his back.

After her body had adjusted to his size, the searing pain changed over to a dull, pleasurable ache. She found herself grinding her hips with his, meeting each thrust with a loud moan.

"Oh shit, Tomi." Dante's pace increased to the point where the bed was loudly banging against the wall. He grunted with each bang that the bed made, and called out Tomi's name as he finally came into her like a forty-day flood. She climaxed quickly after him, and he collapsed on her, drenched in sweat and breathing harshly.

Moments later, Tomi said, "Baby. Baby?"

"Yeah?" He had to utter the word between two hard breaths.

"You're squishing me."

Dante laughed and somehow found the strength to move over until only half his body weight was on her. "Sorry," he told her. "Just give me a minute to catch my breath."

"Well, while you're catching your breath, I'm going to go clean up, okay?" Tomi went into the bathroom. Dante entered the bathroom a little later to discard the condom and to pee.

Once they both had finished cleaning themselves, they fell into the bed together, and Tomi cuddled up to his side. Dante wrapped his arms around her and pulled her even closer. He kissed her and felt her smile against his lips.

"Did I hurt you?" he asked.

"A little," she admitted.

"Was I, you know..." he let his question drift off.

"Were you what?" Tomi teased.

"You know."

"No I don't."

"Ah, you really going to make me say it?"

"Yep."

Dante smacked his lips, and she could imagine him rolling his eyes in the dark. "Was I good, Tomi?"

Tomi teased him even more by drawing out her reply. "Let me see. I think you were all right."

"All right? That's it?" Dante sounded like his pride was at stake, and Tomi couldn't help but take the bait.

"Like I said, you were all right. It could've been better."

"Oh, really?" Dante asked, sliding his hand between her legs and lightly stroking her swollen lips. "Feels like I did a pretty good job. But if you need a second go-round—"

"No!" Tomi quickly disagreed, clamping her legs shut. "I think I need a day or so of recuperation before any thing goes back up in there."

Dante laughed and said conceitedly, "Oh, but I thought I was just all right."

"Okay, baby. It was good, real good."

"I know it was, the way you was screaming my name."

"Dante!"

"Yeah, it was something like that, but with a little more moaning."

"You punk!" Tomi beat him in the chest for picking at her, and he held on to her wrists to keep her from hitting him anymore.

"You are violent as hell, Tomi. That's how I get treated for giving you this good loving?"

"No, that's how you get treated for picking at me."

"I'm sorry, baby." He kissed her forehead. "I won't pick at you anymore."

"Okay. You still a punk."

"And you still my baby."

This time, a comfortable silence fell between them and no more words were needed. The silence was a cocoon that embraced and exemplified the intensity of their lovemaking. In the dark, Tomi traced patterns on Dante's hairless chest with her pointer finger while she relived their sexual encounter in her mind. "Dante," she said in a soft voice, "I think I'm falling in love with you."

He didn't make any reply except for a few soft snores. Tomi smiled, laid her head on his chest, and drifted off into a content sleep.

*   *   *   *

Denise eyed Tomi as Tomi locked up the shop and hopped in her champagne-colored Altima. She had half the mind to follow the little bitch, but she didn't want anything to ruin her plans. For two weeks straight, Dante had been ignoring the hell out of her. He didn't return any of her calls, he wouldn't answer his door when she came over, and when she just happened to coincidentally run into him, he was always in a rush or had somewhere really important to be. Denise knew for a fact that it had to be another woman, but she didn't know who. With a few of her own investigations and a little detective work, she finally found the root of the problem. It was that bitch, Tomi. And now she had a face to go with the name.

Denise clicked her tongue against the roof of her mouth and shook her head disapprovingly. If Tomi thought that she was going to take her man this easy, she had another thing coming. She flicked open the dashboard to make sure that the pregnancy test was still there. It gleamed brightly in the obscure glove compartment.

Yes, her period had been two days late, but no, she was not pregnant. Dante would never know that. She had persuaded her pregnant home girl Tamika to take the test for her—but Dante wouldn't know that either. She glanced at the back-seat to make sure her Victoria's Secret bag was still there. She could see a piece of the lacy, cherry-red material hanging out the top of the bag. Her smile was slow and sneaky, and she had to bite her lip as she recalled how weak Dante became whenever he smelled Love Spell. She had bought the whole Love Spell set: bath gel, bath oil, body lotion, body mist, and body cream—the whole nine yards.

She dialed Dante's number on her cell and, as she expected, he didn't answer. "Today's the last day I'll have to put up with this shit," she avowed as she cranked up her car. "From this day on, I will have Dante's black ass wrapped around my finger." She laughed and drove off.

CHAPTER EIGHT

Niya turned on some soft, aroma-therapeutic music that she had purchased from Avon and grabbed the magazine that had came in the mail a few days ago. It was her July's subscription of *Brothas and Sistaz of Color*. Kadeesha was upstairs playing tea party, Elijah was spending the weekend with his two best friends, and Phillip wouldn't be home until a quarter to one.

She settled down into the cushiony couch, reclined her feet on the ottoman, took a small sip of her green tea, and opened the magazine. She turned to her favorite pages first, the "Get Your Laugh On" section. She laughed at a few of the "Yo mama" jokes and almost died when she read the cracks on celebrities, especially the ones about Marques Houston's sprayed on fade and Ashanti's wolverine sideburns. She read the Dear Iesha section next, although she didn't agree with the majority of Iesha's advice.

"She's so quick to give her two cents on something as if her life is picture-perfect without one single imperfection." Niya scowled and flipped the page. She read a few of the other articles, and for the most part, they were interesting. She flipped the page and smiled when she saw her sister's name under the article's title, *Why Must We Play the Fool*. Even though Kelise was the founder of the magazine, she usually didn't write any articles, unless it was about some issue that meant a lot to her. Niya knew she had to read this.

After reading the first few sentences of the magazine, she felt boiling, red rage well up inside of her. The article read:

Black women, what's going on here? Why are we constantly allowing these trifling ass men to run over us? We are always crying about how we want a good man, and how we will make sure our man respect us, yet we don't even respect ourselves. In many cases, we black women willingly put ourselves in stressful situations because we think the man will eventually change, or that he has finally come to his senses, or that we love him too much to let him go. Ladies, how many times do we have to find our man in bed with another woman to say that's enough? How many times do we have to cry on our home-girls' shoulder, the very home-girls that told us to leave his trifling behind alone from the get-go? We can find a woman's hair in our curling iron, a woman's earring beneath the bed, a used condom under the floor mat, another woman's perfume entrenched in his clothing—but it's not enough. Ladies, what will it take for us to open our eyes, close our heart, and kick his no-good ass to the curb?

With her hand covering her mouth, Niya blinked a few times in disbelief. She could not believe that her sister had the nerve to air her dirty laundry out in the open like this. So what if she hadn't literally stated her name? Every sentence that she read had been a ridiculing statement directed at her. She had entrusted Kelise with her darkest, deepest, most private secrets, and Kelise had laughed at her on a magazine page, allowing the entire black community to laugh along with her.

How dare she try to point the finger as if her love life was all peaches and cream! She didn't know what all Ricardo was doing when he was gone for months at a time. He was trifling, too, because if he loved Kelise as much as he said he did, he wouldn't put his job before her, and he would've *been* had married her.

Niya's boiling point was off the meter. Without a second thought, Niya angrily grabbed her house phone and punched in her sister's number. No answer. She hung up and dialed her sister's cell number instead. Kelise answered on the first ring.

"What's up, girl?"

"Don't you 'what's up' me," Niya replied tartly. "Who do you think you are, Kelise?"

A slight pause. "Excuse me? Niya, what's your problem? I know you ain't drinking again."

"Don't try to change the subject," Niya barked at her sister. She angrily paced the living room floor, unable to keep still. "I read your little article, Kelise. That was wrong. That was completely uncalled for."

Kelise sighed audibly through the phone. "Oh, so that's what this is about. The article."

"Yeah. *Your* article." Niya was so angry that she accidentally stubbed her toe on the corner of the center-piece table. "Shit!" she exclaimed, hopping around on one foot until the pain lessened. "Kelise, when I came to you with my problems,

I came to you and only you—not the whole entire black community that reads your damn magazine! How dare you air my dirty laundry like that—"

"Niya, enough! I've heard enough." Kelise was tired, she'd had a long, trying day at work, and she didn't feel like hearing all of this right now. "I wrote that article because I was sick and tired of women like you who cry, and boo-hoo, and cry some more over a trifling dog, only to take that trifling dog back whenever he can come up with any excuse good enough to cover his ass! I'm tired of it. When I wrote that article, I wasn't talking directly to you; I was talking to every woman who stays with a dog, even when she knows he's a dog, and she knows that he will always be a dog!"

"Well, when I read your damn article," Niya cut in, "I felt like you were pointing directly at me!"

"If the shoe fits, wear it!"

"Oh, no you—"

"Ma, is everything okay?" Kadeesha was standing at the top of the steps, holding her baby doll in one hand and a tea cup in the other.

Niya covered the phone's mouthpiece with one hand. "Everything's okay, sweetie. Auntie Kelise and Mommy are having a little argument. Go on back to your room."

"Okay." Kadeesha hurried off to her room, anxious to get back to playing tea party.

Niya returned her attention to the phone, and this time, her voice had lowered a few octaves. "Kelise, first off, I don't understand how you can sit up here and try to tell anyone what they need to do with their man when you never even see yours. Where's Ricardo right now?"

"In Canada!"

"Exactly! Not with you. He's never with you. For all you know, he could be laid up with some female right now as we speak."

Kelise gasped into the phone. "So what are you trying to say? That Ricardo is cheating on me?"

"I'm saying, don't try to tell me and other women how to take care of our man, when, half the time, you don't even know where your man is at! Worry about your relationship first. How long have y'all been engaged, Kelise? Think about that!" Niya knew it was a low blow, but she felt like Kelise deserved it.

"Niya, don't try to make this about me. We're talking about you right now."

"No, we're talking about how wrong you did me by—"

"Stop blaming me, dammit! You did yourself wrong!" Kelise was hot. "That no good piece of shit that you call your husband is a nothing, Niya. And you seem to not even care! He cheated on you, in your marriage bed—"

"He did not! He told me—"

"He told you a lie, that's what he told you!" Niya had never heard her sister sound this angry before. "Niya, you graduated from NYU; you are beautiful, intelligent—the only black sister at your law firm! I thought you were smarter than this, but when it comes to Phillip, you're as dumb as a mule. He can tell you that shit smells good, and you would believe him. You want to know why, Niya? Because you want him so bad that you are willing to overlook his every fault, believe his every lie, because you want to make what y'all have last. But the thing you need to remember is that it takes two, okay? If you're giving your all and he's giving nothing, it's not going to work. You can be mad at me all you want, but I just want you to open your eyes. And as far as I'm concerned, this conversation is over." Niya's mouth dropped as she was greeted with the dial tone.

She had half a mind to call her sister back, but she decided against it. As far as she was concerned, she had nothing else to say to her either. With that thought in mind, Niya yanked the magazine from the floor, stomped over to the fireplace, and ripped the magazine into shreds. She tossed the glossy pieces into the fireplace, along with a fire-starter log, and lit it with a household blow-torch.

When Phillip arrived home later that night, he sniffed the air and glanced over at the fireplace. "Did someone make a fire?" he asked confused.

"I got cold," Niya stated.

"A fire in the middle of July?" he asked, even more confused.

"I said I got cold!"

And that was the end of that conversation.

*   *   *   *

"Okay, Kelise. But girl, you better be glad I love you." Tomi flipped closed her cell phone and replaced it on her nightstand.

Dante was knocked out sleep, and he had his arm thrown across her waist, and one leg thrown across both of hers. There was no way she could slide out of bed without waking him, so she shook his shoulder, attempting to wake him up.

"Dante. Dante, baby, wake up."

Dante mumbled some indecipherable words in his sleep and tightened his hold around her.

"Dante!" She shook him harder, and he finally blinked awake.

"What? What?" he groggily asked.

"Baby, I have to run over to the pharmacy and grab Kelise some medicine. She thinks she's caught this summer bug that's been going around her workplace, and she's sick as a dog. Can't even get out of bed."

As she was saying this, she untangled herself from Dante and walked over to her dresser to pull on a sweater and a pair of jogging pants. Dante watched as she walked across the room. She was completely naked, wearing nothing but her birth suit. Her shoulders were softly rounded, her back long and slender with a low curve above her buttocks, and her cheeks were high, full, round, brown and beautiful. Dante felt like the luckiest man in the world to have Miss Tomi Thompson holding his arm. And even though Tomi was a wildcat in the bedroom, setting no boundaries for their lovemaking, Dante still felt as if she was holding back a part of herself from him. He knew it had something to do with this guy Jonathan and those flashback episodes that she had. Though he'd heard a little about the incident that had happened, he wasn't bold enough to ask Tomi straight out to reveal that part of her life to him. Until she opened herself to him, there would always feel like something was missing in their relationship.

But Dante couldn't completely blame Tomi for the 'missing piece' in their relationship. He was also hiding something—some *things*—from her. The most important thing that he was holding back was the fact that there was a possibility that Denise could be carrying his child. His other secret was about his past, specifically, his mother. He had never told anyone about that before; not even Denise.

"What are you thinking about?" Tomi asked as she slipped into a pair of navy blue jogging pants.

"You're sexy ass," he replied, which was only half the truth. "Come here."

Tomi pulled the matching navy blue sweater over her head and sauntered over to her man. Dante pushed up onto his elbows, and Tomi leaned over him, giving him a gentle kiss.

"Eww, morning breath," Tomi exclaimed, scrunching her nose.

"I know you ain't talking," Dante tartly replied, leaning over for another kiss. "Both our breaths smell like we ate hawk shit."

Tomi laughed and Dante lay back, pulling Tomi atop him.

"Baby, I got to go," she reminded him, even as she snuggled closer against him, reveling in the feel of his hands running through her mane of hair. "Dante…"

"Yeah?"

"I…like you."

He opened one big eyeball and looked down at her. "I hope you do like me."

"No, I mean, I really like you a lot."

"I really like you a lot, too," Dante replied, ambiguity apparent in the sound of his voice. He tilted her chin up. "Tomi, is there something you want to say?"

"I've already said it. I like you."

He probed deeper. "Is there anything else you want to say?"

Tomi knew what he was getting at, and she didn't want to go there with him. Yeah, she could tell him that she loved him while her body was still flushed with his lovemaking, and her mind was three clouds high in the sky, but now, laying atop him, fully clothed and in her right mind, she couldn't take that chance. Telling him that she loved him would open a door that had been closed too long, and she didn't think she could handle that.

She removed herself from his embrace and grabbed her keys off the nightstand. "Don't you go no where. I'll be back in about thirty minutes."

"Okay, babe." They shared a quick kiss and she left.

Dante tried to lay down and go back to sleep, but he couldn't. He flipped over on his stomach and buried his face into Tomi's pillow, inhaling her peachy fragrance. His mind went over the events of last night. He had taken her to the movies, then they had went to the skating rink, and Tomi had had the time of her life laughing at him because when it came to skating, he was like a baby learning how to walk on two left feet.

After leaving the skating rink, they had came back to her place and he had asked her for a massage since his body was aching from all the falls he had taken while trying to impress her on skates. She had agreed, and what had started off as a massage quickly got heated, and next thing he knew, he had her chanting his name to the rhythm of his strokes.

"Oh my God," Dante exclaimed, gritting his teeth as he felt himself harden by just thinking about the sweet sounds Tomi had made as he moved inside of her. He had to turn on his back again for fear of busting a hole through Tomi's mattress.

Just then, his cell phone started to ring. Dante leaned over the side of the bed and pulled his discarded pants off the floor. He dug into his back pocket and retrieved the flip-phone. The number displayed on the screen was one that he didn't recognize.

Curiously, he answered his phone. "Yo?"

A slight pause, then a woman's voice said softly, "Dante?"

The blood in Dante's veins stood still. His entire body went as stiff as a piece of plywood. "What do you want?"

"Dante, give me a chance before you hang up on me, okay, baby?"

Every part of his conscious mind was screaming for him to hang up on her. Why did she even waste her time calling him? After all she had done to him, did she really think that he could ever forgive her that easily?

Dante worked his jaw, trying to decide if he should hear her out or just end the conversation now. Finally, after much indecision, he finally snapped, "What do you want, Ma?"

"I want a second chance, Dante."

He made no reply. There was no point. She already knew what he was going to say.

"Dante, I was sick."

Did she think sickness was an excuse? "You left me hanging. You left and you never came back." His accusations were bitter confirmations of his pain that still existed even after all those years.

"I'm sorry, Dante. I've apologized a thousand times, baby, and I'll apologize a thousand more if that's what it'll take to get you back in my life. I need you Dante. I don't have nobody else."

"Ma, you hurt me."

"I know I did baby, and I'm sorry."

"You said you were coming back and you never did."

"Baby, I'm so sorry. I was sick, and I needed help. But now, I've been healed. Dante, I even go to church now, every Sunday. And I preach on every fourth Sunday. And on the first Tuesday in every month, I host a 'speak sister' conference to help other women who are recovering addicts." She talked fast for fear of him cutting her off with the dial tone. "See, Dante. I'm trying, sweetie, I'm trying hard. I'm getting my life together, Dante, but I need you. I can't do it by myself. I don't have any family but you. I need my son."

"Your son is dead." Dante pressed the end button and tossed the phone away from him. He leaned forward until he could rest his elbows on his knees, dropped his head between his legs, and allowed the tears to flow.

He no longer felt like a twenty-five-year-old man. He felt like that lonely, frightened seven-year-old boy that he use to be, hiding in the closet from his mother's abusive boyfriend, waiting for his mother to come off her high.

He thought about the night that his mother had kissed him ever so gently, and tucked him into bed. He was happy for once in his life because his mother hadn't lit up that whole day. They had gone to the fair together, and afterwards, she had taken him to Toy Palace and let him pick out any two toys in the whole store that he wanted. Afterwards, they had gone to Pizza World and filled their bellies with pepperoni, sausage, mushrooms, olives, cheese, and tomato sauce.

Now, as she tucked him into bed and kissed his forehead tenderly, she whispered, "When you wake up, I'll be gone. But I'm coming back. I'll be back. I promise."

"Where are you going?" he had asked.

"Shhh." She kissed his forehead again. "Just go to sleep, baby. Close your eyes and sleep."

When he awoke that morning, she was gone. He got himself ready, and got on the school bus, expecting his mother to be laid up on the couch with her boyfriend, Robert, when he returned home. But when he entered the house, it was vacant; neither Robert nor his mother was there. He sat on the couch, patiently waiting for his mother to come, but she never did.

Dante tried his best to remain optimistic. He kept hope alive, everyday going to school and returning home to wait for his mother. Two days passed by, then five, then one week, two weeks. By the two weeks mark, his teachers were beginning to question his poor appearance and change in attitude, there was nothing to eat in the house—not in the refrigerator or the cabinets—and the bills in the mailbox had notified him that by that following week, he would be without food, lights, and water. And his mother was still no where to be found.

Finally, he broke his piggy bank and used those pennies and nickels to catch the city bus to his grandma's house. When his grandma saw him, she ran outside and threw her arms around him. His face was covered with tear streaks.

"What's wrong, baby? What's wrong?"

He wiped at his eyes with two little balled fists. "Mama gone," he told her, "and she not coming back."

The next time he saw his mother was three years later on the news when her body was found in someone's backyard, a block up from a notorious crack-house. She had overdosed on crack and a seizure had followed, causing her to foam from the mouth. The hospital pumped her stomach and was able to revive her.

His grandma took him to visit her once, and she didn't even look like the same woman that had kissed his forehead and had promised to return. She looked like the dried up shell of what use to be.

Dante took one good look at his mother and turned his back on her. He walked out her hospital room and never looked back. From that day on, he never saw or heard from her again, except one other time, when he was twenty-two. She had called to let him know that she was turning herself in to a rehabilitative center. Dante had said, "Good luck," and hung up on her.

And now, for her to call out the blue and actually believe that he would forgive her for the way she had abandoned him. Was she out of her mind? She was the reason that he couldn't be whole in any of his relationships, because when she had left him the way she had, she'd taken a part of his soul with her as well.

"Dang, baby, you could've at least cooked breakfast while I was gone," Tomi teased upon entering the room.

Dante quickly jumped off the bed and tried to wipe the tears away, but it was too late. Tomi had already seen them falling.

She went to him and cupped his face in her hands. "Baby, what's wrong?"

"Tomi." Dante wrapped his arms tight around her waist and hid his face in the curve of her neck. He couldn't let her see him breakdown. God, if she only knew how bad he was hurting on the inside.

Tomi understood that he needed her touch more than he needed her words, so she held him and stroked his head, reminding him that she was there for him, and that everything would be okay.

When he had regained some of his composure, he sat on the edge of the bed and pulled Tomi between his legs, resting his head on her stomach.

"Tell me about it?" Tomi asked.

Dante shook his head. "Don't want to talk about it."

Tomi took a deep breath, then said, "Tell me your secret, and I'll tell you mine."

Dante looked up at her, stared in her eyes to see if he could trust her. Her eyes were wide, open, and showed the path into her soul. He saw a kindred spirit there, one like his own in those oval-shaped, golden-brown eyes. Without a shadow of a doubt, he knew he could trust her, but he wasn't ready to strip his wound. Not just yet.

He shook his head, declining her offer. "Maybe one day."

Tomi decided not to push the issue. She stroked his head like a mother cat would her kitten, and repeated his words, "Maybe one day, then." They shared a sweet kiss, and already, Dante felt some of his throbbing pain melt away.

CHAPTER NINE

"What?"

"Nothing."

"Niya, what?"

"Nothing."

Phillip sighed audibly and gave his wife an exasperated glare. "Don't you think I know by now when something is bothering you? You haven't touched your plate, and I slaved over that kitchen all day just to make sure that our anniversary night would be extra special."

Niya twisted her fork in the angel-hair spaghetti and took a large bite. "There, I touched the plate. Are you happy?"

Phillip sighed again, this time more abjectly. He dropped his knife and fork on the table and crossed his arms against his chest. "What now?" he asked, his voice borderline anger and frustration. "What has you so pissed with me this time?"

"Nothing."

"Is that the only word in your vocabulary, 'nothing'?"

Niya smacked her lips and said not a single word.

Without using proper etiquette, Phillip leaned forward and rested his elbows on the table. "What else do I need to do, Niya? I remembered our anniversary day without you having to tell me. I bought you a Vera Wang dress, and, baby, you best believe *that* put a dent in my banking account. I cooked you a spaghetti and lobster dinner, and after dinner, I had planned to give you a full body massage and make passionate love to you. What am I doing wrong? What is the problem?"

Finally, Niya did away with her reserved demeanor. "Phillip, the problem is I'm not happy."

"What do you mean, 'not happy'?"

Niya pushed away from the table and walked over to the radio in the living room, lowering the volume on Al Green's *So in Love*.

"I'm not happy, Phillip," she repeated. "I feel like you're just going through the motions. You're not doing these things because you love me; you're doing them because that's what's expected of you."

"If I didn't love you, do you think I'd damn near put my banking account in the red just to buy you a two thousand dollar dress? If that's not love then—"

"Material things do not equal love, Phillip. Money is not love." Niya pulled the yellow silk scarf from her neck and shrugged out of her banana-yellow jacket. She sat on the arm of the couch, but turned so that she could face him. "If it was all about the money, Phillip, then I wouldn't need you. With all the money I have, I can buy all the love in the world."

"What are you trying to say, that I don't love you?" Phillip walked over and sat down on the couch beside her, wrapping his arms around her waist.

Niya pushed his arms away and walked over to the other side of the room. Facing the wall, she said over her shoulder, "I love you, Phillip, I swear I do. But I can't keep doing this."

"Doing what?" Phillip had moved across the room so that he was standing behind her. He embraced her from behind and placed a tender kiss behind her ear.

"This," she repeated, removing herself from his arms once again. She returned to the sofa and tucked her legs beneath her. "Phillip, I know you're cheating on me."

"Here we go again."

"I'm not stupid. I can read the signs."

"What signs?"

"I washed clothes last night."

"And what are you going to say now?" Phillip pulled one of the chairs from the dining table, turned it backwards and straddled it. "What? Did you find lipstick on my collar? Make-up on my shirt? Or how bout this one, my clothes smelled like another woman's perfume? Which one is it?"

"How bout this one, I found your wedding ring in your pants pocket."

Phillip was silent.

Niya looked over at him and her eyes dared him to lie about it. "My wedding ring never comes off, Phillip, not even when I'm taking a shower."

"Oh, yeah, about that," Phillip began, "I was washing my h—"

Niya held up a hand to cut him off. "No, no, no. Not tonight. I don't want to hear anymore of your lies or pathetic excuses. Not tonight, Phillip. Not on what is supposed to be our anniversary night."

Niya stood to her feet and stalked pass him towards the bedroom. Phillip got up to follow her, but she slammed the door in his face and locked it.

"Niya, open the door." No response. "What about the dinner I cooked?" Still, no response. "What about that damn two thousand dollar dress I bought? That shit wasn't cheap, Niya."

Suddenly, the door came open and the silver-sequined Vera Wang dress flew out the room and drifted to the floor.

Phillip leaned down and picked the dress up off the floor, holding it as if it was a fragile flower. He leaned his forehead against the bedroom door. "So this is the way our anniversary night is going to end?"

Still no response.

"I do love you, Niya," he avowed loud enough for the entire neighborhood to hear. "I might mess up now and then, but I do love you."

Biting his lip to dam his anger and frustration, Phillip turned away from the bedroom door. He crumpled the dress in his hand and flung it across the room in a fit of rage. Then he stormed out the house, wondering how what had started off as a perfect anniversary had went so wrong.

$$* \qquad * \qquad * \qquad *$$

"I miss you."

"I miss you, too, baby." Tomi smiled at the sound of Dante's voice. He had constantly been on her mind, but she hadn't had the chance to talk to him all day.

"I'm only gone for two days, and you'll be up here Saturday for the party," she reminded him.

"That's too long," Dante told her in his deep sexy voice. He closed his eyes and pictured how she would look now, driving down the road to her mother's house.

"What are you doing tonight?"

"I was going to go to Pete's house and lay down some tracks, but his sister called today and left a message on my answering machine. She said something about him having a date tonight so he had to cancel our plans. That was a bit strange 'cause Pete usually calls me if there's a change of plans."

"Well, baby, sleep tight and dream about me."

"You know I will. Give me a kiss."

She kissed him through the phone, and he sent her a kiss back, then they hung up. Dante grabbed his gym bag and swung his towel around his neck. He had played a rough game of basketball with the boys, and every muscle in his body was tight and tense. The shower in the gym room had helped a little with easing his sore muscles, but he wanted a real massage. He wished Tomi was here so she could give him a full body massage, but he understood that she had to help her parents get everything ready for the surprise birthday party for Niya and Kelise that would be taking place in a few days.

When he pulled up at his house, he felt that something wasn't quite right, but he couldn't place his finger on it. That feeling intensified when he twisted his front doorknob and it smoothly came open.

Now I know for a fact that I locked my front door, he thought as he warily stepped inside. He gave the room a quick inspection and was happy to see that his floor-model TV was still in place, his surround-sound stereo system still covered one whole wall, and his prized Muhammad Ali picture was still hanging on the wall intact.

So I haven't been robbed, he thought with a huge amount of relief. As he closed the front door, he heard a sound come from the back room. His body tensed and his ear sensors became acute. The fight-or-flight sensation dissipated as Denise sauntered in from a back room.

"What took you so long to get here?" she purred.

"Denise?" Dante sighed and dropped his gym bag on the floor. "Didn't I tell you about showing up at my house unannounced? And how the hell did you get in here?"

As she moved closer to him, he caught a whiff of her perfume. Love Spell. He could recognize that scent anywhere. The smell was so strong, he figured she had to have drowned herself in it. His penis began to respond to that seductive scent on its own volition.

"Denise, what do you have up your sleeve this time?" he asked, simultaneously aroused and annoyed.

"Why do I have to have something up my sleeve?" Her voice was that of an angel as she flicked on the light.

Dante's breath caught in his throat, and he felt the blood rush down to his already half-aroused manhood. She had on lacy, cherry-red lingerie trimmed in black lace. The tight corset cris-crossed up her tiny waist, barely cupping her breasts. He just could see her dark areolas over the top of the breast cups. She wore black stockings that were hooked to the bottom of the corset with suspender clips, and her feet were encased in a pair of shiny black, spike-heeled stripper shoes.

"Denise. Don't do this." Dante's plea was weak and held no conviction as she held his head to the side and bit softly into his neck. That was his spot, and she knew it, too. He groaned and pulled her hard against him, letting her feel the hard rock that she had awoken.

She laughed at his weakness and slid herself down his body, unbuttoning and unzipping his pants. He did nothing to stop her. When his penis had been freed from its bondage, she fell to her knees and pulled him deeply into her mouth.

"Oh, shit." Dante let his head fall back against the door and placed his hands behind his head as Denise sent him to four different kinds of heaven. Her mouth felt like a hot, wet furnace as she sucked the length of him. He looked down at her as she teased the tip with the tip of her tongue, then took him fully into her mouth, testes, and all.

"Damn!" Dante had forgotten how she could deep-throat it. He felt the release coming, and grabbed her head, pushing deep into her throat, then pulling out. In and out. In and out. In and…out. In…and…

"Aww, shit!" Dante came hard into her mouth before falling limp against the door.

Denise went to go spit, then returned seconds later to find him still lifeless against the door panel, his penis drooping, hanging to the side. She walked over to him and seductively rubbed her breasts against his chest. "Don't fall out on me now. I'm not through with you yet." She reached behind her to undo the corset, but he held out a hand to bring her to a stop.

"Denise, I can't do this. We can't do this."

"Yes, we can," she told him, proceeding to undo the corset anyway.

Dante stopped her by binding her arms to her sides. "I'm serious, Denise. I can't have sex with you. I can't do that to Tomi."

She rolled her eyes. "It's always Tomi. Tomi, Tomi, Tomi. I'm so tired of hearing her damn name." She thought about how gratifying it would feel to bust the bitch's face in with a jack hammer.

"You might as well get use to hearing her name because I'm in love with her," Dante told her. He decided to prod her some more. "You hear that, Denise? I'm in love with Tomi. That's why I can't have sex with you because I love her too much."

Denise looked at him, her quick temper and anger getting the best of her. "Oh, so you're too in love with her to have sex with me, but you don't have a problem with me sucking your dick and you nutting all in my mouth? What kind of sense does that make?"

"I ain't even going to lie," he told her. "I bit into Eve's apple; I shouldn't have let you do what you did. My body responded before my mind did. But we're not having sex, Denise. And I mean it."

Denise stared down at his penis, which was starting to become erect again. "That may be what your mind says, but your man here doesn't seem to agree." She stood close to him and cupped his outstretched manhood with her hand.

Dante bit down on his bottom lip and reluctantly pushed her hands away. "Go put on some clothes, Denise."

"No."

"Go put on some clothes, Denise."

"No!" She stumped her foot and poked out her lips like a little child throwing a temper tantrum.

What had went wrong? she thought to herself. She'd had him in the palm of her hands, or should she say, the pit of her mouth. Either way, the bedroom was supposed to be the next stop, but he was letting the head on his shoulders get in the way of the head between his legs. And she wanted it so bad.

She decided to change tactics. "Dante, just stick it in once, and I'll leave you alone. I promise." He shook his head. "Just one time, Dante, damn."

"No, Denise! Get out!"

"Please, Dante. I need it—I want it so bad. What do you want me to do? Do you want me to beg?" She fell down on her knees and hugged herself around his legs. "I'm begging Dante. Please, baby, please!"

Dante couldn't believe his eyes or ears. Denise was begging for his dick. She was on her knees, arms wrapped around his legs, begging for his dick. He shook his head in disbelief, disgust, and disappointment. "Get up, Denise. I thought I knew you better than this. You don't have any respect for yourself. Right about now, you're acting worse than a hoe off the side of the street."

Denise stood to her feet and looked at him, her face red with shock and anger. "That's some way to talk to the mother of your child."

"Oh, shit. Here we go again." Dante tucked in his privates and zipped up his pants. "Do you really have to start this shit about Destiny again? That's over and done with. Seriously, Denise, how long do you—"

"I'm not talking about Destiny," she interrupted him.

He turned around to face her. "Then what are you talking about?"

She placed one hand over her flat tummy. "Dante Myles McKoy, I am carrying your child. Right now. As we speak."

Dante's stomach hit the floor, bounced up, and hit the floor again. He looked down at her flat stomach, then back up at her face. *Can she really be serious?* he thought. He remembered the morning he had awoken from what he had thought was a wet dream with Tomi, only to find out that he had just given Denise a powerful dose of good-loving, along with an even more powerful dose of his little soldiers. She couldn't be serious. Or could she?

"What do you have to say about that, Mr. McKoy?" She crossed her arms beneath her chest and tapped her foot impatiently. "You nutted in me, I missed my period, and now I'm pregnant. What do you have to say about that?"

Dante finally found his voice—or at least a part of it. "I…I think you're bluffing."

"I figured you would." She walked off to the back, then returned with a small white stick in her hand. "Is this proof enough?" She thrust the stick into his hand and stepped back so she could observe his reaction.

Full of rage and anger, Dante flung the pregnancy stick across the room. It hit his TV screen, then bounced onto the floor. He stumped off to his bedroom and slammed the door behind him before collapsing on his bed.

Moments later, Denise tip-toed into the room. She placed one hand on his back and he shrugged her hand away. "Don't touch me." His voice held a threat that Denise wasn't willing to test.

"How am I supposed to tell Tomi this? She won't want anything else to do with me."

That's the whole point, she thought to herself. *With Tomi out the picture, I can have you to my self.*

"If you want me to," Denise added softly, "I'll get an abortion—"

"You know I don't believe in that shit," he told her hotly. "But what I want you to do is get the hell out of my house. Now."

"Dante—"

His voice was icily calm. "Denise, get your shit and get out. I've never hit a woman before, but I swear to you, if you don't get out my face right now…" He shook his head and cracked his knuckles.

"I can tell you need some time to yourself. I'll call you tomorrow."

CHAPTER TEN

"Tell me about him right now," Tomi's mother demanded as she dipped her paintbrush into the bucket-sized aluminum can of pale-peach wall paint.

"What are you talking about?" Tomi feigned ignorance. She dipped her paintbrush into the paint and finished up her side of the storage-room wall with three large strokes.

"Every since you got here you've been nothing but smiles. Go 'head. Tell me about him. He must be a mighty fine young man, inside and out."

"He is, Ma," she admitted. Her voice and facial expressions were wistful and dreamy. "He's everything I ever wanted in a man. Ma, we connect on a whole different level. I can be myself around him, and we're always laughing and joking with each other.

"He's too sweet to me, Ma. And he's sensitive and caring, too. No matter how upset I may be, he always makes me smile. Ma, I can talk to him about anything, even boring stuff, and he listens. He's one of the best listeners I've ever met. And did I tell you how sweet he is?"

"Yeah, you mentioned it." Her mother smiled as she finished painting her side of the storage room. "You didn't tell me how he look. Is he handsome?"

"Handsome? Ma, handsome is an understatement. This man is gorgeous." She described his appearance to her mother while they cleaned up the mess they'd made with the paint.

"I can't wait to meet this man," her mother told her with a smile.

"Me either," her father added as he stepped into the storage house. He put his arm around his daughter and pulled her close. "Your mother and I haven't seen you this happy in a long time. The young man will be coming to Niya and Kelise's birthday party, right?"

"And you know it," she assured her father.

He looked around the storage room and nodded his approval. "You two did a real good job with the paintwork. This doesn't even look like a storage house anymore. What's next?"

"Well," Tomi began, wiping her hands on her pants, "after the paint dries, we'll drag in the tables and chairs and put up the decorations."

"Have you ordered the birthday cake?" Cathy asked Matthew.

"Yes, I have, darling. A double-chocolate sheet-cake with whipped butter cream frosting, right, honey-bug?"

"That's right, poo-bear." They hugged and kissed and Tomi thought it was the sweetest thing in the world. For someone to be with the same person for that long and still remain in love, that was something special to be envied by many. She wondered if that's how Dante and she would be thirty years from now.

"And are you sure that Niya and Kelise are completely unaware of this surprise birthday party?"

"Completely unaware," Tomi promised her daddy.

The three of them headed into the house to take a rest break.

*   *   *   *

Kelise parked her hunter green Ford Explorer in her mother's side yard. As she stepped from the car, she was greeted with the welcoming sight of her mother and father resting against the frame of the front door. She hugged and kissed them both before she was able to step foot in the house.

"I haven't eaten a thing all day," she told her parents, "and something smells *good*. Is that fried chicken or potato salad I smell?"

Cathy quickly glanced at Matthew and did an over exaggerated laugh. "Girl, what you talking bout? We haven't cooked a thing. You must be so hungry that you're imagining smells."

Kelise gave her mother and father a shady stare, then shrugged her shoulders. "Whatever." She looked around the house for something big, covered with birthday wrapping paper. "So where is it?" she finally asked. "Where's my big birthday surprise that I had to come all the way down here to get because it was too big for y'all to bring to me?"

"You'll get it as soon as Niya gets here," her father promised her.

Kelise made a face. "What does Niya have to do with my birthday gift?"

"Well, you know that since your birthday is only a day a part, we usually get your gifts together. The big birthday surprise is a gift that you two will have to share."

Kelise rolled her eyes, tempted to say forget it to the whole thing and return back home. Just as she was about to open her mouth, they heard a car pull up. Niya and her family came to the door.

"Happy Birthday!" Cathy and Matthew exclaimed to their daughter, hugging and kissing her first.

Kadeesha jumped on her grandpa, and Cathy squeezed and tugged on Elijah's cheeks. "My, how big you two have grown!"

"The doctor said I grew four inches!" Kadeesha exclaimed before placing a kiss on her grandma's cheeks. "Grandma, I learned a new word at the doctor's office," she bragged in an excited voice.

"And what word was that, sweet-pea?"

"Pository."

Her grandma frowned. "Pository?"

"Spository," Kadeesha tried again.

"Spository?" her grandma asked with a deeper frown. "What in the world is that?"

Kadeesha put a finger in her mouth, pondering for a minute. Her face lit up as a light bulb went off in her head. "Suppository!" she happily exclaimed.

Niya clamped a hand over her daughter's mouth. "Kids say the darnedest things," she apologized with an embarrassed smile.

"How are you doing, sir?" Phillip asked, displaying manners and respect as he shook Matthew's hand. He gave Cathy a small hug.

Niya looked over at her sister and rolled her eyes. *What is she doing here?* she thought to herself. They still hadn't spoken since the night that they'd had their heated discussion over Kelise's 'disrespectful' article.

"Niya." Kelise acknowledged her sister's presence.

"Kelise."

Cathy eyed her two daughters suspiciously, but decided not to say anything. "Okay, you two," she told them, "your birthday present is pretty big, so we had to put it in the storage house."

"It's that big?" Kadeesha asked, her eyes wide with expectation. "I bet it's a dinosaur," she told Elijah.

"All the dinosaurs are dead," Elijah informed his little sister, shaking his head at her naiveté.

"No, it's not a dinosaur," Matthew told his granddaughter. "Come on and I'll show you what it is. Follow me." The crew fell in line and followed Matthew and Cathy to the complex-sized storage house that took up nearly half of the backyard.

Matthew unlocked the door with his key. The building was dark inside.

"Come inside everybody," he ordered them, stepping to the side so that they could all come through the door.

Once everybody was inside, he built up the suspense by asking, "Are you ready?"

Their unanimous answer was a tentative, "Yes…"

Matthew flicked the light-switch, and the small crowd was taken aback by the sudden, unexpected, thunderous chorus of, "Surprise! Happy Birthday!"

Kelise was clutching her heart; Kadeesha had practically crawled up Elijah's back; and Niya had an iron grip on Phillip's shirt. They all let out a relieved sigh once saw the familiar faces.

"We got you!" Cathy exclaimed, hugging her daughters again. "We got y'all good, too, didn't we?"

"Yeah, you got us," they both admitted.

The party turned out to be a success. There were orange and tangerine balloons, ribbons, and streamers everywhere, which went along perfect with the peach tinted storage-room walls.

Cathy and Matthew had invited everyone they could possibly think of: neighbors, childhood friends, friends from high school, friends from college, every relative on the family tree, including members from their home church.

On one side of the room, the younger kids played pin the tail on the donkey, took turns swatting at a candy-stuffed, sun-shaped piñata, and did finger-painting. On another side of the room, the older attendees played cards, chatted about the good ole days, and talked about how much everyone had grown or aged since they'd last seen them. The teenagers and middle aged folk danced in the middle of the floor, played karaoke, and cracked jokes on each other.

Cathy had slaved in the kitchen for hours and her results proved well worth the sweat and time. The tables against the back wall were covered with mashed potatoes and gravy, macaroni and cheese, field peas, mustard greens, yams, deviled eggs, potato salad, broccoli and cheese, macaroni salad, corn-on-the-cob, green bean casserole, chitlins, fried chicken, honey-baked ham, homemade cornbread, and made-from-scratch, buttermilk biscuits.

Clear dessert plates covered the dessert table, and the plates held a variety of fruit desserts, including apple pie, crumble-top cherry pie, key lime pie, and lemon meringue pie. Three large glass bowls occupied the table as well. One bowl held Grandma Maybelline's famous banana pudding, another held Aunt Brenda's chocolate mousse, whipped-cream pudding, and the third bowl was none other than Aunt Carolyn's prize-winning, punch-bowl, strawberry short-cake. But the center piece of the dessert table was the orange, white, and yellow, 60 by 36 inch, sheet cake that read: Happy Birthday Niya and Kelise!!

Over all the noise, Cathy yelled out, "If everyone can be quiet for a sec, I'll say grace and then we can eat." The room fell silent in record time. Cathy said a quick but moving grace, and immediately, a long line of hungry black people seemed to materialize from nowhere.

It was during this time that Tomi presented her sisters with their birthday presents. Since she knew how much Niya adored aromatherapy-related items, she had purchased her an aroma-therapeutic set. The set contained candles, oils, sprays, bath items, tranquilizing CDs, and a bundle of incense sticks.

"Thank you, Tomi," Niya said, hugging her sister tight. "Now this is the way a sister should act," Niya applauded her, "caring and thoughtful, not back-stabbing and trifling."

"No comment," Tomi replied, deciding against involving herself in their dispute. Tomi hurried over to Kelise before she could get missing. "Happy Birthday, sis. I hope you like it."

Kelise took the rectangular box that her sister held out and smiled before opening it. Inside was a personalized silver tennis bracelet with her name in the middle. The box also contained matching earrings that dangled the letter K encroached in diamond rhinestones.

"Tomi!" Kelise shook her head, then hugged her sister. "You shouldn't have! I know this must have cost you a fortune."

"Actually, those are rhinestones, not diamonds," Tomi informed her sister. "Got it from Avon, so you know my girl gave me the hook-up."

"You ain't good for nothing. I thought you actually spent some money on me," Kelise teased.

While Tomi was talking with Kelise, Matthew grabbed a hold of Dante. "So you're the young man who's stolen our daughter's heart?" he asked.

"That depends on if you've heard good things about me, or bad." The two men sat down in white lawn chairs and began to talk.

Moments later, Tomi sashayed over to steal Dante just in time to hear her daddy tell him, "If you hurt her, I'll have to kill you."

"Daddy, stop threatening him," she scolded her father. "I know y'all are having a great conversation, but I need to borrow him for a minute." She pulled Dante to his feet and they headed outside. "Was he real bad?" she asked.

"No. Actually, your pops is mad cool. I like him."

Tomi sent a prayer of thanks up to heaven. Her dad could be a beast when he wanted to be.

Dante asked, "Baby, is there anywhere we can go to have a little privacy? I really need to talk to you."

Tomi paused in mid-step and threw a questioning glance his way. She tried to read him to get an idea of what he might have to say, but he was unreadable. He seemed nervous, anxious, and uncertain all at once.

"Is it good or bad?" she inquired.

"I don't know."

Tomi smacked her lips. "What you mean, 'I don't know'? Either it's good or it's bad."

"Tomi," Dante said in a low voice so that the few old women who were obviously eavesdropping wouldn't hear him, "let's go somewhere private where we can talk."

Noting the fact that they had drawn a small audience, Tomi submitted to his request. Taking his hand in hers, she led him into her parents' house through the back door, then up a narrow stairwell into an empty bedroom.

Tomi shut the door and leaned against it, crossing her arms and looking at him anxiously. "You wanted privacy, here we go. Start talking."

Dante walked over to the small, double bed and took a seat on the edge of it. He didn't know where to begin. There were so many things that he needed to tell Tomi, but none of them that he actually wanted to tell her.

How was he supposed to tell her that he cheated on her within the two days that she was out of town helping her parents prepare for the surprise birthday party? How was he supposed to tell her that one morning, he accidentally awoke having sex with his ex, and as a result of it, he had a little Dante on the way? And how was he supposed to tell her that this man whom she cared so much about would never be able to love her completely because his mother's neglect had left what seemed to be a permanent scar on his heart?

"What is it Dante? Tell me. I'll be understanding," she promised, already preparing herself for the worse.

Dante looked over at this woman whom he had came to care about above anything else. She looked beautiful with her hair layered and framing her face. She wore a cotton-candy pink, spaghetti-strap blouse, a khaki skirt that stopped at mid-thigh, and a pair of pink, delicate stiletto heels that laced up to her calves. Her attire didn't matter to Dante. She could've been wearing a paper-bag for all he cared, and she would have still been the most beautiful woman in the world to him.

"Why are you looking at me like that?" Tomi asked. "Do I have something on my face?" She wiped at her nose, her chin.

"No. You're just that beautiful," Dante admitted, leaning back on his elbows so that he could get a better view of her. "I feel like the luckiest man alive to have you on my team."

Tomi smiled modestly and pushed away from the door, walking over to him and sitting sideways on his lap. "Baby, what is it?" she asked softly, cupping his chin with her hand. "Talk to me."

Dante moved her hand up to his lips and placed a kiss in her palm. Should he tell her about his slip-up with Denise? Should he tell her about the unintentional baby on the way? Could he tell her about his mother?

"You remember when you said if I tell you my secret then you'd tell me yours?"

Tomi paused for a second, then nodded her head. "Yeah." She moved from his lap and crawled onto the bed until she was sitting behind him. Opening her legs and placing one on either side of him, Tomi wrapped her arms around him and rested her head on his back, listening to the sound of his heartbeat. "Yeah, I remember."

He pulled her arms across his shoulders and held her hands against his heart. "Okay, well, I'm going to tell you something I've never told anybody before. Nobody. Not a single person."

Tomi wondered what in the world was he going to say that was so arcane. She remembered the time she had returned home to find him sitting on her bed crying. Whatever had happened, if it could make a grown man cry, it had to be something real bad.

"I'm all ears," Tomi assured him, hugging him tighter from behind.

"Okay. Here goes."

Tomi felt Dante's body tense as he began the story of his painful childhood, and as he continued, his body became more and more tense until he felt like a marble statue in her arms. When he finished his story, for a minute, Tomi didn't know what to say. Any mother who could abandon her child like that both earned and deserved the animosity that Dante felt for her. Tomi knew Dante didn't want her pity, but she couldn't help it.

As Dante revealed his story to her, it was obvious that that neglected, sad little boy was still inside of him, was still crying out for his mother, but was being repressed by an angry Dante who was unwilling to forgive or forget.

"Baby," Tomi whispered, holding him tighter, "Baby, I'm so sorry."

Dante turned around so that he was facing her. His eyes were glistening with unshed tears, and his shoulders seemed to carry the weight of the world.

"Tomi, I need you."

"I need you, too, baby."

"I know I've hurt you, but please forgive me baby, please."

Tomi's brow furrowed with confusion. *Forgive him? For what? He'd hurt her? What was he talking about?*

"Dante, baby, what are you talk—" Her words were cut off by Dante's passionate kiss. His kiss took her breath away. He was kissing her like she was his water, and he was a man lost in the desert, dying of thirst.

Tomi returned his kiss with every part of her being, spreading her fingers against the side of his face and deepening the kiss.

"Tomi, don't leave me," he repeated, placing kisses along the length of her neck. "Baby, please don't leave me."

"I won't leave you," Tomi promised, lifting her chin to give him better access.

Dante slid her spaghetti-strap down one caramel-brown shoulder, and placed a feather-light kiss on her collar bone. He pulled her shirt lower until her braless breasts were revealed.

Suddenly, the door flew open and Tomi's Uncle Thomas filled the doorway. Tomi quickly threw her hands across her chest to mask her nudity.

"Ooh, I'm telling on y'all!" Uncle Thomas declared in a teasing, sing-song voice.

"Uncle Thomas!" Tomi exclaimed, putting her arms through her shirt straps and pulling her shirt up, "Are you spying on us?"

"No, but I should be." His tone was reprimanding. "Your mama told me to come find y'all because Kelise and Niya are about to cut the cake. Thank God I got here when I did, or who knows what might've happened."

"Uncle Thomas, it ain't even like that," Tomi told him.

"You in here half-ass naked, but it ain't like that?" Her Uncle Thomas let out a dubious humph. He pointed a finger at Dante. "Touch her again and I'm gon' whoop that ass."

Dante opened his mouth to defend himself, but Tomi interrupted him, smacking her lips. "Uncle Thomas, quit threatening my boyfriend. Didn't I tell you it ain't even like that?"

"Save it, little miss thang." He pushed the door open. "Y'all come on so these girls can cut this cake. I've been eyeing it every since the party started."

Tomi took Dante's hand in hers and gave him a look that told him that they would finish what they had started later. The three of them returned to the storage house, and Cathy was standing up once again, asking for everyone's attention.

"As you all know," she began, "since Kelise and Niya's birthday is only one day a part, we've decided to throw this surprise party together for both of them. I am very proud of my two beautiful daughters. Niya is now considered partner at her law firm, the only black woman in that law firm, might I add. And Kelise's magazine, *Brothas and Sistaz of Color*, is thriving like never before. I wish you two the happiest birthday and many more to come. Now, y'all come on and cut this cake. Everyone's been waiting to sink their teeth into a piece." She held up a large knife that had orange and peach-colored ribbon tied into a bow around its handle.

"What are you waiting for?" she asked when neither sister budged. "Come and cut the cake."

"Niya, you can have the honor of cutting the cake first," Kelise politely stepped down to her sister.

"No, thank you, Kelise. You can do it," her sister courteously declined her offer.

Kelise's smile was artificial and her tone was non-negotiable. "Since, technically, it *is* your birthday, I *insist* that you cut the cake."

"I *said* no thank you. *You* can do it." Niya's voice held just as much of a challenge as her sister's.

"I have an idea," her mother cut in, "why don't you two cut the cake *together*?" She gave them both the you-two-better-stop-embarrassing-me-in-front-of-all-these-people-before-I-skin-you-alive look.

"I don't see what's the big deal," Kelise stated. "Today is her birthday. Why can't she cut the cake? It's not like—"

Niya cut her off. "It's only a cake, Kelise, damn. Why do you have to act so childish all the time—"

"Childish? For you to be the oldest, you sure as hell ain't acting your age."

Everybody was quiet and their eyes jumped from one sister to the next; they were literally leaning on to the sisters' every word.

"I don't want to cut the damn cake," Niya gritted between clenched teeth. "Stop arguing with me, and just—"

"Well, I think you need to—"

"Maybe that's your problem, Kelise; you think too damn much," her sister finally exploded. "Maybe, if you could keep your thoughts to yourself, you and I would be on speaking terms right now. Putting my personal life on blast, what the hell is wrong with you?"

"Nobody didn't put your personal life on blast. I simply wrote an article that—"

"Maybe, if you had a personal life with your fiancé, you wouldn't be all up in mine."

"Correction. Maybe, if you could open your eyes and quit letting your husband treat you like dog shit, then maybe—"

"Excuse me? Dog shit? If Phillip treats me like dog shit, then Ricardo must treat you like—"

"Ladies!" Their father barked that one word and it echoed throughout the storage room like an ominous burst of thunder. "Both of you. Outside. *Now.*"

The sisters stared at each other, daggers of lightning dangerously flashing in their eyes. Finally, they turned and followed their father outside.

"Ooh, they in trouble now," Uncle Thomas stated. He walked over to Cathy. "Hand me the knife. I'll cut the damn cake. They sound like Ike and Tina up in here." He mimicked Tina's voice, "I-I-I, I don't want the cake Ike!"

CHAPTER ELEVEN

"You what?!"

"Tomi, baby, please. Give me a minute. Let me explain."

"There's nothing to explain, Dante." Tomi was flabbergasted. Here she was, in love with this man, and he just told her that his ex-girlfriend, Denise, was pregnant with his child.

At the birthday party, she had wondered why he'd kept saying please don't leave him. Now, she understood. "Dante, get out my house."

"Tomi, I'm not leaving until you give me a chance to explain."

"I don't want to hear anything else you have to say. Just leave." There were so many tears in her eyes, she could barely make out her surroundings. Fumbling against the wall, she made her way to her bathroom and shut and locked the door.

Dante stubbornly pursued her. "Baby, give me a chance to explain," he begged, knocking on the bathroom door.

"I'm not your baby, dammit. Your baby is inside of Denise's stomach. Dante, I can't believe you. I finally open my heart to somebody and this is what happens? Shit, man."

"Let me explain."

"What is there to explain?" she cried, slamming down the lid before plopping onto the toilet. Her body racked with the intensity of her sobs. "Get out my house, Dante! Get out, get out, get out before I call the cops!"

"I'm not leaving." Dante was stubborn. He refused to let Tomi slide through his fingers this easy because of one little mistake. He knocked repetitively on the door. "Open the door baby. Let me in."

"What part of no don't you understand? Get out and leave me alone!"

He leaned against the door, resting his forehead against his forearm. "Tomi, don't do this to me. I want to be with you. I want us to make things work."

Her only reply was muffled sobs.

With every sob that came from her beautiful lips, Dante felt as if someone was punching him in his gut. If anything at all, he hadn't meant to hurt Tomi. He hated to hear her crying, hated to see her like this. But she had to understand that it wasn't all his fault.

"Tomi, Denise set me up," he tried to explain, refusing to give up.

"She set you up, Dante?" she asked from the other side of the door. "What did she do, rape you? She held you down and climbed on your dick for the ride of her life, and you were too weak to stop her? Is that what happened, Dante?"

"Baby—"

"No, not that. Maybe she was laying naked on the floor and you just so happened to trip and fall inside of her. Is that what happened? Is it?"

"No, it's not like that. Baby—"

"I am *not* your baby, Dante. Will you please just leave? How many times do I have to ask you to get…away…from…my…door?!" With each word, she banged her fist against the bathroom door before collapsing against the door-frame.

"Tomi, don't do this to me." Dante was begging. "I need you. Open the door."

"No," she told him, leaning against the door, "I don't even want to look at you right now, Dante. Please get out. Don't make me ask you again."

Her eyes were watery, swollen, and red; tear streaks covered her face and tears puddled at her chin. She closed her eyes and prayed that he would leave without saying another word. She couldn't take hearing the pain in his voice as he begged for her to hear him out.

On the other side of the door, Dante was angry, frustrated, desperate—he didn't want to lose Tomi, but he felt like it was already too late. "Tomi, shit, I know I messed up. I know I was in the wrong, but baby, don't do this to me. Don't do me like this. Tomi, I…Tomi, baby, I love you."

There. It was out. He had said it. He held his breath, fearful of how she would react to his confession.

Tomi broke down crying harder at the sound of those three words that she had waited so long to hear. She slid down the door, all the way to the floor, until her cheeks rested on the cold linoleum. She had fell in love with him the night they'd ran into each other at the store and he had handed her that ceramic casserole dish off the top shelf—maybe even before then. She knew he cared a lot about her, but she had needed him to say those three words. And now he was saying them, but under the wrong circumstances.

"Did you hear me, Tomi?" he asked, his voice cracking with emotion. "I love you."

Tomi didn't recognize her voice as she said loud and clear, "Dante, it's over. Go away."

It took Dante a second to digest her words. But once her words had been registered in his mind and in his heart, he pushed his body away from the door. He looked at the door once more, pain and hurt etched into his handsome features. One tear escaped his eye and plummeted to the floor. Dante left, slamming her front door hard enough to make her windows rattle. Not once did he look back.

Tomi jumped as she heard her front door slam. She balled her fists and put them against her mouth, trying to muffle her loud sobs. With one hand holding her stomach, she crawled on hands and knees across the bathroom floor, pulled up the toilet seat, and retched the dinner that Dante and she had just shared into the toilet.

✳   ✳   ✳   ✳

"We have an intern, Mrs. Browning."

Niya looked up as Billy ushered in a young white girl, no more than fifteen or sixteen years of age, wearing a two-piece gray suit. She had thick, chocolate brown hair, which was pulled into a ponytail, and soft, blue eyes that stood out behind her oval shaped glasses.

She held out her hand towards Niya. "Hi. I'm Charlotte Parker." Although she seemed nervous and young, her voice was that of a confident adult.

"Nice to meet you, Charlotte. You can call me Mrs. Browning."

"Okay, Mrs. Browning."

"I'll leave you two alone," Billy said, giving Niya a thumbs up sign. He closed the door behind him.

"Is this your first time working in a law office?" she asked the young lady. Charlotte nodded her head.

"Well, first, I'm going to teach you how to file these papers. Then, I'll show you how to pull up files on the computer. Each client that we have is color-coded. In here," she put her hand against an army-green filing cabinet, "are the folders, which are also color-coded. Simply drop the client's file into the folder that matches its color. That's not too difficult, is it?"

"Not at all." Niya appreciated the girl's alacrity.

"Here you go." Niya pulled an armload of unsorted files from a lower drawer. "File these for me." She dropped the stack of files onto her desk and a whirlwind of dust whooshed from the stack. "You should be done no later than three, four at the latest."

Niya looked down at her watch. It was five minutes pass one. She had time to run and get something to eat.

"If I don't be back by the time you finish," she told the girl, "press this button right here." She pointed to a button on her desk phone. "That's Billy's line. Tell him that you're finish filing the papers, and he'll give you some work to do until I get back. Okay?"

"Yes, ma'am," the girl said, already sorting the mountain of files into color-coordinated stacks. Niya gave her a pleased smile and left.

She hopped into her all white Infinity 2005 and cranked up the car while she thought about where she would go for lunch. She thought about McDonald's, but lately, she had been putting on a fair amount of weight in her hips. A burger sounded too greasy and fattening. She thought about Taco Bell, then shook her head when she remembered how intense her gas was the last time she'd eaten there.

"I'll go home," she decided. She still had plenty of food left over from the big seafood dinner she had cooked the night before.

Fifteen minutes later, she pulled into her driveway and was shocked to see Phillip's gray pick-up truck parked in the garage. *Isn't he supposed to be at work?* she thought, killing the engine and stepping out the car. *Maybe he called in sick. Yesterday he was complaining about a killer headache.*

Niya didn't think anymore about it as she turned the key in the lock to let herself into the house. She was greeted with pure silence. Figuring he was probably in the room sleep, she walked into the kitchen and retrieved a pre-made plate from the refrigerator. After removing the aluminum foil, she placed it in the microwave and turned the timer to five minutes. She filled a glass with tap water from the sink and downed it before heading for the bedroom. She wanted to make sure that her baby was okay. If he was sick, she was willing to run to the store and buy him some Dayquil or extra-strength Tylenol.

Opening their room door, Niya stood frozen to that one spot with her mouth hanging ajar. Yes, Phillip was in the bed asleep, but, no, he wasn't alone. A light-skinned, young lady, with hair the same color of the bright, reddish-pink strand that had been found in Niya's curling iron, lay curled up in their marriage bed, arms wrapped around her husband. They both were sound asleep.

Slowly, Niya backed away from the door, shocked beyond belief. She couldn't utter a single sound, say one single word. The hurt that was clutching at her heart was almost unbearable.

How can he do this to me? How can he sleep with that slut in the same bed that he made love to me in last night? How can he be so heartless? How can he be so cold?

Refusing to allow a solitaire tear the opportunity of rolling down her beautiful face, Niya quietly rushed to her office room. Phillip kept his hunting rifle there, and now, she was going to put it to use. She ran over to the long trunk and tried to pry it open, but couldn't. Then, she remembered the key he kept in a small box in the top drawer of her desk. She jerked the drawer open and removed the small, cube-shaped box.

"Damn," she whispered. The box had a combination lock on it. She racked her brain for the combination. First, she tried his birthday. Nope. She tried her birthday. Nope. She tried Kadeesha's birthday and then Elijah's, but neither of those were the combination either. She tried the last four numbers of her social security number. Nope. She tried the last four numbers of his social security number. Bingo! The locked popped open and she removed the key.

Hurriedly, she returned to the rifle box and jammed the key into the keyhole. It turned and made a beautiful clicking sound as it came open. She held the rifle in her hands, and it felt heavy, cold, and merciless, just like her heart. She quickly loaded the rifle, doing it with ease from the many times she had watched Phillip load it. She cocked the hammer back and headed for the bedroom with a confident, brisk stride.

So what if I kill him, she thought to herself. *It will be considered a crime of passion. I might get five years at the max. But seeing him dead will be well worth it.* Today was the last day that she'd ever play the role of his fool.

She opened the bedroom door. They were both in bed, both asleep, both completely unaware of their impending doom. She pointed the gun at Phillip's head, closed one eye, aimed, and fired.

The recoil of the gun almost jerked her shoulder out its joint, causing her to miss her mark. A hole the size of a grapefruit appeared in the wall, right above Phillip's head. The loud noise had awakened both Phillip and the light-skinned chick.

"Oh shit!" Phillip exclaimed. "Niya?"

They both scrambled out of the bed, trying to cover themselves and duck for cover at the same time. Niya loaded the gun and fired at him again. The recoil jerked her arm again, but this time, she missed by mere inches; a grapefruit-sized hole appeared in her armoire instead of his head. She fired again, and this time, the bullet struck the window; the discordant tinkling of broken glass showered the room. She had grown somewhat accustomed to the recoil of the rifle, and her last shot had missed him by the width of a hair.

The red-headed bitch was hiding in the bathroom, screaming like a stuck pig. Niya aimed at the bathroom door and was just about to blow the bitch to hell when Phillip grabbed the gun's barrel and pointed it towards the ceiling. The rifle went off and blew a hole in their ceiling instead. Plaster fell from the ceiling, covering them both so that it looked like they had been fighting in flour.

"Give me that damn gun before you kill somebody," Phillip ordered her, spitting out a mouthful of plaster and shaking even more of it from his face while attempting to pull the rifle out her hands.

"That's the whole point, Phillip." She blinked plaster from her eyes and refused to let the gun go. "I *am* trying to kill someone, preferably you, but the bitch will do."

Phillip was finally able to remove the gun from her hands, but that didn't stop Niya. She bum-rushed the bathroom door and banged on it hard with her fists. "Open the door, bitch! Don't be scared, now! Open the goddamn door!" She kicked at the door, but it wouldn't give.

Cassandra couldn't stop screaming. "Phillip! Get her! Phillip!"

"Baby, calm down. Just calm down for a minute, and then we can sit down and talk." Phillip tried gently to pull her away from the door, but when she turned around and saw his two-timing, trifling ass with the bitch's lipstick smeared all across his face, she pulled back her fist and slammed it into his eye.

"In our marriage bed?" she asked him, as he held the throbbing eye in pain. She grabbed the lamp off their dresser and, with a yell of frustration, shattered it across the side of his face.

At the crashing sound of the shattering lamp, Cassandra screamed from in the bathroom, and Phillip grabbed his face, which was bleeding profusely from a cut that stretched from his cheekbone to his ear.

"Aww, shit," he moaned, tenderly holding his throbbing face with the palm of his hand. "I think you broke something." He spit out a mouthful of blood.

"Not good enough," Niya yelled at him, "I want you dead!" She grabbed an antique flowerpot that her mother had bought for her several years ago and slammed it down on top of his head. Like a crunched aluminum can, he crumpled to the floor. She ran to retrieve the rifle from the other side of the room, but he grabbed her ankle, and she fell to the floor.

Bleeding and in tons of pain, he crawled atop her, pinning her to the floor with his bodyweight. Niya had a field day on his already throbbing, bloody face with her hard little fists. He tried to hold her wrists, but she was too fast for him. A punch to his mouth, a punch to his swollen eye, a punch to his bruised cheek. One punch after another, she just couldn't stop herself. She was hurt, angry, frustrated, and each punch helped her feel that much better.

Cassandra was still screaming from in the bathroom.

"Cassandra! Cassandra!" Phillip bellowed, trying unsuccessfully to dodge his wife's hard blows, "I have her pinned down. Run while you can."

Cautiously, Cassandra cracked open the door and, when she saw that Niya was really pinned to the floor, she scooped up her clothes and shot across the room to the bedroom door, wearing nothing but a daffodil-yellow bra and thong set.

"Let me at her!" Niya demanded, reaching for Cassandra. She caught the girl's ankle and twisted hard. The girl fell to the floor with an ear-piercing scream, and Niya tried her best to wrench the girl's leg from her body, but Phillip's hold on her arms was as unyielding as stone. The girl scrambled to her feet, and Niya was pleased to see that she was limping hard on her twisted ankle; she half-limped, half-ran from the house as if Satan himself was giving her chase.

Once the girl was gone, Niya calmed down somewhat. "Let me up," she told Phillip after she had tired from bashing his face in.

"No." He sounded completely worn out, but his grip on her was still strong.

"Let me up," she ordered him again.

A blood droplet dripped from the cut on his forehead and plopped on her cheek, rolling down the side of her face like a red-tinted tear. Blood oozed from the cut she had caused with the blow from the lamp. And blood rolled from his mouth and dripped on her chin as he whispered, "Promise me you won't kill me. Promise you won't go for the gun and shoot me dead, then I'll let you go." He sounded utterly exhausted.

After a few moments of indecision, Niya finally gave up on her quest to kill. "I promise I won't kill you." She didn't sound convincing.

"Put it on our kids."

"I will not!"

"Put it on our kids."

Niya rolled her eyes and sighed. "I put it on our kids."

Hoping he was making the right decision, Phillip rolled off her, and she sprung to her feet. She looked down at his body, which was completely depleted of all energy and strength, and she couldn't help but to kick him one good time in his gut with her pointed shoe. He didn't have the strength to cry out in pain.

"You better be glad that I have a little mercy on your pitiful ass," she spat at him. "Because if I didn't, you'd be dead by now." She glanced in the mirror at her appearance and didn't recognize herself. Her hair, face, and clothes were covered in thick plaster from the ceiling; it looked as if someone had used her to make biscuit dough. She stripped naked and jumped in the shower to take a quick wash-off and to shampoo her hair.

Once she was out the shower, Niya noticed that Phillip was still lying on the floor in the exact same spot. He hadn't budged an inch. She looked at him to see if he was still breathing and saw his chest gently rise and fall. Niya dried off and covered her body in sweet-smelling lotion before switching into a rose-colored pantsuit. She blow-dried her hair and ran a brush through it, mad that all the curls that she had so painstakingly fixed were gone.

"I'm going back to work," she told Phillip who was lying almost lifeless on the floor. "When I get home, I want you and all your shit gone. Everything. Pack your little shit on the back of your pick-up truck and get ghost. I want you out of my life."

"Who's going to pick up the kids?" he asked, licking his crusted, bloody lips.

"Don't worry about that. I've got it all under control." She stepped over him and headed for the door. She was about to leave, but then turned around and yanked her wedding ring from her finger. "Take that little piece of shit." She flung it at his head, and it made a good, loud cracking sound as it bounced off his forehead. She pulled off the anniversary ring and flung it at him, too. "And take that shit, too. Pawn it all. Trust me, you'll need the money."

She went into the kitchen, took her plate out the microwave, covered it with aluminum foil and headed outside after checking the time. It was almost half past two, which meant that she still had enough time to eat before returning to work. She entered her office just as Charlotte was putting away the last client's file.

"All done, Mrs. Browning."

"Mrs. Browning? Did I tell you to call me Mrs. Browning?" she asked.

The girl's big blue eyes widened behind her spectacles, and Charlotte nodded her head 'yes'.

"I change that," Niya told the girl, patting Charlotte's head thoughtfully. "It's *Ms.* Browning—better yet, just call me Miss Thompson."

The girl smiled, relieved that she hadn't done or said anything wrong. "Okay, Miss Thompson. I see you've changed your outfit."

"Yeah, I got tired of wearing that old skirt," she lied. "And plus, I look pretty in pink. Don't you agree?"

The girl nodded her head. "You look beautiful."

"Thank you, Charlotte."

"What do I do next?" she asked, ready to get back to work.

"Think you can make a few copies of these?" Niya asked, holding up a stapled packet of papers.

The girl gave her an iffy look. "I haven't used a copy machine in a while. But I think I can give it a shot."

"Give it a shot, huh?" Niya asked, repeating the girl's words. She thought about how she had given her husband a few shots only minutes ago and couldn't help the bubble of laughter that escaped her. Charlotte looked at her confused.

"If you only knew," Niya said, shaking her head. "Girl, if you only knew."

CHAPTER TWELVE

"Yes, Dante. Yes! I feel it. I feel it! Dante, I can't...Dante, I...Dante!" Denise came hard at the same time that he climaxed. He collapsed on her, breathing harshly. He hadn't meant to be so rough with her, but all the built up anger inside of him seemed to come out of him every time they had sex.

What had him angrier than anything else was the simple fact that no matter how much time he spent with Denise, he couldn't take his mind off Tomi. Whenever he went out with Denise, he was missing Tomi. Whenever he had sex with Denise, Tomi was always the face he saw when he closed his eyes. Tomi was the first thing on his mind in the morning, and the last thing on his mind at night. She was like a ghost haunting him, and no matter how much he tried to erase her from his thoughts, he couldn't seem to completely wipe her out his heart.

Gently, Denise rubbed the top of his head. "What's wrong, baby?" she questioned him.

"Nothing," he lied. He kissed her before pulling out of that tight warmth. "Did I hurt you?" he asked, remembering again how rough he had taken her.

"I like it a little rough every now and then," she admitted with a cat-like growl, drawing circles across his collar bone. "You didn't hurt me much."

"Good." He kissed her again, then went in the bathroom to discard his condom and clean up.

Although Denise was pregnant by him, he still used condoms because he didn't trust her fully; he was not about to hit raw and end up with some venereal disease. His homeboys had informed him about some of her sexual escapades, and though he'd never caught her in the act, he knew Denise's sneaky personality left no room for chances.

While he was in the bathroom cleaning up, Denise crossed her hands behind her head and looked up at the ceiling with a content smile on her face. She knew Dante would come around eventually, but she was shocked how fast it had happened. One day, they weren't on speaking terms; the next, he was busting down her door, practically throwing her against the wall, and taking her without any foreplay, any unnecessary words, or any false promises. For two weeks now, she had been floating on a cloud called Ecstasy, and she loved it.

She had to admit, she felt a little bad about lying to him about being pregnant; but sometimes, you had to do what you had to do. Her ends had obviously justified her means because, number one, she had her man back, and number two, that bitch Tomi was no longer a part of the equation.

Dante returned from the bathroom and crawled in bed beside Denise. He pulled her atop his chest and ran his fingers through her hair.

"I love you, Dante."

"Yeah."

Yeah? she thought. *Okay, so he's not at the 'I love you' point, but he'll get there. It's going to take a little time. Slow and steady wins the race.*

"When's your next doctor's appointment?" he asked, sliding his fingers across her flat abdomen.

"Next Thursday at three." The lie rolled off her lips as smooth as grandma molasses.

"I'll go with you."

Her body tensed. She never thought about him going to a doctor's appointment with her. He never attended one when she was pregnant with Destiny. He was present at the childbirth classes, and he was there when she went into labor; but that was it.

"You don't have to go with me, baby," she told him, wrapping his long arms around her. "Don't you have to work?"

"Yeah, but I'm going to take off," he told her. "I want to keep up with this whole pregnancy, make sure nothing goes wrong. I don't want us to lose this baby, too."

"Baby, that's unnecessary. I don't want you missing work for a stupid prenatal appointment. The only thing they'll do is measure my stomach and probably run a few tests. I'll have to pee in a cup, and maybe give some blood, but that'll be it. I know you don't want to miss work for that."

Dante was resolute with his decision. "I'm going to be there for everything: every doctor's appointment, every childbirth class, every breathing class, everything."

Denise was becoming a bit worried. How was she supposed to pull off this pregnant role if he was going to play the eagle, watching her every move? She shifted uncomfortably. "Instead of trying to be there for every doctor's appointment, you need to be working, making that money so we'll be ready when the baby comes."

"Denise, I have plenty of money in my bank account. The baby will be well taken care of. I'm going with you to that doctor's appointment—unless you have a problem with that." He looked at her curiously. "Do you have a problem with that?"

"No, baby. If it means that much to you, then I want you to come," she lied, putting on a cheerful face. "But let me warn you, it's going to be pretty boring."

"I have a portable CD player."

When Dante's soft snores told her that he had drifted off to sleep, Denise rose to her feet and paced in front of the bed, glancing at Dante every now and then to make sure he was still asleep. Using his house phone, she dialed her home-girl Tamika's number.

Groggily, Tamika answered on the fifth ring, "Hello?"

"I got a problem," Denise whispered, keeping her voice low so as not to wake Dante.

"Who is this?"

"It's me, Denise."

"Dee? Why you whispering?"

"Cause I don't want to wake up Dante. But anyway, I have a slight problem."

"What is it now?"

"Dante wants to go to my 'doctor's appointment' with me. What should I do?"

"Tell him he can't. Make up some type of lie, you know you good at it."

"I tried. He's not buying it."

"I got it. On the day of your 'doctor's appointment,' avoid him every way possible. Then, the day after the appointment, tell him that you were so busy that day that you didn't get a chance to talk to him, but the appointment went just fine."

"Damn you're good, Mika. You're always…"

"Hello? Dee? Denise? You still there? Hello?"

Denise's attention had drifted away from the conversation because she'd heard a very distant ringing sound, like the ringing of a cell phone. Her cell phone was off, and Dante usually kept his phone on silence, but she was almost positive that she had heard it ringing. Who could be calling him at a quarter to midnight? Had to be a female.

"Hey, Tamika, I'll call you right back."

"Why?"

Without answering her friend's question, Denise hung up the house phone and went in search of the ringing cell phone. She had to find it quick before it stopped ringing or before the ringing sound woke up Dante.

Tip-toeing over towards the dresser, Denise used the small amount of light coming from the bathroom to inspect the dresser top for a silver cell phone. She didn't see it, but she heard it. She knew she was close because the ringing sound was growing louder.

Casting a glance over her shoulder to confirm that Dante was still asleep, she quickly but quietly began to pull open the dresser drawers. The little red light on the phone flickered simultaneously with the ringing sound as she pulled open the top dresser drawer. Found it!

The caller ID read: Tomi.

Glancing at Dante, she hit the talk button and said in a low voice, "Hello?"

"Hello? Who is this?"

"Who is this?" Denise asked with attitude, deciding to play with the dumb chick for a while.

Tomi's voice was hesitant. "I'm sorry, I must have the wrong number."

She was about to hang up, so Denise quickly said, "Wait!"

Dante began to move in the bed, and Denise froze, the cell phone still to her ear. Dante lifted one arm high in the air, smacked his lips as if he was savoring the flavor of spicy, fried chicken, and turned over on his side, immediately returning to sleep.

"Who is this?" Tomi asked after Denise's long pause.

"This is Denise, who did you call to speak to?"

Tomi's side of the line was quiet and, for a minute there, Denise thought she had hung up. Then, Tomi asked, "Where's Dante?"

"In bed. He's tired. I think I...wore him out." Denise's smile was wicked, the smile of a devil. "Would you like for me to relay a message?"

"No, that's okay." Tomi's voice shook, and it sounded like she was about to cry.

Denise's smile widened. "Is this Tomi?" she asked.

"Yeah."

"Hey, sweetie. Dante's told me so much about you. Because you mean so much to him, I would personally like to invite you to our wedding."

"To you're what?"

"Oh, Dante didn't tell you? He proposed to me this pass weekend. Said since I was carrying his child and all, he wanted to make things legally official."

Tomi's voice held no trace of sadness, but pure, acidic anger. "You know what, you *can* relay a message to Dante. Tell him I said go fuck his self. Black bastard!"

Tomi's side of the line went dead, and Denise could barely contain her excitement. If there was any hope of Tomi and Dante getting back together, Denise had definitely squashed it now. Dante no longer existed in Tomi's world, and it was simply a matter of time before Dante felt the same way about her.

With a smile that would have made Lucifer proud, Denise slid into bed beside Dante, and snuggled deep into his embrace. Still fast asleep, Dante threw an arm around Denise, pulling her close, as he whispered, "Tomi…"

Denise felt boiling anger heat up her veins, but she told herself to chill out. Tomi no longer existed to Dante. Now, and forevermore, Tomi would be nothing more than a bittersweet memory of what would never be.

CHAPTER THIRTEEN

Tomi followed her last customer into the front and watched him leave out the door. There were no other customers waiting in the waiting room, so she went into one of the back rooms, reclined in the tattoo chair, and looked thoughtfully up at the ceiling.

Wedding? Dante was getting married that fast?

Every since the night that Denise had answered Dante's phone, that was the only thing she could think about. She wondered if it was possible to become brokenhearted to the point where the heart would cease to function properly. Lately, she had been having pains in her chest, and the pains only occurred when she thought about what Dante and she had shared, or whenever she thought about his wedding.

For the life of her, she couldn't understand why he would want to marry Denise. She remembered all the times they had talked about Denise, and how he had told her about Denise's cold attitude, her sneaky ways, and her utter selfishness. Denise was a full-blooded, two-timing, conniving bitch. Who would want to pledge their life to a woman with those types of negative characteristics?

Her first thought had been that Denise was lying. But Denise had to be telling the truth. Why else would she be answering Dante's phone at midnight? She hoped to God that he wasn't marrying her because she was carrying his child. They were living in the new millennium; who married for that reason any more? That left her with only one other option: he was marrying Denise because he still loved her. And if he still loved Denise, that meant that he had never loved Tomi—he might've been infatuated with Tomi, but he never loved her.

That thought alone almost brought her to tears. What about all the good times they had shared, the laughter, their late night phone calls, there lovemaking? He had even revealed to her the story about his tragic childhood, and she had comforted him. Was it all just one big lie?

Her eyes welled with tears, but she forcefully blinked them away. She wasn't going to shed another tear over him. Her pillow was so full of tears, it was leaking. The lyrics to one of Mary J. Blige's songs crossed her mind:

No, I'm not going to cry, I'm not going to cry, I'm not going to shed no tears. No, I'm not going to cry, cause you're not worth my tears.

Max stuck his purple and green head in the door, interrupting her pity party. "I'm running up to Granny's to grab a bite to eat. You want anything?"

Tomi shook her head. "I'm cool."

"You sure?" Tomi nodded. "Okay. I'll be back in about thirty, thirty-five minutes." He hit the door-frame, turned and left.

Tomi dropped her head back against the chair and let out a long breath. She was tired, she was hungry, and she wanted to take a break from life. Every since Dante and she had broken up, she didn't feel the same anymore. She thought about him every single moment of the day, and it pissed her off because she was constantly wondering if he thought about her even half as much as she was thinking about him.

In truth, Tomi yearned to talk to him, to understand why he did what he did, but her pride and stubbornness wouldn't let her. If he wanted to talk, he knew her number; and he hadn't called her yet.

As if on cue, her cell phone ringed. She removed it from the front pocket of her jeans and looked at the small screen. It read: Private. Usually, she didn't answer blocked numbers, but this time, she decided to make an exception.

"Hello?"

She heard soft breathing on the other end, but the caller didn't say anything.

"Hello?" she asked again.

The caller still didn't say anything, and she felt deep in her heart that it was Dante trying to reach out to her. He wanted to talk to her, but he didn't want to make the first move.

"Dante, is this you?" she asked.

Her phone beeped to signal that the call had ended. He had hung up.

Tomi smacked her lips and replaced the phone in her pocket. Her gut feeling told her that the caller was Dante, but if he thought she was going to call him back, he had another thing coming. Her cell phone ringed again, and she hesitated before pulling it from her pocket. When she looked at the screen, she expected it to be a private call, but instead, it flashed the name Kelise.

She flipped the phone open. "What's up, Keli?"

"What's up, girl? What you doing?"

"Nothing really. Sitting in here bored, no customers. Things are a bit slow today."

"I wish it was like that over here. Girl, the office is crazy today. Everybody keep messing things up. Do you know that, thanks to an employee who didn't pay attention to what he was doing, five hundred of my magazines have been printed upside down?" Tomi couldn't help but laugh. "That's not funny, Tomi. Those five hundred upside down magazines set us back a good bit. I was half-tempted to put them through anyway."

"Kelise!" Tomi chastised her.

"I said half-tempted," her sister reminded her. "I didn't do it. But anyway, what are you doing this weekend?"

"It looks like nothing." She sounded somewhat dejected.

"You mean to tell me that Dante and you aren't going out?" Kelise sounded surprised.

Tomi felt her heart grow heavy. She knew it made her look like a coward, but she hadn't had the courage to tell her parents or sisters about their break-up yet. They all knew how head-over-heels in love she was with Dante, and she didn't want their pity or their sympathy.

"No, he's out of town for the weekend," she lied.

"He's out of town? Well, that's too bad," Kelise stated. "I have three tickets to go see Rickey Smiley perform at the comic club this Friday coming up. I was thinking that you, Dante, and I could go, but…"

"Ain't Ricardo home? Why don't y'all go?"

Kelise's sigh weighed a ton. "He didn't come home this time. He said there was a change of plans and he's headed to Quito, Ecuador right now as we speak. He said he should only be there for a week."

"You are a strong black woman," Tomi admired her sister. "I don't think I could handle a relationship like yours."

I don't know if I can handle it either, Kelise thought to herself. "Well, we need to find a third person to go. Ricardo sent me these three tickets because he knows how much I love Rickey Smiley. I'd hate to waste a ticket."

"Well, me, you, and Niya can go," Tomi offered.

The door ding-donged, signaling the entrance of a customer.

"I think I'll pass on that one," Kelise said to Tomi's offer.

"You and Niya are still beefing?" Tomi hopped down from the tattoo reclining chair and headed for the front of the parlor.

"Girl, I don't have anything to say to her."

"Hold on for a sec."

Tomi acknowledged the presence of the nice-looking, light-skinned brother who had just entered. When he looked up at her, her breath hitched in her throat. She had never seen a male as attractively handsome as he.

"Can I help you, sir?" she asked, her voice barely masking the way she was feeling on the inside.

She could tell that he was attracted to her by the expression written across his face. He walked over to her and leaned his elbows against the counter. "You can help me in many ways, ma," he told her in a sexy, deep baritone. "But I think a piercing will do for now."

Tomi tried to swallow, but all the saliva in her mouth had dried. "Give me one second," she croaked, hurrying off to the back.

When she was out of his hearing distance, she put the phone to her ear. "Kelise, are you still there?" she whispered.

"Who was that guy I heard?" her sister nosily asked. "And why are you whispering?"

"Lord have mercy, Kelise, you have to see this guy standing at the front desk." Tomi fanned herself with her free hand. "Girl, he is sexy as hell! He looks like a freaking male model or something! Keli, his eyes are green—*green*! And he has that butter-colored complexion." Tomi fanned herself even harder. "He's tall with wide shoulders, big muscular arms—I think I've found our third person for the comic club Friday night."

"What about Dante?" Kelise asked ambiguously.

Tomi smacked her lips. "What about Dante? I'll call you later, girl."

"But—"

"Bye, Kelise." Tomi flipped her cell phone closed and tucked it into her back pocket. She checked her appearance in the mirror behind her. She patted a few loose curls into place, tugged down her shirt to expose a little extra cleavage, and checked her butt to make sure it still looked round and plump.

She bounced back to the front desk. "Sorry to have kept you waiting so long," she apologized, leaning forward to expose her bosom.

"Your name is Tomi?" he asked, dragging a finger across the name tattooed above her left breast.

Ordinarily, Tomi would be highly offended if a man took the liberty of putting his hands on her without permission, but for him, she made an exception.

There was something about him, she couldn't quite place her finger on it. Maybe it was his style, the confidence in which he carried himself, that hint of cockiness in his smile that attracted her to him.

Nodding her head, Tomi sucked in a deep breath and bit her lip as his fingertip outlined her name. "And your name is?"

"Keith."

They stared into each other's eyes, and the attraction present was intense and undeniable. Finally, Tomi nervously broke the silence. "You said you want a piercing?" Her voice was low and husky. "Where will I be piercing you today?"

"Right here." He removed his green and yellow Roc-a-wear cap and pulled his green and yellow striped shirt over his head in one smooth movement. He made his left pectoral muscle jump and Tomi damn near fainted. Dante had a nice body, but Keith's was chiseled to perfection. His chest was broad and heavily muscled; his biceps were the size of one of Tomi's thighs; and his abdomen was wash-board flat and ribbed with perfect abs. He had a thin line of hair that started below his navel and disappeared behind the waistband of his boxers.

"Damn." Tomi had tried not to say anything about his perfect body, but she proved incapable of doing so. She felt her vaginal muscles clench and mentally told her body to behave itself. Taking his hand in hers, she said, "Follow me," and led him into one of the piercing rooms.

*　　　*　　　*　　　*

Tomi was laughing so hard, she wanted to cry. A searing pain was splitting through her side, yet she still couldn't stop laughing. Rickey Smiley was hilarious with his act of an old woman at a funeral. The 'old lady' had been singing a hymn and in the middle of the song, without any warning, the Holy Ghost had hit her and she had fallen out on the floor, jerking spasmodically.

Keith rubbed a hand up and down Tomi's back comfortingly. "Are you okay?" he asked; he was shaking with laughter himself.

"Rickey Smiley is a fool," she said, once she had regained her breath. She rubbed her side to ease the dull ache that all that hard laughing had caused. Kelise was still laughing even after Rickey had moved on to his next act.

The three of them left the comic club at a quarter to twelve. As they walked to Tomi's car, they were still laughing and talking about how good a job Rickey had done.

"I heard somebody say that those tickets were forty dollars a piece," Keith said as he opened the back-seat car door for Kelise.

"Those three tickets were a gift from my fiancé," Kelise told him as she settled into the back-seat, "but even if those tickets were forty dollars, I think they were well worth it."

"I agree," Tomi added as she cranked up her Altima. It took her almost thirty minutes just to get out of the overcrowded parking lot. "Where to now?" Tomi asked. "The night is still young."

"I don't know about y'all," Kelise stated, "but I am hungry. Let's go to the Waffle House."

"You ain't said nothing but a word." Tomi zoomed off for the nearest Waffle House, and it was already packed full of black folks who had also just left the comic club. "I hope we can find a table," Tomi said, as she stepped out the car.

They went inside and had to wait a full thirty minutes before a table was finally evacuated. They had to wait ten more minutes before a waitress came over to take their order.

"I would like a waffle platter with an orange juice to drink," Tomi told the lady. "I want my eggs scrambled, and can I get bacon instead of sausage?"

"You sure can." The woman scribbled onto the small pad that she held in her hand. "And what would you like, miss?" She directed her question to Kelise.

"I want a breakfast platter with sausage, scrambled eggs, grits, and two pieces of bacon. Coffee to drink, please. And can I get an extra biscuit with that?"

"Yes, you may. And for you, sir?"

"I think I'll take the dessert waffles and an orange juice."

"And which of the dessert waffles would you like?" the waitress asked. "We have peach, strawberry, blue berry, and apple."

"Two apple, two strawberry."

"Okay. Would you like any extra toppings on them?"

"Yes, ma'am. Can I get chocolate syrup, powdered sugar, and whipped cream. A lot of whipped cream." He looked at Tomi, but said to the waitress, "I love whipped cream on everything I eat."

The waitress blushed, catching his double meaning, and Tomi wished she could melt into the floor. She hit his leg beneath the table and he smiled, showing off his picture-perfect teeth.

"I'll be right back with your drinks," the waitress told them. She returned a few minutes later and placed their requested drinks in front of them.

They sipped on their drinks and chatted while waiting for the waitress to return with their plates.

"So Keith," Tomi asked him, "what do you do for a living?"

"I play keyboard. Right now, I'm playing for this little group called One Voice."

"Really?" Kelise looked surprised. "Ricardo taught me how to play the keyboard. My favorite thing to play is *Moonlight*. Do you have a favorite?"

"Yeah, but it's an original song called *Sexual*."

"Can you sing, too?" Tomi's interest was piqued.

"I can hold a tune, but I'm no K-Ci and JoJo."

"I hear that," Kelise said. "I'd like to hear you play something, one day."

"One day."

The waitress returned with their plates and extra words were unnecessary as they dug into their steaming piles of food. Suddenly, Tomi had to pee really bad, and she excused herself from the table. "I have to run to the ladies room," she explained.

She hurried off in search of the ladies room and was almost at the restroom section when her eyes landed on no one other than Dante himself. It was her first time seeing him since their break-up.

He was looking directly at her, and both of them wore surprised looks on their faces. Tomi's eyes wandered over to the woman occupying the seat across from him. It was Denise. She knew it was her because he had shown her a picture of the woman, once. Tomi looked back at Dante, and though she tried to hide it, hurt was visible in her eyes.

Deciding to pretend as if she'd never seen this man a day before in her life, she rushed past him for the bathroom. Once inside the safety of the pale-blue, ceramic-tiled walls, she ran her hands over her face, and looked at herself in the mirror.

Why are you so mad? she asked her reflection. *Why wouldn't he be here with her? She is carrying his child, you know. They are engaged. He has just as much of a right to be here as you do. What is so wrong about him having a late-night brunch with his fiancée?*

No matter how she tried to rationalize it, it still hurt. It wasn't too long ago that they had made passionate sweet love together, that Dante had revealed one of his most private secrets to her, that Dante had confessed his love to her. And now he was sitting up in Waffle House having a late night brunch with this other woman? Tomi had loved him so much—still loved him, if she was to be honest with herself; and he had left her cold for a red-boned bitch?

Tomi stared at her reflection in the mirror and shrugged her shoulders. "It's time to let bygones be bygones," she said aloud, heading for an empty stall.

Even though it would hurt, to save her sanity, she had to bury Dante in the same graveyard where she had buried Jonathan. She emptied her bladder, washed her hands, and took a deep breath before pushing open the bathroom door.

Dante was still sitting at the table with Denise, but she stalked past them, her head held high, pretending as if they didn't exist in her world. She retook her seat and couldn't help but to steal a glance over at Dante's table. His eyes were fixed on her, and he frowned as his eyes drifted over to the man seated next to her.

A devious smile curved her lips as she turned to Keith, who had just finished inhaling his two apple waffles and was now starting on his strawberry ones, and said in a sugary sweet voice, "Keith, those waffles look absolutely delicious. I wonder, do they taste as good as they look?"

"Girl, these things are off the charts! You want to try one?"

Nonchalantly, Tomi shrugged her shoulders. "Sure."

Keith cut her a slice of the waffle, stabbed it with his fork, and brought it up to her lips. She bit the strawberry waffle from the fork's tip and chewed it as if it was some type of exotic aphrodisiac. "Mmm, it *is* good," she exclaimed, chewing with over exaggerated pleasure.

"You have a little whipped cream right here," Keith told her, dabbing the whipped cream from the corner of her lips with a napkin.

She had to see if Dante was still looking, and when she glanced his way, she was shocked to see that he had forcefully yanked Denise up by her elbow, and was all but shoving her out the front door. Tomi smiled triumphantly as she resumed eating her food.

Kelise sat lost in her own thoughts. She had wondered about her sister's change of attitude every since Tomi had returned from the bathroom. After inconspicuously studying her sister for a while, she had followed Tomi's line of sight across the room, and was shocked to see Dante seated over in the no-smoking section.

I thought Tomi told me that Dante was out of town, Kelise thought, wondering why her sister would lie about something as trivial as that. She had seen the beautiful woman that was sitting with Dante…and then it clicked. Everything began to make sense.

That's why she's sweating Keith so hard. Dante and she broke up, and she's using Keith to hide her hurt and to get back at Dante. Kelise shook her head. She would have to have a small talk with her little sister about playing with a man's feelings. Playing with people's emotions was a dangerous game.

They finished up their meal and Keith paid for everything and left a generous tip. They got in Tomi's car and left. Tomi dropped Kelise off first, then headed for the Wal-Mart parking lot where Keith's car was parked.

Tomi pulled up beside his car, allowing her car to remain running. She turned towards Keith and asked, "Does it hurt much?" She gestured at his left breast.

"Oh, this? I ain't even going to lie," he admitted, "it hurts like hell. But I'm a big man; I can take it."

Tomi smiled. "Thank you for coming with us tonight. I had a good time."

"No, thank you for asking me to come with you tonight. I really enjoyed myself." He looked at Tomi for a while, then leaned over and kissed her. She kissed him back, but she felt like she was in the wrong. Even though Dante and she were no longer an item, in a way, she still felt like she belonged to him.

Slowly, Keith moved his hand up her arm, and then over to caress her breast. He gently massaged the soft mound. "You want to come to my crib and chill for a while?" His voice was deep and alluring.

Tomi felt herself grow wetter, and she was unable to sit still. She took his hand and kindly removed it from her breast. She couldn't deny the attraction between them, and she knew for a fact that if she went to his house, he would be between her legs as soon as they walked through the front door, if not sooner. She wasn't ready to make that step yet. She wasn't ready to completely let go of what Dante and she had shared.

"Not tonight," she told him, almost ready to change her mind once she saw the evident bulge straining against the front of his pants.

"That's cool," he told her smoothly. "But can I at least get a number so I can call you?"

Tomi thought for a minute, then nodded. "You can call me." She took his phone and entered her number and name.

"You know, that's the first time I've ever asked for a woman's number," he admitted.

"I can tell," she told him with a laugh. "Looking at you, I bet they write their number on your chest, put pieces of paper in your pockets, stalk you to your house—"

"How'd you know?" he asked, feigning surprise.

Tomi laughed. "Keith, get out my car."

"I'm going, I'm going," he promised her. He leaned over and kissed her again, and this time, he left her breathless. "That's the first time a female's ever kicked me out her car, too," he told her before stepping away. "Drive safe."

"I will." He shut the door and Tomi drove off. She told herself that she wouldn't look back, but she glanced into her rearview mirror to catch one last glimpse of him. Her cell phone ringed, and she looked down at the screen. It read: Dante.

She smacked her lips. "Oh, please. Don't call me, now." She put her phone on vibrate and drove home, listening to her radio, and thinking about fine-ass, sexy-ass Keith. He was attractive, charming, and lovable—what else could a woman want?

When she got home, she checked her cell phone again. She had eleven missed calls. Every single one was from Dante.

CHAPTER FOURTEEN

"Can I help you?" Kelise tartly asked her sister as Niya walked through her office door. She pushed the papers she had been working on to the side and crossed her arms, leaning back in her reclining swivel chair.

Niya sat down in one of the plush chairs seated in front of her desk. "I guess you heard what happened," she stated.

Kelise lifted one eyebrow.

"I caught Phillip in the bed with another woman."

"Oh. That's too bad." Kelise's words were cold and heartless.

Niya knew how stubborn her sister could be, so she overlooked her sister's cold cruelty. "I left him," she said with an air of finality. "I've washed my hands of him. This time I mean it."

Kelise smirked. "I wonder how long *this* will last."

Niya hit her sister's desk with her fist. "Dammit, Kelise, can't you see that I'm trying to call a truce between us? Can you at least meet me half way? I'm really going through right now, and I need my sister."

Reluctantly, Kelise uncrossed her arms and did away with giving her sister the cold shoulder. It was pass time to call a truce with her sister, but she had been determined that Niya would make the first move because, technically, Niya had been the one who'd started it. She knew it had taken a lot for Niya to swallow her pride and approach her, so Kelise decided to cut her some slack.

"Okay, Niya," Kelise gave in, "we can call a truce. But first, I want an apology."

"An apology?" Niya looked bewildered. "Isn't it good enough that I made the first step?"

"Nope. I want an apology."

Niya sighed and dropped her shoulders. "Okay, Kelise. I apologize. I'm sorry for getting so angry at you for your article." She decided to be honest with her sister and herself for a change. "In all honesty," she began, "the reason why I got so angry with you in the first place is because your article was true. It was like a slap in the face. Your article was saying everything my conscious had been telling me, but for me to read it on paper…it was too much. I'm sorry, Kelise. Can you forgive me?"

"Girl, give me a hug." Kelise walked around her desk and wrapped her sister in a tight hug. "I'm sorry, too, Niya."

Niya laughed. "What are you sorry for?"

"For being a total ass. Even though I was mad at the way you came off on me, I think I took some of the anger that was meant for Ricardo out on you. I didn't mean to come at you so hard. You forgive me?"

"What else are big sisters for?" Niya hugged her sister again, then pushed her away. "You smell like mothballs."

"Do I?" Kelise giggled, pulling at her moth-eaten, pea-green sweater. "It was chilly this morning, and I didn't want to end up sick again, so I dug this out the back of the closet."

"Looks like you dug that mess out of Frankenstein's closet. With you wearing that fashion atrocity, I'm embarrassed to claim you as blood."

"Is it that bad?" Kelise asked feeling self-conscious.

"It's that bad and worse," Niya assured her.

"Oh, well. I ain't trying to impress nobody, so it don't matter," Kelise said, shooing away her sister's unspoken comments and pulling up a chair beside her. "Tell me what you did when you found them in bed together. I know you acted a pure fool."

"Put it this way. I have a bullet hole in my wall, my dresser, my window, and my ceiling."

Kelise laughed and shook her head. "Why am I not surprised?"

*   *   *   *

Dante wanted to shatter his cell phone against the pavement. What was Tomi's problem? She wouldn't answer any of his phone calls, and she never called him back. He knew his name had showed up on her caller ID numerous times.

For the pass few days, every since he'd seen her and that nigga together at the Waffle House, he had been trying in vain to get in touch with her—they needed to talk. Twice he had gone by her house, but she was never there. He had showed up at her job a few times, too, but she'd had so many customers, he knew he wouldn't get a chance to pull her to the side.

Angrily, he slammed his fist against the hood of his car, then grimaced when an imprint formed in the blue metal. He shook his throbbing fist and cursed aloud. After he had calmed down a bit, he dialed Denise's number. She answered on the first ring.

"Hey, sweetie. What's up?"

"Nothing. I got a lot on my mind, that's all."

"When you getting home?"

"Probably around six, six-thirty."

"Okay. I'm in the kitchen now cooking dinner for us—you're favorite, supreme pizza-lasagna and garlic bread."

Usually, the thought of his favorite food bubbling in the oven would make every worry melt away, but not this time. The mentioning of food made him sick.

"Okay, babe, I'll talk to you later."

"Bye, sweetie."

Dante flipped his cell closed and remained in the same position, thinking. Looking up at the sky, he saw that the sun was already hidden behind the clouds, and dark storm clouds were slowly but surely rolling in from the east. He could taste the rain in the air. The foreboding weather mirrored his mood.

He couldn't believe that Denise didn't realize how bad he was hurting. Could she not see the pain in his eyes? Or did she choose not to see it? He hadn't hurt this bad since the doctor came in the waiting room to announce to them that their daughter was dead, since the time he walked in the hospital room and saw his mother's dried up shell resting on those white sheets.

The pain was mentally excruciating. He missed Tomi so much, he felt sick to his stomach. He wanted her back—had to have her back, no matter what it took.

The time on his watch told him that his thirty minute break was over, but he didn't care. Hopping off the hood of his car, he jumped inside, cranked up the engine, and backed out the parking lot. Fuck this job. Yeah, he was going to get in big trouble for not returning after break, probably might even end up fired, but he needed to talk with Denise. Talking over the phone wasn't going to cut it;

they needed to converse face to face. It was pass time to let her know that he didn't have to be with her just because she was carrying his child. It was pass time to admit to her his feelings for Tomi and bring an end to their tryst. Every time he kissed Denise, every time he went inside of her, it felt like a part of him had died. He couldn't take it. He couldn't do it anymore. He was going to end things with Denise, and, even if it took the rest of his life to do it, eventually, he would win Tomi's heart back

Dante pulled up at his flat, and instead of pulling in his front driveway like he usually did, he circled around the house and pulled up in the backyard beside the water-hose. His car was in dire need of a good washing, and his rims needed to be shined. Under normal circumstances, he made sure to it that his car and rims were taken cared of every weekend. These pass two weeks had left him physically and emotionally drained, and he hadn't had the energy to do it.

Using the back door key, he let himself into the house and pulled off his heavy work boots, placing them beside the dryer. The smells of pepperoni, tomato sauce, garlic, and other tantalizing herbs and spices wafted through the air, and though his stomach growled aloud, he didn't feel like eating. He couldn't see Denise from the small laundry room where he was located, but he could hear her bustling around in the kitchen and talking on his house phone, her mouth moving a mile per minute.

"Girl, yeah!" she was saying, "I didn't think it would be *this* easy, but maybe luck is on my side after all. I might have been wrong for what I did, but Dante needed this. He needs me."

Dante was about to turn into the small hallway that led to the kitchen, but at the sound of those words, he froze. Something told him to hold his position a little while longer, and a great revelation would be revealed unto him. He could hear Denise chopping something on the wooden chopping board, probably cucumbers for the salad, but even that loud noise didn't help mask the sound of her voice.

"Tamika, I don't know why you lying. You know for a fact if Jeffrey was to pull some stunt like that on you, you would do the same thing I did...What? What?" Denise laughed. "Okay, okay. Well, let me ask you a quick question. If I'm so wrong, then why did you help me out by peeing on the stick for me?"

Peeing on the stick?

Suddenly, it clicked in his head, and it took all Dante's willpower not to blow his cover. Tamika! That was Denise's six-months-pregnant home-girl. Denise had used Tamika's pee to make a positive result on the pregnancy test and had passed it off as if it were her own. That meant that Denise wasn't pregnant. She wasn't carrying Dante's child!

The feeling of relief was indescribable. Dante felt his knees buckle, and he had to hold on to the washing machine to keep from crumpling to the floor. It felt as if the weight of the world had been lifted from his shoulders. He no longer had any obligation to Denise. He had been freed! He was a free man! Thank you God!

Dante had every intention of heading into the kitchen to let Denise know that she had been cold busted, but her next words stopped him in his tracks.

"Yeah, I told her stupid ass that we're engaged. And she fell for it, too! Didn't even doubt my words for one second. That's how you know that she knows Dante is still mine. She said some stupid shit like, 'tell him to go fuck his self.'" Denise burst out laughing again. "That Tomi is one dumb bitch!"

"You did what?!" Dante exploded, huffing and puffing as if he had finished running the mile run rather than only coming around the corner.

He had taken Denise by such surprise, she had not only dropped the phone, but the scalding pan of supreme pizza-lasagna that she had just removed from the oven as well. The lasagna lay like a steaming pile of slop on the kitchen floor, but Dante could care less. The only thing on his mind was Tomi, Denise, and murder.

"Baby!" Denise exclaimed, looking as guilty as a convicted felon, "I didn't hear you come in. I thought you were at work."

"You did what?!" Dante demanded again, taking three menacing steps towards her.

Denise staggered away from him, bumping into the kitchen table and nearly crawling on top of it. She had never seen Dante's eyes look so murderous before, and she feared for her life.

"Baby, how—how much of, of the conversation did you—hear?" she choked out, still backing away from him.

"I heard it all," he barked at her. Dante was so angry, he could taste the emotion in his mouth. "You lied to me. You lied about every fucking thing! You ruined my relationship with Tomi, you made me think you were carrying my child, and you—and you—" the words were so painful, he couldn't make them pass his lips, "—you told Tomi that I was going to *marry you?*"

"No, it wasn't like that," Denise tried to calm him with more lies. "I told her that we could possibly be contemplating thinking about trying to slightly consider the idea of *maybe* weighing the option of getting married."

Completely ignoring her babbling foray of lies, Dante continued, "No wonder why she don't answer any of my calls and absolutely refuses to see me. She thinks I'm engaged to you on top of the fact that you were supposedly pregnant with my child."

"Dante—"

He held up his hand. "Don't fucking say my name. You don't have the right to say my name."

"Dante—"

"Denise, don't touch me."

"Dante—"

"I said *don't fucking touch me.*"

Denise jumped at the sound of his voice and her body began to shake with fear at the look in his eyes. "What about dinner?" she whispered.

He said only two words. "Get. Out."

The look in his eyes told her that if she didn't disappear at that very moment, *she* would be dinner—dinner for the worms.

Without saying another word, Denise disappeared in the back room, returning mere seconds later with her purse in hand. She looked over at Dante as if she wanted to say something, but wisely decided against it. She turned and left, looking sad and somewhat remorseful for once in her pitiful life.

*   *   *   *

"Checkmate." Tomi knocked over Keith's king and smiled at him.

"How the hell did you do that?" he asked, leaning back in his chair and eyeing the board carefully. "I knew I had you this time."

"Come on, now, Keith," she said, sliding the chess pieces back into their case, "I'm the queen of chess. You may come close, but you'll never beat me."

Keith accepted his defeat like a man. As Tomi walked pass him to put the game away on the shelf, Keith pulled her into his lap.

"Keith!" she exclaimed, laughing aloud. "Stop before you make me drop this game."

"What's more important, me or the game?"

"The game," she teased, setting the game to the side and straddling one leg on either side of his chair. She took his face in her hands and kissed him deeply, rolling her tongue against his. Keith wrapped his arms around her, pulling her closer.

She felt him become aroused, and his penis pressed through his sweat-pants into her belly. "What's this?" she goaded him, wrapping her slim fingers around the length of him.

"Tomi…" Her name slipped from his lips like a small warning as he watched her fondle his hardness.

She freed his penis from his pants and her jaw dropped at his large size. "Damn, Keith. Is that normal?"

He laughed. "It's a little bigger than average, but yeah, it's normal."

Tomi leaned forward and kissed the tip of his penis.

Keith growled and his hands tightened on Tomi's upper arms. "Tomi, I'm a grown man. Don't tease me."

She looked up at him and smiled. "I was just having some fun," she said innocently. "But I'll put it away because you ain't getting none of this tonight." She tucked his male hardness into his sweatpants.

Keith wanted to cry. "Tomi, damn, how long are you going to make me wait?"

She wrapped her arms around his neck and kissed him gently. "Keith, please, we've only been dating for two weeks now."

"Two and a half," he corrected her.

"Same difference."

"You won't let me go up inside you, but you'll let me eat you out of house and home. How's that fair?"

"Nothing's fair in the game of love."

"Are you going to make me wait forever?"

"Not forever. But I am going to make you wait, because then, when you finally do get to sample my goodies, it'll be that much better."

He groaned and kissed the pulse beating in the hollow of her neck. "I want you so bad," he admitted. He groaned again in frustration. "This is hard for me, Tomi. With all the other females, I usually hit on the first night."

"Well, incase you haven't noticed, I'm not your average chick."

"You right about that." He held her close to him and moved his lips over hers. As they deepened the kiss, there was a knock at the door.

"You expecting company?" he asked, his eyes hazy with evident desire.

"Nope," Tomi told him, standing to her feet and stepping away from his chair. "I don't know who it is. Probably my sister."

She walked over to the door and swung it open. Her breath caught in her throat when she saw Dante. It was raining outside, and he didn't have an umbrella or a coat. He was soaking wet; rain water dripped from his eyelashes, nose, and chin. In his hands, he held a bouquet of twelve white roses, the same roses he had bought for her on the night of their first date. He held the roses out to her.

"These are for you." With his free hand, he wiped at his nose and sniffed.

"Dante…" Tomi didn't know what to say. She took the roses from him and shook her head in disbelief. "I don't know what to say," she admitted. "What are these for? And what are you doing here?"

"Can I come in?" he asked, gesturing at his drenched clothes. "I need to talk to you."

Tomi was at a loss for words. She couldn't let him in because Keith was inside, but she couldn't leave him standing outside in the pouring rain, either—no matter how pissed she was at him, that just wouldn't be right.

"Dante," she began, still unsure of what to say, "I, uhm…well, I'm a little busy right now. Can you come back la—"

The door swung open wider as Keith appeared behind her. He wrapped a strong, possessive arm around her waist, pulled her back against him, and eyed Dante challengingly. "What's up, bro? Can I help you?"

When Dante saw the man, he instantly remembered him from the Waffle House, feeding Tomi and dabbing at her lips with a napkin. The swell of anger that rose in him was chokingly thick.

"What the hell is he doing here?" He kept his eyes on Keith, but directed his question to Tomi.

"The question is, what the hell are *you* doing here? Obviously, you weren't invited." Keith stepped forward and his big shoulders seemed to fill the doorway.

"You got a problem with me, my nigga?" Dante asked, never the one to back down from a fight. The way he was feeling right now, a fight was exactly what he needed. "You got a fucking problem with me, my nigga?" he asked again, his eyes and choice of words daring Keith to jump to his bait.

"Dante, what is wrong with you?" Tomi asked, appalled by his satanic anger.

Ignoring Tomi, all his attention focused on the bigger, taller male, Dante taunted him relentlessly, "You got a problem with me, you yellow punk-ass bitch?"

Dante's last word had barely left his lips before Keith had forcefully shoved Tomi to the side and cracked his fist into Dante's left jaw. The cracking sound was sickening, but it didn't slow Dante for a second. His fist cracked against Keith's jaw, and the two men were at it, going blow for blow.

For the first ten seconds, Tomi was speechless. She didn't quite understand what was happening. One second, she was in her house, spending quality time with her male companion, the next second, she was opening her front door to be greeted with the drenching wet sight of her ex-boyfriend, and in those following seconds, her boyfriend and ex were now on her front-lawn, fighting as if their life depended on it.

"Stop you two!" she ordered, wanting to jump in to break them up, but deciding against it for the simple fact that she would probably succeed more in damaging herself than in breaking up the fight.

Inspite of the fact that it was pouring down raining outside, nosy neighbors had materialized out of nowhere, some with umbrellas, some without, watching the fight and rooting for whichever one they chose to win.

"Don't just stand there and stare!" Tomi demanded, dropping the bouquet of white roses on her porch. "Somebody, break them up before they kill each other!"

But none of the men in the surrounding crowd was brave enough to interrupt the fight.

Keith had Dante pinned to the ground and he was repeatedly landing hard blows across Dante's face. Dante was finally able to get on his feet, and he head-bunted Keith in the stomach, sending the taller man sprawling on his back in the mud. Immediately, Dante was on top of him, throwing constant blows to Keith's face until he tired to the point where he actually collapsed on Keith.

Keith was equally tired out, and he didn't have the strength to push Dante off of him. As the two men wore themselves out, finally, three other men from the crowd of onlookers jumped in and pulled them apart.

"Thank you!" Tomi exclaimed with relief. "Look at you two," she reprimanded them in a voice that a mother would use to scold her children. "You look like two stupid fools, muddy, bloodied, and bruised, and what did that accomplish? What did you prove? Did that fight make you any manlier than you were before?"

"Hey…he started it," Keith said between harsh breaths.

"Fuck you, bitch."

"Stop it!" Tomi demanded.

Keith leaned against a tree, completely out of breath, and Dante sat in the mud, taking large gulps of air, but still breathing heavily. The rain water sloshed down their faces, mixing in with their sweat and blood.

Now that the fight was over, the neighbors returned to their homes, animatedly reenacting and retelling to one another the events that had just taken place. Most of them were angry because neither of the men had actually won; it was an even fight—both of them throwing equal blows, both of them receiving equal bruises, and both of them tiring out at the same time.

Angrily, Tomi turned to Dante. "Why did you come over here, anyway, Dante? You know you weren't invited."

"Don't try...to turn it on me," Dante breathed at her, staggering to his feet, "you the one...over here...spending time...with high-yellow, pretty boy."

"Dante, whoever I spend time with at my house is none of your concern, okay? Why don't you go back home to your pregnant fiancée?" Her words were sharp and scathing, but the anger in her voice was only a cover up for the pain.

"That's what...I came over here for. To explain." He limped over to the front porch and leaned against the cold cement, taking a second to catch his breath. "Me...and Denise....are not engaged. Denise...is not pregnant. She lied...lied to you and me...about everything."

Tomi felt a flash of hope flare to life in her heart, but she immediately quelled it. He was only telling her what her heart longed to hear. He wanted her, and he was willing to do or say whatever it took to win her back. She couldn't succumb to him. She had to be strong.

"I don't believe you," she whispered. Her words were barely audible over the rain.

Dante had almost fully caught his breath, and with desperate eyes, he pleaded, "Tomi, you have to believe me, baby. I wouldn't lie to you. I love you."

"Dante, leave," she told him.

"Tomi..."

She was resolute in her decision. "Dante, leave."

She watched anger cross his handsome face, then frustration, and then a profound sadness. He glanced back at Keith, who was still recovering over at the tree, and when his eyes returned to hers, they were the eyes of a defeated man.

"You won!" he yelled behind him at Keith. Dante bent down, retrieving a large rock from Tomi's drive way, and flung it with all his might at the stormy sky. "You fucking won!" he repeated.

As if forgetting about his car, he turned and walked off in the pouring rain. Tomi wanted to run after him, apologize, and tell him that she wanted him back...but she couldn't. Dammit, why was she feeling like the bad person when he was the one who had hurt her?

Turning to look at Keith, she told him, "I think you should go, too."

"Me? What did I do?"

"What didn't you do?"

Keith's brow was furrowed. "What's that supposed to mean?" He limped towards her, favoring his right leg. "That nigga came over here and started with me. He called my bluff. What was I supposed to do? Stand here and let him punk me like I'm some scared little bitch? And especially in front of what's mine?"

"What's yours?" Tomi rolled her head to the side and put her hand on her hips. "What you and Dante fail to realize is that I am not an object to be won. I'm a human being, not a trophy."

Keith's frown deepened. "I know that. But you're still my woman."

"You just don't get it," Tomi said, shaking her head. "You need to go. I need some time alone, time to think."

"What is there to think about, Tomi? You're my lady, now. That nigga is old news."

"It's not that simple!"

"The hell it is! What's the difficult part?"

"The difficult part is that I still love him. There, I said it. I am still in love with Dante. Yeah, he hurt me in so many ways. Yeah, he broke my heart and ripped it to shreds. And yet and still, I still love him."

"What about me?" Keith's voice was so tender, it struck a nerve in Tomi, and she reached out for him, placing a hand against his soaking wet, sweaty, bruised face.

When he looked up at her, she whispered in a soft voice, "Go home, Keith."

He took a few steps back, and his handsome face was distraught with the same emotions that Dante's face had displayed earlier. "So what are we going to do about us?"

"Give me time. I need time to think."

Tomi knew that if she looked at him, his eyes would mirror the betrayal that his voice portrayed. Because of this, she turned from him and, without looking back, entered her house and closed the door behind her. As the door latch clicked into its place, Tomi's cell phone ringed. It was her mother.

"Hey, sweet-pea. How's my baby doing?"

"Ma, I don't know," Tomi replied truthfully, plopping down on the couch and flipping the TV to BET. "Ma, I honestly do not know."

"What's wrong, baby?" She sounded concerned.

"It's about Dante."

"What about him?"

Tomi hesitated, wondering if she should tell her mother or not. She finally said, "Ma, we broke up. About a month ago. I should have been done told you, but I didn't want you guys feeling sorry for me."

"Sounds like to me you're feeling sorry for yourself."

"I don't know how I feel right now. Confused. Frustrated. I just feel like screaming," she admitted, completely understanding the emotions that Michael and Janet were feeling when they made the song *Scream*.

Bluntly, her mother asked, "Y'all broke up? Whose fault was it, his or yours?"

"Ma! Duh, it was his fault."

Her mother didn't sound persuaded. "What exactly did he do?"

"He got another female pregnant, and now they're engaged."

"And you really believe that?"

"Well, yeah." She paused, gathering her thoughts. "I mean, he told me himself that he had gotten Denise pregnant. And then Denise told me that they were engaged. But today, he came by here and told me that Denise had set him up and that she's not pregnant, and they're not engaged."

"And if he told you that, Tomi—in the words of you young people—then why are you tripping?"

A music video came on filling the screen with girls in tiny bathing suits, shaking ass everywhere to the beat of the song. Tomi flipped the channel to the news where they were giving the exclusive on a murder trial that had made national headlines.

"Why I'm tripping?" Tomi repeated her mother's question. "Are you even listening to me? I'm tripping because Denise is pregnant by Dante, *my* Dante. Now, I'll give him the benefit of a doubt, Denise may have lied about them being engaged, but she's not lying about being pregnant. I know that for a fact."

"Now, you listen to me," her mother began in a no-nonsense voice, "when I met Dante, we had a nice, long talk. He told me how much he cared about you, and he told me all about that little heffa named Denise. Denise is sneaky; she's a liar, and she's always up to no good. Call it mother's intuition, but I can bet you all the money in the world that that little hussy made up that lie about being pregnant by him to break y'all two up. And it seems to me like she succeeded in doing so."

"Ma, you don't understand," Tomi tried to enlightened her.

"No, *you* don't understand," her mother interrupted her. "I know love when I see it, and that boy loves you just as well as you love him. Don't allow someone's jealousy to tear apart a good thing. A love like that doesn't come around often."

Tomi didn't say anything. She knew her mother was probably right.

"But Ma, there's more to it than that."

"What else is it, baby?" Her mother's voice was laced with loving care.

Tomi hesitated once again before she confided in her mother. "I met this other guy and…" She let her unfinished sentence hang in the air.

"You love him, too?"

"No…not the way I love Dante." She quickly added, "But I do care a whole lot about him, and I don't want to hurt him. I feel like I used him as a rebound guy, and now, we've gotten deeper than what I'd intended."

"Tomi," her mother began, "don't play with a person's heart. Love is a very strong emotion, and it should be taken seriously. You can't love two people at once; that only causes more problems. And you have to remember that this guy—"

"—Keith—"

"—Keith, has feelings, too. I'm not telling you who to be with, because that's your choice, but I am telling you to do this: pray about it. Prayer changes things. We serve a God that is understanding, merciful, and full of grace. God says any two He put together, let no man tear apart. When God made you, Tomi, He made your soul mate, too. And if you pray, stand still, and wait on his voice, he will lead you in the right direction. God will put the answer in your heart."

Tomi nodded her head as she listened to her mother. She knew her mother was right, and she knew what her heart wanted. Her heart yearned for Dante, but her pride and stubbornness wouldn't allow her to willingly admit her own transgressions, nor forgive his. She liked Keith, but he didn't hold that special place in her heart—that special place was for Dante and Dante only.

After schooling her daughter on love, her mother informed her that it was almost a quarter pass ten. Cathy wished her daughter a good night and told her to give her a call if she needed someone to talk to.

"I love you, Tomi, no matter who you choose to spend the rest of your life with."

"And I love you, too, Mama. Tell Dad I said goodnight."

"I will definitely do that. Sleep tight honey, and try not to worry yourself too much."

"Okay. Love you."

Tomi hung up the phone and headed for the front door. She threw open the door, half expecting Dante to be standing on the other side of the threshold, but he wasn't there. His car was still parked about a block up from her driveway where he'd left it, and his rain-washed rims glistened in the street-lights.

With a heavy sigh, Tomi took a seat on the cement porch steps, and her mother's earlier words echoed in her mind: *When God made you, Tomi, He made your soul mate, too. And if you pray, stand still, and wait on his voice, He will lead you in the right direction.*

Folding her hands together in prayer, Tomi looked up at the starlit sky and said, "God, I haven't prayed in years. To be honest, I really don't know what to say. I know I've sinned and fallen short of your glory. I'm no where near perfect, and you probably don't want to hear from a little sinner like me, but God, I'm lost right now. I feel like love is right at my fingertips, yet I still can't reach out and grasp it. Mama said that if I pray and listen for your voice, then you'd lead me in the right direction. Well, God, I'm praying. I'm turning the situation over to you. Give me direction. Amen."

Tomi sat there and waited, and waited, and waited. She didn't know exactly what she was waiting for, and eventually, she started to feel stupid.

"What am I doing?" she asked aloud, standing to her feet and swiping dirt from her bottom. "God's not going to answer me. There are people out there who really need Him right now, and I'm asking Him to get involved in my stupid love affairs. What was I thinking?"

As she was about to enter her house, something white caught her eye at the edge of her porch steps. Curious, she walked over to the other side of the porch to find out what it was. It was the bouquet of white roses that Dante had brought her.

Somehow, the roses had withstood Dante and Keith's macho contest, had held up through the intense, relentless rain, and had survived the night while retaining an innocent, pure, radiant beauty of its own.

Tomi ever so gently retrieved the bouquet from the steps and held it against her chest, inhaling its sweet, fragrant scent. A smile touched her lips as she looked up at the sky and said, "Thank you, God."

CHAPTER FIFTEEN

"All done," Tomi told her nephew as he jumped out the chair and began to knock hair from his shoulders. "Don't knock that on my floor," Tomi scolded him. "You know you sweeping that up."

Using one of Tomi's hand-held mirrors, Elijah viewed his fresh new shape-up and smiled from ear to ear. "Aunt Tomi keeps me looking hot for the ladies."

Tomi rolled her eyes. "Boy, please." She heard something clatter against the floor and hurried into the kitchen to see what Kadeesha had gotten into this time. She knew it was only a matter of time before something went down, because the little girl had been too quiet for too long. Her suspicions proved correct.

"Sweetie, what did you do?" Tomi asked, looking at her chocolate-battered floor and her cake-splattered walls.

"You told me to beat it until all the lumps was gone. I did." Kadeesha looked like the perfect angel, covered from head to toe in rich, chocolate cake mix. She licked some of the batter off her pointer finger and gave her aunt a wide-eyed, innocent stare.

"Did you turn off the mixer before lifting it out the mixing bowl?" Tomi asked her niece, trying to remain calm even though she was about to lose it.

"No. You didn't tell me to."

Tomi sighed aloud. "Well, come on and help Aunt Tomi clean this mess up." Tomi tried to figure out what was it again that had possessed her to ask her sister if she wanted her to keep the kids for the weekend. Tomi knew what it was. Somewhere between the kids worrying the hell out of Niya, repairs being made to her house, meeting with a lawyer concerning her divorce, and the cases she was handling at the law firm, Tomi knew her sister needed a break. The plan was to surprise Niya with a triple-chocolate extreme cake, but things weren't turning out quite how she'd expected.

"Grab a rag and help me clean off the walls before that chocolate dries," Tomi told her niece.

While on her hands and needs, scrubbing at the delicious smelling chocolate, Tomi heard a loud crash from her living room. "Oh, hell." She ran into the front room to see what the problem was now. Her family portrait was laying on the floor in front of the fire place, shattered to smithereens.

"Ooh, you in trouble," Kadeesha told her brother in a foreboding, sing-song voice.

Tomi put a hand against her forehead and counted backwards from ten. "Elijah, how did this happen?"

"It was an accident, Aunt Tomi, I swear. I was practicing doing some back flips and my shoe flew off and hit the picture. Then it crashed. I'm sorry, Aunt Tomi."

"Why were you doing back flips in my—" Tomi had to bite the inside of her cheek to keep from cussing him out. "You and Kadeesha go in the kitchen and finish cleaning up that mess in there. I'll handle this."

Elijah quickly disappeared into the kitchen, appreciative that he had been spared the wrath of Aunt Tomi. Cautious, so as not to cut herself, Tomi began to pick up the large slivers of sharp glass and place them in the metal firedog. Just then, there was a loud, unexpected knock at the door, which caused Tomi to jump and cut her hand on the piece of glass she had been holding.

"Aw, shit," she exclaimed, dropping the piece of glass and cupping her injured hand with the other to keep her blood drops from decorating her white carpet. *Can it get any worse?* she wondered.

"Give me a sec!" she called out to the unanticipated visitor. She grabbed a half-towel out the bathroom closet and gently wrapped her hand in it, then went to the door.

When she saw that it was Dante, she felt little butterflies come to life in her belly, and her throbbing hand suddenly didn't hurt as bad. "Dante," she said his name as she opened the door.

"Hey…did I…interrupt something?" He couldn't help but ask after seeing the smear of chocolate across her cheek and forehead, the glob of chocolate threaded through her hair, and the smudges of chocolate covering her clothing.

"No, you didn't interrupt anything at all," she lied. She opened the door wider. "Please, come in. Have a seat."

He walked into her living room and was taken aback by the shattered picture and the pieces of glass showering her fireplace. "Is everything okay?" he inquired.

"Everything is just fine," she lied again, glancing into the kitchen to make sure Elijah and Kadeesha hadn't managed to get into anything else. Elijah was mopping the floor, and Kadeesha was working hard on cleaning the counter top.

She made her way back into the living room to find Dante on his hands and knees, picking up the jagged pieces of glass. "Dante, you don't have to do that," she told him, kneeling beside him.

"I got this," Dante told her, gently nudging her out the way. "How did you manage to do this, anyway?"

She sat on her love seat and held her throbbing hand against her heart. "It wasn't me. It was my nephew. His shoe hit the picture." Dante glanced over at her, but she shook her head. "Don't ask."

After he finished placing all the pieces of glass into the firedog, he sat the glass-less picture against the side of her couch. Looking over at her with a concerned expression, he asked, "Tomi, what's wrong with your hand?"

"It's nothing," she lied again, but was unable to keep from flinching when he took her hand in his.

As he unwrapped the injured hand, she bit down on her bottom lip and let out a low, sss-ing sound. "Damn, baby."

"Do I need stitches?" she asked, almost on the verge of tears.

"No, it don't look deep enough for stitches. But you do need it properly bandaged. Where's your first aid kit?"

"Behind the mirror in the bathroom."

Dante left and returned only seconds later with the first-aid kit in hand. He cleaned the wound with peroxide and applied Neosporin with a Q-tip. Then, he placed a large bandage over the cut and wrapped the palm of her hand with gauze. A piece of water-proof tape held the gauze in place. "Does that feel better?" he asked.

"Yes." She looked up at him, and the feelings that she had harbored from him for so long came forth in such a rush, she felt smothered by them. Even with his face slightly puffy, bruised and discolored all over, he looked as attractive as ever. God, she never knew how much she'd missed him until now.

As if reading her mind, he kissed her forehead gently before saying, "I missed you, too."

"Oh, Dante." She wrapped her arms around him and pulled him against her, resting her head on his shoulder. She felt so safe, so whole. She thought about the sign that she had received from God last night, and she knew deep in her heart that this was where she belonged.

"Dante," she began, "about yesterday—"

"Who are you?" Kadeesha's voice broke the magic of the moment. "And what's wrong with your face? Why it's so swolled?"

"Kadeesha!" Tomi's voice was both appalled and reprimanding. "How disrespectful! Apologize right now."

"Nah, it's okay." Dante held out his hand to her. "Allow me to introduce myself. My name is Dante. And my face is a little sore; I got in a scuffle yesterday."

"I'm sorry your face hurts," Kadeesha apologized while shaking his hand. "My name is Kadeesha. But my mama was gonna name me Katie at first, but Grandma said that Katie sounded too white, I think I would've liked Katie, but I like Kadeesha, too, I like your name, too. Mama said my name is unique, you know what unique means? It means one of a kind. My name is one of a kind, don't you think? You don't meet too many people with the name—"

"Kadeesha." She noted the tone of her aunt's voice and quickly ended whatever else she was about to say.

"Why is everybody covered in chocolate?" Dante asked.

Kadeesha bounced over to the sofa and sat down beside Dante. "Because, we was making Mommy a triple-chocolate ex-scream cake, but it didn't turn out right cause I messed up. Elijah said I'm always messing something up. That's my big brother, he gets on my nerves, he's in the kitchen helping me clean up the mess."

"Well, why don't we try to make this cake, again? You know the saying, 'second time's a charm.'"

"Ooh, can we? Can we, please, Aunt Tomi?"

"It's 'third time's a charm,'" Tomi corrected him. "But," she added before Kadeesha could say anything, "I guess it'll be alright if—"

"Yeah! Come on, Dante," Kadeesha said, grabbing his hand and dragging him into the kitchen.

"Come here, Elijah!" Tomi called. Her nephew came sauntering into the living room. "Go get the vacuum cleaner and vacuum over that area. I don't want anyone getting glass stuck in their feet."

"Yes, ma'am." He sounded remorseful.

It wasn't long before her house was under control again. The rich smell of chocolate cake wafted through the air like an exotic fragrance, and her front room was glass-less once again. If only her hand could magically heal, everything would be perfect.

"Can you ball?" Elijah asked Dante as they put away the last mixing utensil.

"I've been told I'm nice on the court." Dante sounded every bit conceited.

"Well, let's see what you got." Elijah ran into the guest room and returned with a basketball. "There's a court up the street. Each shot, one point; we going to twenty. Can you handle that, old man?"

"Old man? I'll show you an old man. You might have to take it easy on me, cause I'm a little on the sore side."

"I wanna go! I wanna go!" Kadeesha whined.

"No," Elijah told his little sister. "You'll only get in the way. You don't even know how to play."

"Yes I do." Kadeesha crossed her arms and stuck out her bottom lip a mile and a half. Her eyes were brimming with tears, and Elijah knew she was about to have one of her crying fits.

"Kadeesha, you can come," Dante quickly intervened. "You can be our cheer-leader," Dante told her.

"Yeah!" Kadeesha exclaimed, her eyes immediately clearing. She ran off to find her sandals.

"I guess I'll just stay here," Tomi said, motioning at her injured hand. "There isn't much I can do besides get in the way."

"You can referee," Dante told her, referring to the black-and-white striped blouse she wore.

"Oh, shut up," she told him, but couldn't help the smile that made its way across her face. She was glad he had figured out a way that she could participate, too. She didn't want to be left out.

Before leaving, she removed the three pans of chocolate cake from the oven and placed them on the cooling racks. Moments later, the four of them walked up the street towards the basketball court. Dante and Elijah played make-it take-it to see who'd get the ball first, then the game began. Tomi was on point with her refereeing. She called every travel, every double-dribble, and every foul.

Kadeesha stood on the sidelines with some make-shift pom-poms that Tomi had helped her create, and called out little cheers. "Stomp 'em down, make 'em scream, beat that player, beat that team!"

At first, Dante took it easy with the small boy, but by the time the score was 13-16, with Dante losing, he became more serious.

"Foul!" Tomi called as Elijah fell to the ground.

"What?" Dante was mad. "I didn't even touch him!"

"Foul!" Tomi repeated, daring him to challenge her. "Two free shots."

"What?" Dante was astounded. He put his hands on his hips and paced the court with sweat dripping down the column of his neck.

Elijah made both shots with ease, knocking his score up to 18.

"Okay, I see how y'all want to play," Dante told them. He swept off his shirt in one graceful movement, and Tomi unconsciously licked her lips. She couldn't take her eyes away. His chest glistened with sweat and Tomi wanted to use her tongue to wipe the sweat away. She shook her head, trying to clear her thoughts, but her attempt was unsuccessful.

Dante made five shots back to back, quickly making it a tie game. Elijah made the next shot.

"Eighteen to nineteen. Game point," Tomi announced.

Kadeesha cheered them on. "You can do it! You can do it! Just put your mind to it! Shake it to the left, bounce that butt; shake it to the right, bounce that—"

Tomi sent a warning stare at her niece, and she quickly changed her tune. "You can do it! You can do it! Just put your mind to it!"

Dante didn't make the final shot easy for Elijah. Elijah was able to steal the ball twice, but missed both shots. Finally, Elijah caught Dante's rebound and made a lay-up, bringing an end to the game.

"Go Elijah! Go Elijah!" Kadeesha shook her pom-poms and jumped up and down. "That's, my brother; that's, that's, my brother!" she sang.

Dante was mad that he'd lost, but he was a good sport. "Good job, man," he told the younger boy, limping over to pat him on the back.

"You didn't do too bad, either, for an old man," Elijah told him with a smile.

"Old man?"

Tomi walked over to Dante and took the shirt off his shoulder, mopping his forehead with it. "Let it go, Dante. It was a good game."

"Yeah, it would've been better if the referee wasn't making so many false calls," he said on a sour note.

"Oh, don't be a sore loser," she teased him, popping his butt with the twisted shirt. Whispering so that only he could hear, she told him, "Besides, you look sexy when you sweat." She tossed his drenched shirt back over his shoulder and gave him a wink.

By time they made it to her street, the sky was dark and the street-lights were bright.

"Well, I think I'm going to head on home," Dante told them as they entered her house. "I need to go get cleaned up, and plus, it's getting late."

"Don't go," Kadeesha whined. "I want you to play tea party with me."

"You can't spend the night?" Elijah asked.

"Nah, guys. I think I need to get going before it gets too dark."

"Aw, man," Kadeesha whined. "Well, that means you have to play tea party with me, Elijah."

"No, I'm not. That's gay!"

"No, it's not. And Mama said not to use that word."

"Hey, you guys, cut it out," Tomi told them. She turned to Elijah. "Can I trust you two to ice the cake while I walk him to his car?"

"Yes, ma'am," he promised. "Come on, Kadeesha." His sister followed him into the kitchen, and Tomi followed Dante outside.

"They sure seem to like you," Tomi told him as they walked slowly towards his car.

"Yeah. They're a good bunch of kids."

Tomi never realized how short her front-yard was until she realized how quickly they made it to his car. She walked over to the driver side and leaned against his window, delaying him from opening the door.

"So, Dante, why did you come over here? I know it wasn't to help make a chocolate cake and play a game of ball."

Dante stretched out beside her against the car. "Are you forgetting that I left my car over here yesterday? I had to return to get it eventually."

"That's the only reason why you came over here? For your car?"

Dante brushed a stray lock of hair from her face. "You know why I came over here, Tomi."

She fell quiet, and he took her uninjured hand in his, lightly kissing her fingertips. "I miss you and I want you back. Denise lied about everything, Tomi. She isn't pregnant—she never was pregnant. She just wanted to destroy us…but I'm not going to let her do it. Will you take me back, baby? Please? Give me another chance to win your heart back."

"Dante, I…"

"Tomi, just listen to me for a second." Dante took her hands and looked deep into her eyes. "Baby, I've come to realize that you are my everything. These pass few weeks have been a living hell for me. Everyday, I live, but I feel dead on the inside. I need you in my life, Tomi. You are all I have. And without you, I am nothing."

A flashback struck like lightning through her body, and Tomi started involuntarily shaking. She was eighteen again, seated in the passenger seat of Jonathan's car. Jonathan was staring at her the same way Dante just had, and he was saying similar words.

"Can't you see, Tomi? Without you, I am nothing. My life doesn't make sense; it has no meaning. I just need to—I need to get away. If I can't be with you, there's no reason to live."

Tomi felt her breakdown coming, but something in her head said, *No! Fight it! You do not have to keep reliving that moment. Fight it!*

And she did.

Jonathan's last words were jarringly loud in her mind, echoing again and again like a never ending horror story: *"When you look back on this night, remember that you could've saved us, Tomi. I gave you the chance. You could've saved me…"*

"It is not my fault," she whispered, and though his words were repeated again, they weren't as loud as they had been before. When Tomi noticed this, she gained an inner strength and stated again with force, "It is *not* my fault!" She said this over and over again until Jonathan's words became as soft as a whisper, then finally disappeared all together.

While this was going on, Dante had been holding her in his arms. He knew she was having one of her flashback episodes so he held her tight and kept telling her that she was okay, and that he was there for her.

Once the flashback had passed away, Dante continued his hold on her, and she didn't object. Dante wanted to ask, but he knew that when she was ready to tell him she would. They stood there for ten minutes or more not saying a word, just holding each other. Finally, Tomi took a deep, calming breath, and broke the silence.

"At school," she began, "I was the most popular girl walking the hallways of Sheridan High. To be my friend was a privilege; to be my man was an honor. Jonathan was my first love, but he was also my friend. Together, we were unstoppable. Everybody was jealous of our relationship, because that's how real we were with each other.

"Eventually, I lost that feeling of being head-over-heels in love with him. I don't know what happened. It just wasn't…that feeling wasn't there anymore. So I broke it off with him, but I told him that I still wanted us to be friends. He said he was cool with it. But then one day…"

"It's okay," he encouraged her in a soothing voice.

"One day," she continued, "he took me out. I was so pissed because he had promised not to come on to me, and that whole entire day, all he did was beg and plead for a second chance. Finally, I told him to take me home.

"We were on our way home when, all of a sudden, he pulled over in this abandoned parking lot—this was where the kids who weren't old enough to get into a club hung out at on the weekends. Jonathan sat there, professing his love for me, but I didn't want to hear it. He told me that he loved me and that he couldn't live without me. And then…"

She paused again, and Dante pulled her tighter into his arms, comforting her with his embrace. "And then he pulled out a gun." Her voice began to crack with emotion. "I thought he was going to kill me, I swear. He put that gun to my head, Dante, and I pleaded for my life. Then he told me that he could never hurt me. He said he loved me and that I could've saved him…then, he—then, he…he stuck that gun in his mouth…and pulled the trigger."

"Oh, my God." Dante held her, rocking her in his arms.

To her surprise, Tomi wasn't crying. Yes, she was hurting because of the vividness of the images, but she wasn't a puddle of tears like she usually was whenever she relived that incident in time.

"Baby, I'm so proud of you," Dante told her with admiration in his voice. "I know how hard it was for you to tell me that, and that really means a lot to me. You are a strong woman. Many people would have been left permanently scarred by something that traumatic."

"I was scarred," she admitted. "Not only did I lose, Jonathan, I lost everything, Dante. A part of me died the night that Jonathan took his life. I lost my self-esteem, my understanding of life, my motivation to live. With time, I regained the power to do the habitual things of life, but those things that I'd lost, I never quite gained back. I hid behind my beauty and my work. I put my passion for life into piercing and creating tattoos. I was alive, but I wasn't living…until I met you."

She looked into his brown eyes, looked into the gateways to his soul, swallowed, then said, "You want it? Here it is. Here's my big confession. I'm scared to love because I'm scared I'll kill again. Don't you see, Dante, I'm a murderer—he pulled that trigger because I couldn't save him."

"That's where you're wrong, Tomi. Like you said earlier, it wasn't your fault. Even if you were superman, you couldn't have saved him. Only he could have saved himself, and he chose not to. He chose to take the easy way out."

Dante stepped away from Tomi and leaned forward, resting his elbows on the hood of his car. "I know how he must have felt. In a way, I can relate to him. Thoughts of suicide have crossed my mind more than a few times. For a mother to walk out on her son, leave him completely by himself knowing that she was all he had, that's some fucked up shit, Tomi. Then, to grow up thinking how anybody can want me when my own mama didn't even want me, that shit hurts Tomi."

"I know baby." Tomi leaned on the hood beside Dante.

"I don't think I can ever forgive her."

Tomi stared at him until he looked at her. "Baby, she might have messed up, but she's still your mother."

Dante looked away. "You don't understand."

"Yes, I do understand. I understand that she hurt you really bad, just like the way Jonathan blaming me for killing himself hurt me really bad, too. But if I was somehow able to talk to Jonathan again, I'd forgive him for what he did. Because if you never forgive, you will never be able to move on with your life. And I'm ready to move on."

Dante looked over at her and threw an arm around her waist. "After telling me about what happened with Jonathan, how much lighter do you feel?" he asked her.

She smiled. "If there was a breeze in the air, I'd blow away."

Dante pulled her to him and kissed her forehead, her nose, her chin, and lingered on her lips. "Tomi, I love you. I swear I love you so much."

"I love you too," she whispered.

"I want to give you all of me," he confessed, "but I can't because there's a part of me missing. It's the part of me that my mom took away when she left and never came back."

"I'm going to find that missing piece for you," Tomi promised him, crossing her arms around his neck and pressing him against the car with her body. "And when I give that missing part back to you, I want you to love me with all of your heart and soul, with every fiber of your being."

Her mouth closed over his and her tongue searched for his. When he met her kiss with equal passion, Tomi knew without a doubt that he was her soul mate. They were two wounded souls who God had brought together so that they could begin the healing process for each other. Tomi felt that she had already started her healing process the moment she'd decided to confess the truth to Dante. Dante wouldn't be able to start his healing process until he made amends with his mother. Tomi made a solemn vow to herself that she would do whatever it took to see Dante healed, whatever it took to find his missing piece.

Chapter Sixteen

"Who is it?"

"Keith."

"Keith?" Kelise wondered what in the world could have possessed him to come knocking at her door at such a late hour. She pulled on her white terry cloth robe and patted her thin dreds with a towel.

When she swung the door open, she asked, "Keith, what do you want? Do you know what time of night it is?"

"I need someone to talk to." He looked like a lost little boy as he stood there on her doorstep with his hands stuck deep inside his pants pockets.

"You couldn't talk to Tomi?" she asked, pulling her robe tighter as a cool night breeze chilled her skin.

"It's about Tomi."

Kelise hesitated for a second. It was a quarter after eleven and she had to be up at five in the morning. Her plan had been to take a shower then pass out in her bed, but she guessed she could make an exception. The five o'clock shadow and the creases in his forehead told her that whatever Keith needed to talk to her about had been weighing heavily on his shoulders for a while.

She opened the door wider. "Come in."

Keith ducked as he entered her house so as not to hit his head on her door frame. "I'm sorry to be bothering you at such a late hour," he apologized, "but I really needed to talk to someone."

"It's no problem," Kelise lied. She shut and locked the door behind him and followed him into her den. "Can I get you something to drink? Water, tea, soda?"

"You got any alcohol?" He plopped down onto her black leather sofa. "I need a *drink*."

"I have five o'clock gin—"

"Perfect," he interrupted her, wiping a hand across his weary features. "Do you have any juice to mix it with? If not, just hand me the gin."

"Wow. Is it that bad?"

He nodded his head. "That bad."

Kelise entered her kitchen and mixed his drink. For herself, she was going to have a club soda, but passed that drink up in favor of a gin and juice as well. She returned to the den and handed him his drink before taking a seat across from him.

"I don't even know where to start," he admitted.

She had half the mind to say, "Start from the beginning," but she didn't know how long his story would last, and she didn't have all night. She thought about saying, "Take your time," but again, time was a virtue. So instead, she said nothing.

"I mean," he continued, "Kelise, I've never had feelings for a girl the way that I'm feeling Tomi."

"So what's the problem?" She took another swig of her drink.

He paused, gathering up his thoughts. "It seems to me as if she's brushing me off like I'm a flea. Every since that day that me and that nigga fought on her front steps, I haven't heard from her. Kelise, she don't answer any of my phone calls, and she never returns any of them either. And yesterday, when I rolled by her house, I saw that nigga's car parked over there."

Kelise finished her drink and sat her glass on the table in front of them. "It seems to me, Keith," she began after a moment of thought, "that she chose Dante over you."

"But if she still had feelings for old dude, why did she start talking to me in the first place? I feel like I was used as a front."

"It wasn't like that," she tried to take up for her sister. "Tomi...Tomi has some sensitive issues with men. To be honest, she's just recently resumed any type of dating life, period. In other words, Tomi is a little rusty with the proper dating etiquette. Charge it to her head, not her heart."

"I'm just not used to getting treated this way. Being pushed to the side like this is new to me—"

Kelise rolled her eyes towards heaven. "I know, I know. A guy who is as fine, sexy, and charming as you is used to getting whatever he wants, whenever he wants, however he wants. Well, things didn't quite turn out how you expected, did they, Mr. Keith? And now your pride is hurt. Poor baby. Trust me, this may be the first, but it definitely ain't the last time something like this will happen. Get use to it and get over it."

Keith blinked his eyes twice. "Damn! I can see when my presence isn't wanted. I'm sorry for taking up your—"

"Keith." She put a hand on his arm. "I didn't mean it like that. I'm sorry I snapped at you—PMS. Plus, my life…my life is a bit crazy right now. First, I took out my anger and frustration on my sister, Niya, and now I'm taking it out on you. I'm sorry."

"It's alr—"

Her phone rang, and she looked at her caller ID. "Ricardo."

"Can I..?" he motioned at his glass, and she shrugged her shoulders.

As Kelise answered her phone, Keith headed for the kitchen to refill his glass. "Ricardo, I don't even want to talk to you right now."

"Mi amor," Ricardo began, after hearing the anger in her voice, *"Lo siento mucho."*

"You're sorry, my ass," Kelise interrupted him hotly. "What happened to you only being in Ecuador for a week, Ricardo?"

"Yo sé, yo sé," he told her. "But it's not my fault, *chiquita.* Give me one more week, and I promise I'll be home."

"One broken promise after another. Ricardo, when is all this nonsense going to end? Do you even care about what's happening to our relationship?"

"You know I care, *señorita,* but there's not much I can do about it right now."

In a soft voice, she said, "Yes, there is. You can find another job."

"Chiquita," he sounded hurt, "don't ask me to do that. I didn't make you choose."

"You didn't have to."

Keith had returned from the kitchen, and he was seated at her keyboard, which was stationed in the corner on the opposite side of the room.

"The meeting is about to start so I'll call you tomorrow, okay, *mi amor?"*

Kelise sighed. "Bye, Ricardo."

"I love you, *mami."*

"Yo tambien, papi." Kelise hung up the phone, but remained in the same position with the same forlorn expression on her face. Her mood perked up somewhat when Keith began playing her favorite song—*Moonlight.* She made her way across the room and took a seat beside him. She started playing the song along with him, and when they hit the final key, she turned to face him with a smile.

"Ricardo taught me that song when we were in the ninth grade. We were in the same keyboarding class."

"Oh, y'all were high school sweethearts?"

She nodded her head, looking down at the hand which wore her engagement ring.

Before she knew what had happened, tears were streaming down her face. Keith didn't know what to do; he was no expertise when it came to a crying woman. He patted her back, trying to console her the best way he knew how.

"I don't know what's happening to us," she admitted on a hiccup. "We were the perfect couple until he got that damn job. Keith, he's never here. He flies all around the world, calls me whenever he can, and drops by to see me every now and then. But that's not enough. I know he loves me, but...I get terribly lonely, sometimes. We use to be so in love with each other. We were inseparable."

Keith put an arm around her and pulled her against his chest, rubbing her back in a circular, reassuring motion. He had to struggle to keep his balance on the keyboard seat because the alcohol in his system had him a bit unsteady.

"You came over here to spill your problems out to me, but I guess I have too many problems of my own," she told him, untangling herself from his arms. She wiped at her teary eyes with the back of her hand, giving him a strained smile. "My sister doesn't know how lucky she is. She has two men who are head over heels in love with her, and she don't even know what to do with them. Keith, I'd give anything to have Ricardo show me half as much of the attention as you and Dante show her."

Keith was listening to her, but it seemed like someone had thrown a cover over his head. Her voice sounded fuzzy and far away to him. His head was swimming—it felt like his brain was a pool of mushy gray matter. When he had gone in the kitchen to refill his glass earlier, he had taken a swig or two...or three...or four of gin directly from the bottle. The gin in his system was starting to work throughout his entire body. He had forgotten the effect that liquor had on him, but the hardening bulge in his pants was a quick reminder.

Sitting there with nothing on but her bath robe, Kelise looked inconceivably desirable to him. The realization of exactly how attractive she was hadn't hit him until he'd pulled her into his arms a moment ago. He hadn't noticed how full and succulent her lips were either, but suddenly, he wanted to taste them oh so bad.

"...and I tried to tell him how I feel about the whole situation," she was saying, "but it's like he doesn't even care, you know what I'm saying? If he loves me as much as he says he do—"

Kelise's sentence was abruptly cut short as Keith's lips covered hers. She was shocked into silence as his warm mouth moved over hers, coaxing her to return his kiss.

"Keith, what are you doing?" she asked, pulling back just a tad.

"Shhh," he said, straddling the keyboard seat with both legs, and moving towards her. With his arms wrapped around her waist, he pulled her to him; and though she resisted, it was only a half-hearted attempt. "Kiss me, Kelise."

Kelise knew she was wrong, felt in her very soul that she was wrong, but she couldn't help herself. Everybody else got to experience some type of happiness, except for her. She had been completely faithful to Ricardo, even when one of his business trips had taken him away from her for half a year. She yearned for Ricardo to look at her the way Keith was looking at her now, yearned for Ricardo to say her name the way Keith had just said it. She just wanted to feel…wanted.

Even as she leaned forward, offering him her lips, she knew she was wrong. He was drunk, and though she had indulged in a few sips herself, she was still in her right frame of mind. A fleeting image of Tomi's face interrupted her thoughts, but she shook it away. Yeah, she may regret this; yeah, she may hate herself in the morning, but for now, she was going to live in the moment.

She dipped her tongue into Keith's mouth, tasting the gin that flavored his tongue, and he moaned, crushing her closer to him. She didn't protest as he undid her robe, allowing it to slip to the floor. She didn't object as his fiery mouth found her hard nipple, suckling strongly as his other hand slid up and down her bare thigh. An objection was the last thing on her mind as he went down on his knees, spread her legs, and buried his tongue deep inside that hot, wet spot that needed to be touched.

"Keith!" She threw her head back, trapping her bottom lip between her teeth as she trapped his head between her legs. "Keith…Keith…oh, Keith…"

He brought her almost to the point of climax, only to stop just before she reached it. In a sexual haze, she looked at him through half-opened eyes. She was breathless as she asked, "What are you doing? Please, don't stop."

He said nothing as he moved the keyboard seat out the way and pulled her down to the floor with him. "Do you want it?" he questioned her, his voice low, husky, and enticing.

No turning back now, she thought. "I want it," she admitted in a throaty voice. She helped him unbutton and unzip his pants, and pulled him atop her. He softly bit the tender flesh of her neck, and she twisted and turned beneath him, unable to lay still.

"Keith," she groaned, guiding his rigid flesh to the one spot that wanted him the most. When he entered her, she screamed out in pain mixed with pleasure. "Oh, yes! Yes, Keith. Keith. Oh, Keith." It took her only five minutes to cum, but it was the most explosive climax that she had ever experienced in her life. He came moments later, and fell on top of her, breathing harshly.

They looked at each other, and turned their faces in shame, looking in opposite directions. Already, guilt was eating at both of them, but neither had the courage to face it. Once the throes of passion had completely faded, Keith rose to his feet and tucked his privates away.

"Kelise…"

She stood to her feet, retying her robe and looking at the floor, the couch, the TV—anywhere, but him.

"Have a good night," he told her, smoothing out the wrinkles from his shirt.

"You, too," she mumbled, still unable to look at him.

"I'm sorry," he apologized. Giving her one last forlorn look, he turned and left, gently shutting the door behind him.

As she locked the door and headed for her bedroom, she asked herself in disgust, "What in the hell have I done?"

*   *   *   *

"Have you talked to Keli lately?" Niya asked her sister, pulling a black silk skirt from off the rack. "What do you think about this?"

Tomi scrunched up her face. "I don't like the ruffles on it. The ruffles make it look too 70s for me." Niya put the skirt back on the rack.

"I don't know what's up with Kelise," Tomi continued. "Every time I talk to her, she's oh so busy working on a story for the magazine. I told her if she don't want to talk to me, just say it."

"Now that I think about it, Keli has been acting a little strange these pass few days. What do you think about this?" Niya held up a gray and white shirt to her chest, and Tomi snatched it away from her.

"That shirt is so me. It goes perfect with my new Air Force Ones."

Niya smirked. "I didn't know they made Air Force Ones with stiletto heels."

"Forget you!" Tomi exclaimed, giving her sister a light shove. "You need to hurry up and find something to wear because I'm starving! I'm ready to eat."

Niya arched a questioning eyebrow at her little sister. "You've been having a mighty healthy appetite lately."

"What's that supposed to mean?"

"Don't play stupid."

"I'm not pregnant."

"Do you and Dante use condoms?" she asked, pulling another shirt off the rack.

"What Dante and I do in the bedroom, Niya, is none of your business," Tomi told her, inconspicuously glancing down at her stomach. She didn't think she was pregnant, but she wasn't a hundred percent sure. Her period hadn't come on last week like it should have, but then again, her period had a mind of its own. Some times it came a week or two early, at other times, a week or two late. So she wasn't too worried. As long as she didn't get a case of morning sickness, she figured she was good.

"I found it!" Niya exclaimed. "Tomi, what do you think of this?" Niya shook the scarlet-red skirt in front of her sister. It was made from a shiny, clingy material and looked as if it probably wouldn't even cover her goodies.

"It's a little short, don't you think?"

"I'll go try it on and we'll see. Doesn't it go good with this shirt?" She held up a black spaghetti strap shirt with a crimson-red rose embroidered in the middle. Niya pranced off to the dressing room, and Tomi rummaged through the racks, looking for nothing in particular. Dante had taken her on a shopping spree the pass weekend and had bought her a whole new wardrobe. Later that night, she had put on the naughty, pearly white teddy that he had bought her, and they had made love with Jagged Edge playing in the background.

While Tomi was waiting on her sister, she decided to run over to the drink machine to purchase an Aquafina. Her mouth was so dry, she didn't have enough saliva to moisten her throat. She slid a dollar in the cash slot and pressed the Aquafina button. As she retrieved her drink from the machine and turned around, she accidentally bumped into the man who had been walking pass behind her.

"I'm sorry sir," she apologized, holding out a hand to steady him. Her breath caught when she realized who the man was. "Keith."

"Tomi." He didn't look too happy to see her. Actually, he seemed extremely nervous and paranoid, and he had a look on his face that said he wanted to be anywhere except right here, in this mall, at this precise moment.

"Keith, are you okay?"

"Yeah, yeah. I'm fine. But look though, it was nice seeing you. I got to—I'm kind of in a hurry. I got to go. Bye Tomi." He gave her one last look before quickly walking away. He didn't look back.

Tomi stood there, **her** mouth wide open. *What the hell was all that about?* she wondered. *Damn, why **didn't** he just slap me in the face? At least that would have implied that he had some type of emotional feelings.*

Shaking her head, **Tomi** returned to Body Rock clothing store and leaned on the clothing rack while **she** waited for her sister to finish in the dressing room. She still couldn't figure out how Keith could act so nonchalant towards her. Had he lost feelings for her that fast? And if he had, didn't that mean that he never really cared about her, that it was all about getting laid from the start? For some reason the thought saddened her, and she tried to clear her mind and think about something else. About Dante. About the love of her life.

"How does it look!" Niya came bursting out the dressing room, bursting through Tomi's troubling thoughts, while twirling around in her teeny tiny skirt. "Tomi, I like it so much! I feel ten years younger!"

At the sight of her sister, Tomi's jaw dropped and hung there. Niya looked stunning! Tomi hadn't seen her sister look this good since she was eighteen years old. Her skin seemed to glow. Here was her sister, two years away from being thirty and looking more like her twentieth birthday had just passed the day before.

Niya's smile lit the whole room. "Do I really look that good?"

"You look amazing," Tomi promised her sister. "Tonight, it's going to be all about you. If Phillip could see you now, he'd lose his damn mind."

"Don't say his name. His name is forbidden from now on." Niya twirled around in front of the body-length mirror. "Phillip didn't deserve all of this anyway."

"You ain't lying about that. Now can you please go change so we can get something to eat? I could eat a whole cow right about now. My stomach is over here talking to me."

Niya looked down at her sister's flat stomach again, gave her a skeptical look, then headed back into the changing room. Moments later, she returned and purchased the shirt and skirt. Her total came up to $73.24.

"See, that's why I don't shop here. That was damn ridiculous," Tomi exclaimed, looking at her sister's receipt. But she knew for a fact that that was only chunk change to Niya.

Once they had entered the food court, Niya asked her sister where she wanted to eat. "It don't matter, Niya, as long as I eat something."

They ended up eating at Subway. Tomi ordered a foot-long meatball hero, and Niya ordered a six-inch veggie sub.

Once they were seated at the table, Tomi said, "Guess who I bumped into while you were in the dressing room."

"Who?"

"Keith."

"Really? What did he say?"

"Nothing." Tomi took a large bite of her sub and chewed angrily. "He acted like he didn't want to be no where near me. Said he was in a hurry and left."

"What?" Niya lifted one eyebrow. "What was all that about? I thought he was really feeling you."

"I thought so too. Guess I was wrong." Tomi finished her whole sub and went back to order a six-inch cold-cut trio on rye.

Niya watched her sister wolf down her food like it was nothing more than an appetizer. She had never known her sister to have an appetite quite like this. Call it big sister's intuition, but she had a gut feeling that Tomi had a little bean baking in her oven. "Tomi, I want you to take a pregnancy test."

"Why?" Tomi asked with a piece of lettuce hanging out the side of her mouth.

"Because you're pregnant."

"No I'm not!"

"Yes you are."

Tomi lowered her voice after getting an annoyed look from a nearby shopper. "Niya, I'm not pregnant. I don't feel pregnant, I don't look pregnant, therefore, I'm not pregnant."

"Sis, incase you're forgetting, I have two children of my own. I think I know a little something about the whole pregnancy thingy."

Tomi gave in an inch. "If it'll make you happy, I'll take the freaking test."

"Take it now," her sister urged.

"No."

"Why not?"

"Because I'm eating." Tomi finished her whole sub and was still hungry. She didn't go back and purchase another, though; it would have only strengthened Niya's absurd notion that she was with child.

"Come on," Tomi told her sister, heading for the store, Pierre, "we have to find you some killer shoes to wear with that outfit you just bought."

"And then we'll go buy you a pregnancy test."

Tomi rolled her eyes, but said nothing.

CHAPTER SEVENTEEN

"Hello?"

"Oh, so I had to call you with a blocked number just for you to answer my phone call?"

"Tomi, I'm really busy right now. I'll call you la—"

"Keli, put down your pen and paper and come to the club with Niya and me tonight," Tomi insisted.

"Tomi, I can't. I'm very, very—"

"Kelise. Listen to me. Niya actually went through with the divorce, okay? We've always wanted her to ditch that trifling dog, and she's finally done it! Their divorce went through today. Niya is a free woman, and we need to welcome her back into the single life—show her how to live it up, have fun, let loose!" Tomi was dancing around her front room with Dante, and she had to pop his hands as they eased below her waist. "Stop boy."

"Tomi—"

Dante took the phone from Tomi and put it to his ear. "What's up, Kelise?"

"Hey Dante. How are you?"

"All gravy, baby." He loudly kissed Tomi. "Why won't you go out with my baby tonight? Help her celebrate with her sister. It's the weekend; you have all Saturday and Sunday to finish writing whatever it is that you're writing."

"Dante—"

"Look, you're going out with my baby and Niya tonight, and that's end of story. They'll be over to pick you up around ten. Be ready."

"But—"

Dante flipped Tomi's cell closed and twirled her around the front room. "Baby, she said she'd love to go to the club with you and Niya tonight."

Tomi laughed. "Dante, you are a mess. Give me a kiss."

Dante kissed her before reluctantly letting her go. "I have to get going. I promised my home-boy that I'd help him hook his car up today. I'm putting in his speakers and two amps. When I finish with his ride, if you sit in it, his music will be loud enough to make your hair straight." Dante looked at her hair, then said, "You should come with me so I can take you for a ride in his c—"

Tomi elbowed him hard in his side. "Don't try to play me just cause I haven't had a perm in a month. I have good hair; I don't need no perm."

"If you say so."

Tomi elbowed him again, and Dante gave in, hugging her tight against him so she couldn't elbow him anymore. "Okay, baby, okay. I was just playing."

He kissed her lips. "Do you love me?" he asked, rocking from side to side with her as he gazed into her chocolate-brown eyes.

She returned the kiss. "You know I love you, boy. Serious up."

"Just had to make sure," he said. "A'ight, baby, I'm gone."

Tomi looked out the window and watched him as he backed out her driveway. When she saw his car turn the corner, she went into the bathroom and ran a tub full of steaming hot water, then added a cup of creamy milk bath. She had just settled in the tub good when she heard a cell phone ringing. At first, she thought it was her cell phone, then realized that she didn't recognize the tune of the ring.

Rising from the tub, she loosely draped a towel around her and headed towards her bedroom. Once inside her room, the sound of the ringing intensified. Tomi glanced at her cell phone, which was setting on her dresser. It wasn't ringing. She walked over towards her bed and the ringing sound increased in volume. Just as she was about to figure out the exact location of the phone, the ringing stopped.

"Dante must've forgot his phone," Tomi said aloud. Her curiosity got the best of her, and instead of returning to her bath, she decided to initiate a scavenger hunt for Dante's phone.

She lifted up her pillows, looked under the sheets, under the mattresses, by the nightstand. Just then, the cell phone started ringing again. The sound was coming from under her bed. Tomi dropped to her hands and knees and rummaged under her bed until she retrieved Dante's phone.

Whoever was calling wasn't listed in his phone book, because the caller number wasn't identified with a name. Also, the number was long distance.

Suddenly nervous and anxious about what she would find out, Tomi hesitantly answered the phone. "Hello?"

"Hello?" a woman's voice asked. "Is this Dante's phone?"

A powerful surge of jealousy raged within Tomi's chest. *How dare some female have the nerve to call her man. And how dare Dante give out his number in the first place.*

Angry beyond understanding, Tomi snapped, "Who is this and why the hell do you want to speak to Dante?"

"I want to speak to Dante because I love him. I'm his mother."

*   *   *   *

Kelise nervously paced her living room floor as she waited for Niya and Tomi to arrive. "Just be yourself," she ordered, talking to her reflection in the living-room mirror. She was wearing a black scarf around her dreads, a button-down, black dress that hugged her hips and waist, and a pair of black, low-heeled church shoes. Wearing all black had been intentional. It symbolized not only the death of her and Ricardo's relationship, but the death of her friendship with her sister. Black was the embodiment of all the mourning she would endure once the shit hit the fan.

Kelise jumped at the sound of the loud, hard knock on the door. *They're here!* her mind screamed. *Oh God, what if Tomi can look at me and see my guilt written all across my face? What if she can smell Keith on me? What if she can look at the floor and actually see where we had almost burned a hole in the carpet with our lovemaking?*

Oh God, what have I done? I knew I shouldn't have answered the phone.

There were three more hard knocks, then Niya's voice, "Hurry up, Kelise! Ladies get in free until ten-thirty!"

Kelise took three deep, calming breaths, then pulled the door open.

Tomi was the first to speak. "Damn. Kelise, we're going to the club, not a funeral. Girl, if you don't take your ass back in there and change."

"No," Kelise said in a careful voice, "I'm wearing what I have on."

Niya looked at Tomi, and Tomi gave her a wink. "Fine then," Tomi relented. "You can wear that, but I'll have to change it up just a little bit." She reached forward and ripped open the top of Kelise's dress.

Niya burst out laughing and Kelise gasped in shock as the first five buttons to her dress popped off, bouncing around on her cement front porch. "Tomi!" she protested, looking down at her damaged dress. "You ruined my dress."

"Honey, that dress was ruined the day you bought it," Niya informed her.

They looked over Tomi's handiwork. Kelise had gone from being a nun on the way to someone's funeral, to being a sexy *mamacita* who would make a grand entrance no matter where she went. With the first five buttons of her dress removed, Kelise's lacey black bra and the top curves of her breasts were tauntingly exposed.

"That'll work," Tomi decided.

"What about her feet?" Niya asked, staring at her sister's feet with a look of disgust.

"We wear the same size," Tomi told her. "I always keep an emergency pair of stilettos in my trunk. Come on, guys. It's ten-oh-eight. We have to put a move on it."

Moments later, Niya yelled out over the blaring music from the mega-speakers, "This club is jamming! How'd you know about this joint?"

"Dante and me came here one night," Tomi told her sister, throwing her hands up in the air and swinging her hips from side to side. "Loosen up, Keli!" she said, bumping hips with her sister.

"Let's go get on the dance floor!" Niya was excited and ready to get on the floor so she could shake her tail-feather.

"No, not yet," Tomi told her. "We'll wait til the dance floor gets a little fuller. Come on, guys. Let's go get a table before they're all taken."

First, they went to the bar and ordered their drinks—Tomi, a bottle of water (due to the evil eye Niya bestowed on her), Kelise, a sour apple martini, and Niya, a Sex on the Beach. With drinks in hand, they found a vacant table in a corner of the club.

"Guys, I'm having a lot of fun. I can't remember the last time I've actually went out and enjoyed myself like this." Niya sipped on her drink, still bouncing to the beat. "Phillip never—"

"Unh, unh!" Tomi cut her off. "We're not going to mention Phillip's name, remember? We brought you out tonight so you can have fun and forget all about your worries."

"Okay," Niya succumbed, finishing up her drink. "Nothing more about Phillip. I swear." They bobbed their heads to the music for a while, then Niya asked Kelise, "Sweetie, why are you so quiet? You've hardly uttered a word since we've been here."

Kelise shrugged her shoulders. "I have a lot on my mind."

"Like what?"

"Well…"

"Excuse me, ladies," a light-skinned, tall, broad-shouldered male with just-right waves in his hair, approached the chair where Niya was seated. "I don't mean to interrupt or anything, but I couldn't help but notice your exquisite beauty." He took Niya's hand in his, and if she would've blushed any harder, a blood vessel would have popped in her head. "Can I have this dance?"

Niya looked at her two sisters with an unsure, nervous smile.

"What are you waiting for?" Tomi asked her. "Go dance with the man."

Niya smiled at him. "I guess it's okay to dance." She allowed him to help her from the table and they disappeared into the crowd.

Tomi saw plenty of eyes following her sister's long legs as she made her way to the dance floor. "I'm so happy for her," she told Kelise, resting her elbows on the table. "She deserves to be happy."

And you deserve to know what I've done, Kelise said in her mind. She badly wanted to tell her sister about her betrayal. Her guilt felt like a cancerous tumor eating away at her very soul.

"Tomi." Tomi didn't hear her because she was too busy jamming in her seat to Ciara's Goodies. "Tomi," she repeated, a bit louder this time. Tomi still didn't hear her. "Tomi!" she yelled at the top of her lungs.

"What?"

Now that she had her attention, Kelise didn't have a voice. "I need to tell you..."

"Hey there, beautiful. You want to dance?" It was a brown-skinned cutie with corn-rolls that reached his shoulders. He looked like he was mixed with Indian.

"I'd love to," Tomi told him, jumping to her feet. "I'll be right back," she promised her sister before disappearing onto the dance floor with the Indian cutie.

Niya returned to the table, huffing and puffing, sweating bullets. Her tiny red skirt clung to her thighs which were also glistening with sweat. "Girl, I can't remember the last time I've had a workout like this! I danced with three different guys, and this female tried to dance with me, too. I had to tell her I don't play that."

Kelise laughed. "I'm glad you're having fun, Niya."

Niya eyed her sister. "Why are you still sitting here? You should be doing your thing on the dance floor. There's plenty men to go around."

"Naw," Kelise declined. "I think I'll—"

"Can I buy you a drink?" a toasted almond brother with matching toasted brown eyes asked Kelise.

"No, thanks" she politely declined, "I'm good."

"You sure?"

"Positive."

"You can buy *me* a drink," Niya offered, looking appreciatively at the man. There was not one part of his body that didn't portray some type of sex appeal, and Niya was intrigued. It had been so long since she'd had the pleasure of looking at another man and seeing him as something more than just an attractive man who was completely off limits. Phillip had been her all and all, but obviously, she must not have meant as much to him as he had meant to her, or he wouldn't have had that tomato-head bitch in their marriage bed. It was time for her to move on with her life. It was Phillip's lost, not hers.

"What's your name?" she asked the guy, slipping her arm through his as they headed for the bar.

"Myriad," he replied, seductively licking his lips.

They set off for the bar, leaving a disheartened Kelise sitting at the table alone.

On the dance floor, Tomi was getting down with her fourth dance partner. He was a mixed brother with a thuggish demeanor. If she had been single, she wouldn't have mind hollering at him, but since she was in a relationship, she kept their dancing as clean as she could.

The record ended and the melodic beats of Jodeci's *Stay* flowed through the speakers. It was the first slow song that they had played all night.

"I'm beat," Tomi told the guy, wiping a pool of sweat from her forehead. "I think I'm going to sit this one out."

"No," the guy objected, pulling her close to him, "I've been wanting to slow dance with your sexy ass all night." His hands lowered to her buttocks, and he squeezed her cheeks in his palms.

"Get your nasty hands off me!" Tomi hotly demanded, mushing him in his face and twirling from his grasp. "Don't you ever touch me like that again!" She mushed him in his face once more before stalking off the dance floor.

Before she could make it to her table, an oil-spill with a shiny gold tooth reached out an arm and pulled her against him. "Where you headed to, walking all fast, lovely?"

Before she could reply, a female's voice from behind them said, "Damn, Jerome. I can't turn around for two seconds before you're all up in some hoe's face."

"Excuse me?" Tomi asked.

"You heard me, bitch." Denise approached them and when Denise saw who the other girl was, she couldn't help but to show her surprise and displeasure at seeing Tomi again. "Well, hello, Tomi."

"How do you know my name?" Tomi asked, unable to recognize Denise because of the club's obscurity.

"Don't worry about all that," Denise snapped, stepping to her face. "Do you know I could beat the shit out of you right now for taking my man?"

"Your man?" Tomi was confused, but she didn't let her guard down. If this high-yellow bitch wanted to scrap, she wasn't about to punk down from no fight. "Trust me, girl, don't nobody want that black ass oil-spill except for you."

A few people had stopped dancing and were staring over at them to see what was going on.

"I'm not talking about him," Denise snapped at her angrily. She stepped forward until Tomi and she was almost touching noses. "I'm talking about Dante."

"Denise." Tomi crossed her arms and rolled her eyes. "I should've known. Let us get something straight. First off, I didn't take your man, okay? You never had him. Second off, I should beat the shit out of you for lying to him about carrying his child and for lying about y'all being engaged."

Denise turned a little red, but she held her ground. "If you would've stayed out our lives," she told her with scorching animosity in her voice, "I wouldn't have had to lie about anything because he would still be by my side."

"Who the hell is Dante?" Oil Spill asked.

"Mind your fucking business," Denise told him without even looking over her shoulder. "Listen to me, Tomi. You better watch your back. 'Cause I will leave a permanent tattoo all over your beautiful face." Her tone was soft and taunting.

"Oh, really?" Tomi asked, her anger coming to life like a savage beast within her. "You mean a tattoo like this?" With both hands, she used her nails to claw down the sides of Denise's face, drawing blood.

"You bitch!" Denise screamed. She pulled back her hand and pimp-slapped the right side of Tomi's face. Tangling her hands in Tomi's hair, she roughly yanked Tomi's head back and landed two blows across her face.

"Cat fight!" somebody screamed, and immediately, a crowd formed around them.

Struggling to regain her balance, Tomi scratched and pulled at Denise until she was finally able to free herself from her firm grasp, but not before Denise was able to remove a chunk of her hair. Denise held the hair up high enough for everyone to see. "One good thing about the bitch," she said in a loud voice, "she don't wear weave."

Tomi worked her jaw, then spit blood onto the floor. She looked up at Denise with hatred written all over her face. "You shouldn't have done that," she warned. "You don't mess with a black woman's hair."

With that notice, she balled up her fist and slammed it into Denise's throat. Making gurgling sounds, Denise dropped to her knees, holding her throat with both hands.

"Stupid bitch," Tomi yelled at her, "do you know how long it took me to fix my hair?" With that question, Tomi kicked her hard in her stomach, and Denise rolled over onto the floor, scrunching up in a fetal position.

Tomi fell on top of her, landing blows one after another against Denise's once flawless face. Her plan was to mutilate; she wanted to leave Denise with some serious bruises. After she had finished beating Denise's face until it looked like a swollen, bruised tomato, she grabbed Denise's head and banged it on the floor until Denise lost consciousness. Tomi jumped up and modestly pulled her dress back into place before rearranging her breasts into her shirt.

"Stupid bitch made me break my heel," she complained, removing the broken shoe and tossing it away.

"Why you do her like that?" Oil Spill asked, leaning over Denise's motionless body. "You didn't even have to do her like that."

Tomi didn't have time to reply because the bouncers bum-rushed the scene, picking her up at the waist.

"Put me down!" she shrieked, but he threw her over his shoulder and headed for the exit door.

"There's no fighting in this club," he told her. "That goes for ladies as well as men." She continued to scream for him to put her down, but he didn't obey until they were outside.

Roughly, he dropped her to her feet and barked, "And don't come back!" He turned and, with his one million muscles bulging from his arms, marched back inside. A few seconds after he disappeared, Kelise and Niya came running out the club.

"What happened?" Niya asked when she saw her sister's face.

Kelise added, "What in the world happened? One minute, I was sitting at the table, looking at everybody dancing, next thing I know, I see your ass thrown over the bouncer's shoulder, and him marching outside."

Tomi wiped blood from her busted lip before saying, "That dumb bitch Denise."

"Where she at?" Niya asked, looking around as if the girl would be standing out side.

"She's in the club laying on the floor. I beat the shit out of her," Tomi told them, limping towards her car.

"Are you okay?" Kelise asked. "Why are you limping? Did she hurt your leg?"

"No," Tomi muttered, "she broke my heel. Do you know how much these shoes cost me?" Both Niya and Kelise shook their heads at their little sister.

"I'll drive," Niya told her, taking the keys from her as they approached Tomi's car. Niya started up the engine and drove off.

"Niya, I'm sorry about tonight," Tomi apologized, checking out the damage Denise had done to her face in the visor mirror. "We were supposed to make sure you had a good time, and instead, I end up getting us kicked out the club."

"Oh, it's all good," Niya assured her, making a right at the light. "I met this cute guy named Myriad. He's really sweet. And guess what his dog name is?"

"What?"

"Phillip." Niya laughed aloud. "How fitting is that?"

CHAPTER EIGHTEEN

"What does it say?" Tomi asked, sitting on the edge of the bathtub and biting at her thumbnail.

"It doesn't say nothing yet," Dante told her, holding the pregnancy stick in his hand while sitting on the toilet.

"God, I wish it would hurry up. The suspense is killing me!" Tomi had gnawed her thumbnail to pieces, and she had just gotten her nails done a few days ago. *That was a wasted thirty dollars,* she thought.

"Okay, I'm getting something," Dante told her, moving up to the edge of the toilet seat.

"Oh God, oh God, oh God," Tomi nervously chanted. She jumped off the edge of the tub and paced the tiny area of her bathroom. "What does it say, Dante? What does it say?"

After keeping her in the dark for a few intense seconds, Dante finally smiled and stated, "You're a mommy."

"Serious up?!"

"Serious up."

"Let me see it!" she exclaimed, snatching the stick out his hands. The digital sign of the test read: Pregnant. "Dante, I'm pregnant!" she said in an incredulous tone. "I'm really pregnant!"

"I know, baby," he replied, nearly falling off the toilet as she threw her arms around his neck. They kissed three or four times before pulling apart.

"You're going to be a daddy again," she told him, holding his face lovingly in her hands.

"Come here," he told her, pulling her to him and pushing up her shirt so he could place his ear against her stomach, which was a bit pudgy now. "I wonder if it's a girl or a boy," he said wistfully, rubbing her stomach with his hands.

"Which do you want?" she asked, smoothing her hand across his head.

"A little girl. We'll name her Diana Destini McKoy."

"That sounds beautiful," she told him. "And if we have a boy—"

She heard her cell phone ringing from in the kitchen. "Let me go get that," she told him, hurrying out the bathroom. As soon as she picked up her phone, it stopped ringing. Her caller ID identified that the caller was her mom. She hit a button to call her back.

"Hey baby. I just called you."

"I know, ma. I didn't reach the phone in time. But I have something to tell you!"

"What is it?"

"You'd never believe me."

"Try me."

Tomi plopped onto her couch and threw her legs over the arm. "I'm going to be a mommy!" she yelled into the phone.

She had to pull the phone away from her ear as her mother screamed in the background. Finally, when the initial shock from the fact that her baby girl was going to be a mother had passed, her mother said, "I knew it! I knew it! I knew it! I didn't have a dream about flying fish for nothing!"

"Where's daddy?"

Cathy laughed aloud. "Girl, he's gone fishing with your Uncle Thomas. He should be back around six or seven. And how bout we're eating fish for dinner tonight." She laughed again. "I knew I didn't have that dream about fish for nothing. My baby girl ain't no baby no more, huh?"

"I can't believe it either," Tomi admitted. Dante walked into the front room, leaned over her, and planted a kiss on her cheek. "I'm going outside to wash our cars, baby. Let me know when you get off the phone."

She mouthed the word 'okay' and shooed him away so she could finish her conversation with her mother. While she was on the phone with her mom, Kelise beeped in.

"Hey mom," she interrupted her mother, "I'd love to talk with you, but Keli's beeping in and I want to let her know that she's going to be a new auntie."

"Okay then. Call me later. Love you."

"Love you, too." Tomi flipped over and, without missing a beat, exclaimed, "Keli, girl, guess what."

"What?"

"You're not going to believe me."

"What is it?"

"I'm pregnant."

"No you're not."

"Yes, I am. Keli, I promise to God I'm pregnant. I just took a test, and it said 'pregnant' in very clear letters."

"Wow, Tomi. Congratulations."

"Thanks." Tomi paused for a second. "Kelise, why you sound like that?"

"Like what?"

Tomi shrugged her shoulders. "I don't know. You just don't sound like yourself anymore. Do you want to talk about it?"

Kelise took a deep breath. It was now or never. "Tomi, I have something to tell you."

Tomi lifted a questioning eyebrow at her tone. "What?"

"Promise me you won't be mad."

With a serious expression on her face, Tomi sat up on the couch and repeated again, "What?"

Taking a deep breath, Kelise reconsidered telling Tomi the truth. She could tell by Tomi's voice that this wasn't going to go smooth.

"What is it?" Tomi repeated.

"Tomi, I…"

"You what?" Tomi was all ears, now.

"Tomi, I…" Kelise felt tears welling up in her eyes. "Tomi, promise you won't be mad at me."

"What the fuck did you do?" Tomi's voice was loud, and she was on her feet now. "What did you do, Kelise?"

Kelise took one more deep breath. "I slept with Keith."

"You did what?"

There it was. The shit had hit the fan…and it didn't smell good.

"I'm sorry, Tomi."

Kelise's words were a slap in the face. "Yeah, you are sorry. You're a sorry excuse for a sister. How could you do me like that?"

"It was an accident," Kelise pleaded with fervor.

"What about Ricardo?"

"I know, I know," Kelise cried, tears pouring from her eyes. "I don't know what I was thinking. I messed up. I shouldn't have done it. I was so wrong."

"That was real dirty, Kelise. But you know what? It doesn't even matter. I'm with Dante, I love Dante, and I'm pregnant by Dante. Whatever little nasty, fucked up shit that you and Keith are doing, y'all can continue to do it because—"

"It only happened once! I swear!"

"When?"

"When what?"

"When did it happen?" Tomi barked at her sister.

On a hiccup, Kelise said, "A week ago—"

"A week ago?" Tomi exclaimed. "So in other words, when we went to the club together, you had already fucked Keith?"

"Don't say it like that."

"Answer my question!"

Kelise sobbed softly. "Yes..."

"Kelise, I can't believe you! You and Niya beefed for the longest because you thought Phillip was so trifling, but how are you any different? You sat there, smiling in my face, and the whole time knowing that you and Keith had slept together! Just—just—fuck you, Kelise."

"No, Tomi. Don't—"

Tomi hung up on her sister and threw her phone on the couch just as Dante walked in through the back door.

"Everything okay, baby? I heard you yelling outside."

She couldn't stop the tears from flowing as she relayed everything that had just taken place to him. It wasn't the fact that Keith and Kelise had messed around that had her so upset; it was the fact that Kelise was her sister, and she knew that Tomi and Keith, at one time, had had something going on. Never in a million years would she have ever believed that one of her sisters would do her like this. It hurt her to the core.

When Tomi had finished retelling what had happened, Dante stated in a matter-of-fact fashion, "I don't understand why you're so mad about it. If you're in love with me, then why should you care about who she sleeps with?"

Tomi rolled her eyes. "You don't get it, do you? Baby, her sleeping with Keith would be like you sleeping with Niya."

Dante walked to the other side of the room, placing a sufficient amount of distance between them. "So what are you trying to say?" he asked in a loud voice. "Are you trying to tell me that you were in love with that dude?"

"No!" she quickly replied. "But I did care for him."

"Sounds to me like you still care for him." Dante's voice was as cold as his stare. "When you figure out who you want, you call me and let me know."

He turned to leave, but Tomi grabbed his arm, pulling him to a stop. "Dante, I know who I want. I want you! I'm carrying your child, ain't I?"

He turned to face her. "Then why are you so upset that your sister slept with old dude? Why do you even care?"

"Because she's my *sister*." Tomi sighed aloud because Dante still wasn't getting it. "Dante, baby, what I'm trying to say is that it could've been anybody else and I wouldn't have cared, but because she's my sister, it matters."

A long, tense silence settled over them. Then, Dante asked in a low voice, "Did you ever have sex with him?"

Tomi looked down at the floor and mumbled under her breath, "No."

Dante lifted up her chin until her eyes met his, and repeated his question, "Did you ever have sex with him, Tomi?"

"No," she replied again.

A look of extreme relief softened his features. Still holding her chin, he asked, "Did you want to?"

"Did I want to what?"

"Don't play dumb with me."

Tomi tried to look away, but he wouldn't let her. "Does it really matter?" she asked.

"It matters to me."

She took a deep breath to help steady her emotions. "Yes, Dante," she finally admitted, "I wanted to have sex with Keith." The look of hurt on his face was so intense, she almost wanted to take back her words—but she didn't.

"I wanted to have sex with Keith, but we never did," she continued, "but you can't say the same thing about Denise, can you?"

His head snapped around as he looked at her, a confused frown on his face. "What are you talking about?" he asked.

Tomi rolled her eyes towards heaven. "Don't you play dumb with me. When we broke up, I drove pass your house plenty of times and saw Denise's car parked over there at all times of the day—morning, noon, and night. Don't try to tell me that she was just over there for house cleaning.

"And one night I called and she answered the phone. Said you was sleep in bed, and that she had wore you out. What was all that about?"

"Yeah, I was fucking her," he admitted, "but that's all it was—fucking. And the whole time I was in her, I was hurting inside because I wanted you."

"Am I supposed to feel flattered?" she yelled at him.

"Tomi, that's besides the point—"

"Then what is the point of this conversation, dammit?" Tomi was angry enough to spit fire.

"The point of this conversation," Dante enlightened her, "is that I could give a rat's ass about Denise, but it's obvious that you still have feelings for this lame ass nigga.

"When you told me about what happened at the club, and about Denise being there with some oil spill, I didn't trip, now did I? But when you hear that your sister slept with your ex, you go fucking bananas. It's obvious that you still have feelings for dude."

"I don't have feelings for him," Tomi corrected him, "I *care* about him."

"And you wanted to fuck him!"

"But I didn't!"

Tomi and Dante were standing face to face. Fiery fumes were escaping from both their nostrils.

"Get out my house," Tomi told him through clenched teeth.

"You ain't got to tell me twice," he heatedly replied. He stomped towards her door, saying over his shoulder, "I'll get out your damn house. And when you feening for me, when you laying in the bed, wishing I had my arms wrapped around you, you call that other nigga. The one you love so damn much." He slammed her door hard enough to make her involuntarily jump.

She fell onto the couch, covered her face with a pillow, and tried not to cry. But when she thought about how today was supposed to be the happiest day in her life, the day she found out that she was going to soon bring a new life into this world, a baby with the man whom she loved more than life itself—and this was how her happiest day would end because her sister couldn't keep her damn legs closed? She buried her face into the pillow and cried until there were no more tears left to cry.

*   *   *   *

Kelise didn't have an appetite. With the tip of her fork, she pushed the three-cheese lasagna back and forth around her plate while waiting for Ricardo to return to the table. Not even a whole hour after Tomi had ended their phone conversation, Ricardo had showed up at her house. He was ecstatic about the fact that he didn't have to leave again for two whole months. She was happy to see him, but saddened at the same time. She didn't know how to bring up her infidelity. How was she supposed to tell the love of her life that she had slept with another man?

When he had entered their house, he had picked her up in her arms and swung her around in circles. "Baby, I'm going to make up for all the lost time we've had," he had promised, hugging her to him as if he was afraid to let her go. *"Dame un beso,"* he told her, and she did.

Kissing him gently on his lips, her eyes had filled with tears. How could she have cheated on a man who loved her so much with a man whom she barely knew? She felt like the cheapest, lowest tramp that had ever walked the earth.

Ricardo returned to the table and eyed her untouched plate. *"¿No tienes hambre?"* he asked her. "You haven't eaten a thing."

"I'm not really hungry," she admitted. How could she eat when her stomach was so full of guilt?

"Well," he told her, pushing her plate aside, "never mind the food. I have a surprise for you."

"Really?" Her eyes lit up. "What is it?"

Ricardo was a man who loved to bejewel his woman with some of the most expensive jewelry from countries he had passed through during his business trips. Her engagement ring itself ran about five G's.

Ricardo motioned to the maître d´ and seconds later, the chandelier above their table dimmed, casting silhouettes of their wineglasses against the dark-honey tablecloth. Ricardo stood to his feet, taking Kelise's left hand in his as he lowered himself to the floor directly in front of her.

With eyes the size of saucers, Kelise covered her mouth with her free hand.

Ricardo said, "Kelise, I do believe I have loved you every since the day that you stumbled into me, asking me where could you find the cafeteria. When I asked you to marry me, I meant it from the heart. You are my everything, *chiquita*, and without you, I am nothing. I know my job has taken me from you, leaving you by yourself for long periods of time, but I swear to you, all that is about to change. I love you *con total de mi corazón*, and it would do me great pleasure if you would marry me on Sunday, my birthday, August 1st."

Kelise couldn't believe her ears. He had proposed to her almost two and a half years ago, and he was finally setting the wedding date—five days from today!

"Are you serious?" she asked. "We're getting married at the end of this week?"

"I swear it to you."

"Oh, I love you so much," she exclaimed, throwing her arms around his neck. She kissed him deeply as he softly outlined her spine with his fingertips. How was she supposed to tell him her secret now? There was no way in hell that she would jeopardize getting married to the only man she'd ever love.

"We have so much we have to do, baby," she told him, still overwhelmed by the unexpected wedding date. "I have to get fitted for a dress, you have to get measured for a tuxedo, we have to send out invitations, we have to—"

"Kelise!"

"What?"

"Shut up and kiss me."

And she gladly did.

Chapter Nineteen

With a loud sigh, Niya pulled open her front door. She crossed her arms over her chest and gave him a semi-irritated look. "What are you doing here, Phillip?" she asked. "You don't pick up the kids until next weekend."

He looked bone tired and sounded exhausted as he said, "I didn't come here to see the kids."

"Oh really?" With arms still crossed over her chest, she leaned against the door-frame and asked in a challenging voice, "Then what did you come over here for?"

"Can I come in?" he asked, "Just to talk."

"Hell no. Whatever you have to say, you can say it right here." Niya couldn't help but notice the fading bruise she had caused that marred his cheek. He caught her staring and rubbed his hand self-consciously over the mark.

"Start talking," she prompted him.

He rubbed his hands together, something he did whenever he was nervous. "Niya, I know I should've been told you this, but better late than never." He finally looked at her and met her insensitive stare head on.

"Niya, I want to apologize for all the shit I've ever put you through. I apologize to you for the drug problem that I had; I apologize for settling for all those shitty jobs when I knew I could've done better; and I apologize for cheating on you. I know me and you will never have a chance of getting back together, but I want you to know that I love you, I've always loved you, and I will always love you. I just messed up. Big time."

To her dismay, Niya felt some of her cold resolve towards him melting away. No matter how wrong he had done her, she couldn't deny the fact that she did still love him. Why else would she have married him? But she wasn't going to be like a lot of these other women, allowing love to be a curtain over her eyes.

"Apology accepted," she finally said, remembering her mother's words to her the day before: *You can't go to heaven holding no grudge. The Bible says to forgive those who trespass against us.*

"Can I get a hug?" he asked, holding out his arms.

Niya looked at him for a second as if taking his request under deep consideration. Finally, she opened her arms. "Come here, Phillip." She hugged him tightly, not only because he looked like he needed a hug, but because she needed to feel his arms around her once last time.

When they pulled apart, she thought for a minute that he was going to kiss her, and to be honest, she didn't know how she would respond if he did. But he must've changed his mind because he turned and walked down the porch stairs, shaking his head. "I messed up big time, didn't I?" His question was a rhetoric one.

"Drive safe," she told him, and she softly shut the door.

*   *   *   *

Cathy said, "Kelise, we have a slight problem."

Kelise's eyeballs almost burst from their sockets. "Oh, my freaking God!" she exclaimed in a loud, irritated voice. "What? What? What? What now? What could possibly be wrong this time?"

"Baby, somehow the catering service messed up your order."

"What do you mean by 'messed up'?"

"We ordered boneless, skinless chicken, right?"

"Yes."

"Well, we got boneless, filleted fish instead."

It was at times like this when Kelise wished she hadn't chopped off her dreads, so she could run her frustrated fingers through them, grip them, and try to remove them from her scalp. Now, instead of golden-tipped locks, she had a boy-cut with tiny, juicy, brick-red curls covering her scalp—a new look for a new life. Ricardo said he liked it because it fit her face, and it accented the soft curve of her neck.

The wedding was driving Kelise insane. She felt like a chicken with her head cut off, running around trying to make sure that everything and everyone was in order; and it was only one problem after another.

First, Niya's bridesmaid-dress got caught on a nail and ripped. Thanks to their mother's exceptional sewing skills, that problem was quickly fixed. Then Uncle Thomas misplaced his tie, and they had to throw together a last minute search team to find it. And if that wasn't bad enough, Kadeesha tripped and fell, knocking out her loose front tooth. Now, their flower girl had to walk down the aisle looking like a jack-o-lantern because she wouldn't quit smiling.

And to put the icing on the cake, filleted fish instead of boneless chicken. Kelise threw her hands up in the air. "Well, Ma, go buy a few tubs of coleslaw and call it a day. I give up."

"Kelise, your make-up!" her friend/employee, Trisha, yelled from somewhere.

"I gotta go," Kelise told her mother, hiking up the edges of her wedding dress and hurrying after the voice.

Kelise stood in the full mirror, staring with approving eyes at Trisha's handiwork. Her make-up looked like it was done by the hand of a professional; she looked like an exquisite, African princess.

"Trish, I owe you for this one."

Putting away her make-up equipment, Trisha replied, "Give me a raise, and I'll be good to go."

"I'll think about it," Kelise promised her.

Just then, the dressing room door flew open with Cathy marching in followed by her two daughters, Tomi and Niya. They looked amazing in their strapless, rich-honey bridesmaid dresses. All of the bridesmaids had the same hair-do, large kissy curls spilling from a bundle atop their head, with a golden rose pinning back a few curls on the side.

"I got good news," Cathy told her daughter.

"Finally!" Kelise proclaimed.

"Brian McKnight made it. He just pulled up in his limo."

"Thank God!" Kelise sent a prayer of thanks up to the Lord that at least one thing had went right.

"Kelise, you look beautiful." Cathy's tone was wistful and her eyes were full of tears. "All my babies are growing up so fast…"

"Mom, don't cry or you'll make me cry," Kelise told her mother, but she was already carefully dabbing at the corners of her eyes in order not to mess up her make-up.

"Pull it together, girls," Niya told them, a bit teary-eyed herself, "we have a wedding to attend in a few minutes."

"Yes, we do," Cathy told them. "So bridesmaids, go take your places. And Tomi," she added as they headed towards the door, "I know you may not feel too good because of your pregnancy, but try to put on a cheerful face, baby. Suck in that bottom lip, and quit looking like a thunderstorm waiting to happen. This day is very special to your sister."

"Okay, Ma," Tomi told her. "I'll try."

As Tomi followed Trisha and her sister outside, she tried to tell herself to think happy thoughts, but it wasn't easy. She had so much stuff on her mind.

Dante and she still weren't on speaking terms, and she missed him more than she cared to admit. Looking at Kelise was difficult for her to do because every time she saw her face, she pictured Kelise and Keith making love. And mix all that with her crazy hormones due to the pregnancy, she wanted to take a large gulp of corn liquor, crawl into bed, and sleep until next year.

Not only did she want to do that—Tomi wanted to draw blood; she wanted to get even. Her plan was to ruin her sister's big day as much as possible, and so far, she was doing a good job. The food mix-up was no accident—all it had taken was one little phone call, and everybody knew how much her sister hated fish. And that atrocious rip in Niya's dress—that wasn't caused by a nail; it's amazing what a two-dollar eyebrow archer can do. She had 'accidentally' tried to spill her cup of fruit punch on Kelise's train, but Kelise had moved just in the nick of time. Tomi knew what she was doing was wrong in so many ways, but, oh well; Kelise knew what she had done was wrong, too. Retributive justice: an eye for an eye.

Tomi, Niya, and Trisha lined up on one side of the church's vestibule, and the groomsmen, Elijah, Dante, and Uncle Thomas lined up on the other side. Tomi looked over at Dante, and she knew he felt her staring, but he wouldn't look back. She wondered how he would react when she had to put her arm through his in order for him to usher her into the church.

As mad as she was at him, she still couldn't deny how attractive he looked in his suit. Dressed in cream-colored tuxedos with matching ties, the men were looking fresh and on point. Their shoes were also the color of cream and made out of real alligator skin (compliments of Ricardo). The dime-sized diamond stud in Dante's ear shined star-bright, and Tomi's eyes drifted from the diamond to his freshly edged up sideburns, which she had done herself. She felt a slow, dull ache begin between her legs as she thought about all the times she had outlined his sideburns with her fingertips while they made sweet love in the dark.

Forget him, she told herself, forcing her eyes to look at anything besides him. If that's how he wanted to act, then so be it. She wouldn't worry herself over his childishness.

The music began and Brian McKnight's unique, melodic voice strongly sang the words to his song, *Back At One,* as the bridesmaids and groomsmen coupled off down the aisle.

He sang, "It's undeniable, that we should be together. It's unbelievable, how I use to say I'd never fall…"

Dante was nonchalant and cool as he tucked Tomi's arm close to his side. Tomi wondered if their touching affected him as much as it affected her. She just wanted to apologize to him and call a truce, but he didn't deserve an apology—she did!

She looked over at him, trying to get him to look at her, but his eyes were focused straight ahead. It was as if peripheral vision didn't exist to him. With a resigned sigh, she held her pearly bouquet of magnolias high against her chest and plastered a fake smile on her face for her mother's sake.

As they neared the altar and went their separate ways, Dante seemed profusely detached. Tomi had been standing arm in arm with him, yet she felt like they were on two separate sides of a vast ocean.

Brian McKnight brought the song to a beautiful end as the bridesmaids and groomsmen lined up on either side of a nervous Ricardo. He was shifting from foot to foot, and sweat beads decorated his upper lip. Tomi wanted to rub his back encouragingly, but refrained from doing so.

The music started up again and as Brain McKnight began to sing Luther Vandross' *Here and Now* with an added twist of his own, Kadeesha made her way down the aisle, carefully littering the walkway with deep-red rose petals. Kelise appeared in the doorway, and a hush fell over the family and guests as they stood to their feet. Holding her arm tight against his side, Matthew escorted his daughter down the aisle.

The next part of Tomi's plan was to have a coughing fit good enough to win an Oscar award as her sister made her way down the aisle. Just as she put one hand against her mouth to begin the coughing, something stopped her. It felt as if someone had placed a hand on her shoulder and whispered, "Enough."

Grudgingly, Tomi put her hand down and looked up at her sister. Even though she still harbored animosity towards her, she couldn't help but to admire how beautiful her sister looked. She was a magnificent, Nubian queen as she made her way down the aisle with eyes for no one except her man.

Once she made it to the front of the church and took her place beside Ricardo, the preacher told everyone that they could be seated.

The preacher began. "Do you, Kelise Tanner Thompson, take Ricardo Santana Lopez to be your lawfully wedded husband, for richer or poorer, till death do you part?"

Kelise looked Ricardo in the eye as she said, "I do."

The preacher turned to Ricardo, who still looked as if he could pass out at any given moment, and asked, "Do you, Ricardo Santana Lopez take Kelise Tanner Thompson to be your lawfully wedded wife, to have and to hold, through sickness and through health, for richer or for poorer, till death do you part?"

Ricardo wiped the beads of sweat from his top lip and stammered out, "I-I-I do. I do, sir. I do."

Trisha snickered, and Niya discreetly elbowed her in her side.

"Very well. The rings." A ring was put on both Kelise and Ricardo's fingers, binding them together forever in the eyes of the Lord.

The preacher looked up at the church and said, "If there be any man here who have just cause why these two should not be wed, let him speak now or forever hold his peace."

The preacher sent a quick observing look over his spectacles at the crowd. Silence was his only reply.

"Very well—"

"Wait!"

The sudden outburst drew everyone's eyes to Kelise. She looked like a deer caught in the headlights.

"Ms. Thompson?" the preacher asked.

Kelise opened her mouth, but her throat was too dry to utter a word. She ran her tongue over her lips, but her tongue felt like a massive, dried up slug weighing down her words.

"Ms. Thompson?" the preacher asked again.

Ricardo was looking at her with an inquisitive stare. "Baby…?"

She had to tell him the truth. She couldn't allow this man to marry her, give his life to her, oblivious to what she had done.

"Ricardo, I…I have a confession. I have to let you know that while you were gone, I did—"

"—she did a lot of thinking," Tomi cut her off, "and she realized that she loves you with all her heart, and that she has always been foolishly in love with you, and that you are the only man and will always be the only man for her."

All eyes were on Tomi, now. Tomi had no idea what she was doing, had no idea what she was going to say. And even though she had tried her best to ruin Kelise's wedding, she knew she couldn't stand here and allow her sister to tear apart what God was trying His best to put together.

"Kelise was going to run out on this whole wedding, Ricardo. She got cold feet and she was going to quit on you, but I wouldn't let her. She wasn't sure if she was fully in love with you or not, but I assured her that it was just nerves."

"You don't love me?" Ricardo asked, a surprised and wounded look on his face.

"Yes, I love you!" Kelise reassured him, throwing a secretive, questioning glance at her sister.

Tomi stared at her, saying with her eyes, *"Shut your mouth and marry the man."*

Kelise looked back at her husband-to-be. "She's right, Ricardo. I confess. I was going to back out of this whole marriage, and Tomi talked me into going through with it. I just thought you should know before we finalized our vows."

"It's okay," Ricardo assured her, taking her hand in his. "I almost backed out of it, too. But I love you with all my heart, and I know for a fact that you're the only woman I'll ever love. You're the woman I want to spend the rest of my life with, have kids with, grow old with, all that good stuff."

Kelise placed a loving hand on his cheek. "I love you, too, baby. You don't know how much you mean to me."

In a patronizing manner, the preacher looked from Tomi, to Ricardo, and finally to Kelise. "Can we continue now? Please?"

"Yes. Sorry," Kelise laughed.

Tomi let out a pent up breath of relief as the preacher finally finished what he was saying. "By the power vested in me by the state of Georgia, I now pronounce you, husband and wife. You may kiss the bride."

Ricardo's smile was heart warming as he lifted Kelise's veil and gave her a Hollywood kiss. Her face was flushed and beaming as they turned to face the congregation.

"I present to you, Mr. and Mrs. Ricardo Santana Lopez."

Everybody clapped approvingly and stood to their feet as Ricardo and Kelise jumped the broom. She squealed as he swooped her up in his arms, and headed down the aisle. He didn't look nervous anymore; his smile was award-winning.

Once outside, they were covered with bubbles and beige and white streamers. A man wearing a black tuxedo and white gloves brought a small cage up the church steps. Kelise and Ricardo reached into the cage and removed two, pure-white turtledoves. They released the beautiful birds and the doves soared to the sky as everyone gave applause.

At the reception, Ricardo and Kelise slow danced to Jodeci's *Forever My Lady*. Tomi sat alone, taking small sips of her too-sugary fruit punch from a diamond-cut wineglass that probably cost more than her car.

"Is this seat taken?"

Tomi's drink paused half-way to her lips, and she looked up to see Dante's handsome face. Her stomach flip-flopped at the sight of him. Even after being together for this long, he still had the power to make her feel like a little, blushing school-girl.

Boy, was she tired of their fussing and fighting, tired of crying, and tired of all those lonely nights of curling into a tiny ball in her big King-size bed, wrapping her arms around herself and wishing he was at her side. She wanted things to be right between them. She wanted her baby back; but she knew the ball was in his court.

"Be my guest," she told him, gesturing towards the unoccupied seat beside her.

They were both quiet, and Tomi was tense. She knew he didn't come over here only to sit beside her. Obviously, he had something to say, and she wasn't sure if she wanted to hear it.

"Tomi."

"Yeah?"

"Tomi," he repeated her name, and she finally looked over at him. "That was a good thing that you did back there in the church."

She nodded and looked away, taking another sip of her syrup.

Dante gingerly took the glass from her and sat it on the round table beside them. He took her hand that was closest to him and kissed each knuckle. "Tomi, I love you."

"I love you, too, Dante." She gave him a wavering smile.

"I apologize for the way I yelled at you. I was just jealous, baby. I mean, I've always been scared to really hold on to something because I always end up getting hurt."

As she listened to him talking, Tomi realized that her 'surprise' for Dante hadn't shown up. The night that she had talked to Dante's mother on the phone, they had kept in touch, and since then, they had talked on the phone twice more. Their plan was for her to show up at Kelise's wedding, and now, the wedding was almost over with and she still hadn't arrived. Maybe Dante had been right after all. Maybe she never would change.

"What's wrong, baby?" Dante asked, noticing the change in her demeanor.

"Nothing. Nothing." She shook her head. "I was just thinking about what you were saying. And I apologize for yelling at you, too. I don't ever want us to fight like that again."

"Come here, baby." He pulled her into his arms, and she felt relieved to feel his warm embrace around her again. He buried his face in her neck as he whispered over and over again, "I'm sorry. I'm so sorry, baby."

"It's okay," she told him, finally able to run her fingers up and down his thin sideburns.

"From now on," he told her, kissing her lips, "when we get mad at each other, I want us to talk it out instead of barking at each other like cats and dogs."

"Okay," she promised, not caring who saw their loving display, just glad to have her baby back.

He covered her slightly protruding belly with his large hands. "I want to be with you, Tomi. And not only for the baby. Tomi, while Kelise and Ricardo were up there giving their vows, I realized something."

"And what's that?"

"That I want to spend the rest of my life with you. That I want to cook for you, clean for you, buy you anything that money can afford. That I want to massage your shoulders after a long day at work, give you medicine when you get sick, help you start a garden if you'd like. That I want to grow old with you, helping you find your teeth and letting you change my pamper whenever my bladder shuts down on me."

Tomi laughed and lifted an eyebrow at him. "Are you asking me to marry you?"

He smiled. "Yeah, I think that's what I'm trying to get at."

She shoved him gently. "What happened to the traditional way of proposing? You know, getting down on one knee, romantically professing your undying love, and holding up an expensive ring?"

"All that will come in due time," he told her, hushing her up with a kiss. "But first, I need a yes."

"Yes, Dante." She wrapped her arms around his neck and kissed him while gazing into his eyes. "Yes, I want to spend the rest of my life with your stubborn, always trying to make cracks on me, baggy pants wearing, good-sex giving, attitude-having ass."

"Damn, am I really all that?"

"All that and more." She gave him another kiss. "And I wouldn't trade you for the world."

"Y'all need to get a room," Uncle Thomas butted in, jumping in between them. He cast threatening eyes on Dante. "Didn't I tell you if you ever touched her again, I was gonna whoop that ass?"

Tomi took Dante's arms and wrapped them around her waist. "And didn't I tell you to quit threatening my man, Uncle Thomas?"

"You got a good girl," he told Dante, patting him hard enough on his back to make him wince. "Do good by her. Or else I'm going to—"

"—whoop that ass," Dante finished for him. "I know, I know. I'll treat her good, sir. I promise."

"That's more like it," he told him, holding his wine glass up in the air and looking around the room. "Have y'all seen that old lady with the big red hair and no teeth? I've been trying to find her all night long, with her sexy ass."

"She's probably running from you," Tomi told him teasingly, snuggling down into Dante's embrace.

"Uncle Thomas, what do you want with a no-teethed woman, anyway?" Dante asked him.

Uncle Thomas threw an arm over Dante's shoulder and said to him in a loud, man-to-man whisper, "Boy, let me school you on a few things. It be them ones with no teeth that can really make you—"

"Eww, Uncle Thomas!" Tomi cut in before he could finish his statement. She pushed him away. "Go on somewhere with your nasty self."

He started laughing as he walked off. "I'm trying to tell you, boy," he said, pointing a finger at Dante, "a no-teeth one equal jackpot, baby!"

"Please excuse him," Tomi apologized for her uncle's roguish behavior. "Incase you haven't figured it out by now, he ain't got no sense." She turned in Dante's arms so that she could face him. "But anyway, where were we?"

An erotic smile curved his lips as he went in for another kiss. But before they could kiss, the brand-new bride came and interrupted them. "Sorry to interrupt, guys, but I wanted to know if it was alright if I can steal Tomi for a minute."

Dante held up his hands in surrender. "Take her away."

Tomi gave him a quick kiss before following Kelise on to the dance floor.

"Girl," Kelise began, shaking her hips to the beat of the music, "I done just about wore my self out dancing. I think I've danced with just about every man in here."

"You better not wear yourself out too much," Tomi teased, "you know you have a long night awaiting you. I just hope you can keep up with Ricardo; he might try to pull an all-nighter on you."

"Oh, I got this," Kelise promised her. "Pulling all nighters is nothing new for my baby. I'm use to it by now."

"Too much information," Tomi told her, scrunching her face up in an 'eww' expression.

Kelise laughed, and then her face became serious. "Tomi, uhm, thank you for...you know...for how you...you know..."

"Kelise," Tomi cut her sister off, "let's leave the past in the past. We're sisters; we're supposed to have our ups and downs."

"Does that mean you forgive me?"

"What do you think?" she asked, pulling her sister into a tight hug. "I love you, girl." When she felt a faint shaking in her sister's shoulders, she said, "Keli, don't cry, or else you'll end up looking like a raccoon—all that mascara Trisha put on you."

Kelise laughed and hugged her sister tighter.

"What about me?" Niya asked, walking up to them while holding her wine glass in one hand. "I need a hug, too."

"Come, join in," Kelise told her.

Niya put an arm around either sister, and they held each other. "Girls, you know we've been through a lot. One little sister married, the other little sister head-over-heels, pregnant and in love, and me...divorced—"

"With two beautiful children," Kelise quickly added.

"And two wonderful sisters who love you more than life itself," Tomi added in a no-nonsense tone.

Niya smiled and finally released her firm hug on her sisters. "I'm so glad God blessed me with sisters like you two. I'd be lost without you."

Dante tip-toed over to them and snuck an arm around Tomi's waist. "Excuse me, beautiful women. I hate to interrupt but it's getting a little late, and my fiancée and I have some very important business we need to handle."

"Fiancée?" Niya and Kelise asked at the same time.

Niya grabbed Tomi's hand and gave it a good looking over. "I don't see no ring."

"In due time ladies," Dante told them with a charming smile.

Kelise shook her head at them. "I knew it was going to happen. It was just a matter of time."

"Whatever you do, just don't pick the colors peaches and cream for your wedding," Niya told them. "I don't think I look good in peach."

Kelise thumped her sister upside the head. "It ain't about you!" she told her.

Dante laughed and pulled Tomi away from their small circle. "We have to go," he told them again. "Your sister and I have some...very important business that needs to be taken care of immediately."

Niya shook her head. "See, that's why little miss thang here is in the predicament that she's in now. But I don't blame her, handsome rascal."

"Don't hate," Tomi told her with a wink as they headed towards the exit.

As soon as they walked through the exit door, Dante froze in the very spot where he was standing. Tomi turned around and tried to pull his arm again, but he had turned into an immobile statue.

"Dante, what's wrong...?" Tomi stared at his face, and realized that his eyes were transfixed on something across the room. Tomi followed his line of sight, and her eyes fell on what had to be the most magnificently beautiful woman she had ever seen.

The woman looked to be in her early forties. She wore a three piece pantsuit which was pure white and sheer. The arms of the pantsuit drooped low like angel wings, and the bottom was pants with a skirt attached that flowed at an angle. This woman could have easily been an angel that had descended from heaven.

Her hair was jet black, short and shaved at the back, stacked curls at the top. Her skin was a rich, oatmeal brown color, her eyes like those of the Chinese, her nosy tiny and petite, her lips full and colored with iced lipstick. A string of white pearls decorated her neck and long baby-raindrops pearl earrings hung from her ears. Her beauty seemed to radiate from within.

Tomi knew that this was Dante's mother when she saw those cinnamon-brown eyes, almost sheathed by genuine, inch-long eyelashes.

"I, uh, I missed my flight. Had to catch the three o'clock one. But I came. I came." She was talking directly to Dante.

Tomi looked over at Dante who was still standing as stiff as a statue. Tomi feared his reaction. She knew he hadn't seen his mother in twelve years. The last time he had seen her, she'd been laying in a hospital bed, overdosed on crack cocaine, and hanging on to life by the grace of God.

Tomi looked over at Dante's mother. She looked back at Tomi, her eyes glittering with unshed tears. Looking in her eyes, Tomi saw love, fear, anxiety...and, yet in still, a mustard-seed of hope.

As Grace took a step forward, Tomi nodded her encouragement. Grace walked up to Dante, stood before him, and bowed before her son. She kissed both his feet, then, still kneeling on the ground in all her white, looked up at her son and said, "Dante, I love you. All I ask for is a second chance. I can apologize a million times for the wrong I've done you, but nothing can change the past. I can only live for today and try to change our future. Will you give me that chance? If you say yes, from this day forth, I will be the best mother I can be. If you say no, I will spend every single day of my life trying to change your mind."

She rose to her full height, which brought her level to his chest.

Dante looked his mother in the eye, then threw his arms around her, crushing her tiny self against him. He was sobbing, not just crying, but sobbing. "You came back, Ma," he cried, "you promised me that you'd come back. You came back, Ma."

Tomi couldn't stop crying. She was already emotional due to her pregnancy hormones, and now this? The scene was like something out of a movie, touching to even the most cold-hearted person. Tomi stood off to the side and watched as they hugged each other, both reluctant to let go probably for fear of the other disappearing in thin air. Dante was hugging his mother so hard, Tomi knew the woman was probably hurting, but she didn't pull away.

Finally, Grace was able to move her hands up to her son's face so that she could wipe away his tears. She stood on tiptoe so that she could kiss his forehead again and again. "I will never leave you again," she vowed. "And that's not a promise. That's a sacred vow before you and God. I love you Dante."

Unable to hold back any longer, Tomi walked over to them and Dante crushed Tomi against him, hugging her hard enough to break a bone, but she didn't protest.

Tomi turned to Grace and said, "Thank you for coming."

Grace replied, "When God gives you an opportunity like this one, it's either all or nothing. So I risked it all."

Tomi unhooked herself from Dante and stepped off to the side. "I know you two have a lot of catching up to do, so I'm going to disappear back into the reception. Call me if you need me."

Wiping her eyes and sniffing her nose, Tomi tip-toed back to the reception and slid her way into the electric slide, which she could bet money on that her Uncle Thomas had started. About an hour later, a smiling Dante, almost giddy in nature, returned to the reception and ushered Tomi back outside. He threw one arm around Tomi's waist, the other around his mother's, as they headed for his car.

"So," Dante began, his voice holding a smile, "can someone please explain to me how all this was made possible?"

"It was all Tomi," Grace quickly told him. "She went through your phone one day when you left it at her house."

"Oh really?" Dante looked over at Tomi. "A little nosy aren't we?"

"Dang, Grace, you're a tattle-tell," Tomi teased.

"And your a nosy rat," Dante retorted.

"Well, if I'm a nosy rat, then you're a waterhead."

"Oh, we got jokes, huh?"

Grace laughed at both of them. "You two are like peas in a pod."

"No, she's more like pee in a pot."

"What?" Tomi laughed and shoved Dante. "I got you, punk!"

"Why you always hitting on somebody? That's why Denise tagged your head that night at the club."

"Oh, no he didn't." Tomi went after Dante, but he ran behind Grace and put his hands on her shoulders, ducking behind her when Tomi tried to swing.

"Lord have mercy, Dante, after all these years, you would think you'd have grown up by now."

"Men, don't grow up," Tomi told Grace, hooking her arm through the older woman's, "they're just kids trapped in grown men bodies."

"Ain't that the truth?"

Dante laughed as he hugged his mother from behind, kissing her cheek loudly. "Ma, you surprised me today," he told her, "but I have a surprise for you."

"Oh, do you? And what is this surprise."

Dante reached out his hand and palmed Tomi's belly. "You're about to be a grandma—"

"Oh, my God—"

"And a mother-in-law."

"Thank you God!" Grace pulled Tomi close and hugged her tight. She looked up at the sky and said, "God, I thank you! I remember on my dying bed, you told me that if you spared my soul, if you gave me a second chance at life, it was up to me to give myself a second chance at living. My son, a daughter, *and* a grandchild?"

"And I remember," Tomi added, looking up at the night sky, "standing on my front-porch, confused beyond understanding, and you sent me a sign that Dante was my other half, my soul-mate."

"And I remember," Dante added, putting an arm around either woman and looking up at the sky, "thinking that my mom would never come back, and that I'd never be whole again because there would always be a piece missing. But you gave me back that missing piece." Dante sniffed, and Tomi looked over at him, saying up under her breath, "Waterhead."

A horn blared and they all looked over to their left to see what was going on. A taxi was sitting there, and the driver seemed exhausted and impatient. "Lady, you know you're still on the clock."

"Oh, Lord, I forgot all about that," Grace said, hurrying towards the taxi. "I just need to get my suitcases out of the trunk."

"I'll help you." Dante and Grace went over to the taxi. Tomi stood by Dante's car waiting for them to return.

After Dante finished filling his trunk with his mother's suitcases, Dante walked over to Tomi and kissed her gently. "Before we go, I just want to know the answer to one question."

"What's that?"

"Why'd you do it? Why'd you save Kelise's wedding?"

Tomi thought for a while, then said, "Sometimes in life, you have to decide the worth of things. It wasn't worth it to see my sister miserable for the rest of her life just because she had made one mistake. Everybody makes mistakes, but in every mistake, there's a lesson to be learned."

Grace hugged her son and added to Tomi's statement, "Couldn't have said it better myself."

EPILOGUE

Dear Readers,

Being a married woman is a new experience for me, but it's one that I wouldn't trade in for anything in the world. Ricardo treats me like I'm his queen, and I treat him like he's my king. He's even cut his business trips down to one every three months. I still miss him when he's gone, but it's nothing like it use to be—thank God. I finally told him about Keith, too, and guess what? He told me that he still loved me, and though my confession really hurt him, he was willing to work through it. God, I love him so much.

Tomi had her little girl a week ago. They named her Diana Destini McKoy, and she's a beautiful, little angel. Dante and she looks like twins. They're tying the knot next week, and guess who's presiding over their wedding? Dante's mom, Grace. She finally got her license to preach.

Niya is still single, but at least she's dating now. It seems to me like she's enjoying the single life more than she enjoyed the married one. Phillip and she have formed a mutual relationship, and they've actually become friends. I told Niya to be careful when it comes to Phillip, because I believe that some of those feelings for him are still there. I believe that Phillip is a good man, but not the man for her. He finally got a real job (hallelujah, Jesus); he's a bank teller at Bank of America, and because he has a master's degree in accounting, they're talking about promoting him already. I'm happy for him.

My magazine, Brothas and Sistaz of Color, is thriving beyond understanding. I am now CEO of this magazine with three other sister magazines branching off of mine—doing it way big, y'all! Now, I can hang around Niya and not feel as if I'm poor as dirt.

I remember a while back when my sister and I had gotten into a really big argument because she claimed 'I was airing her dirty laundry in front of the whole black community that reads my magazine.' I wonder what she will think after she reads this (ha, ha).

To my wonderful readers, I ask that you keep on reading because it's you that keep my magazine alive. I love you all and God Bless.

Sincerely,
Kelise

978-0-595-39676-4
0-595-39676-3

Printed in the United States
119501LV00017B/117/A